THE
BLACKSTONE
LEGACY

ROCHELLE ALERS

THE BLACKSTONE LEGACY

THE BLACKSTONE LEGACY

ISBN-13: 978-0-373-22994-9

Recycling programs
for this product may
not exist in your area.

Copyright © 2011 by Harlequin Books S.A.

The publisher acknowledges the copyright holder
of the individual works as follows:

THE LONG HOT SUMMER
Copyright © 2004 by Rochelle Alers

VERY PRIVATE DUTY
Copyright © 2004 by Rochelle Alers

www.kimanipress.com

Printed in U.S.A.

CONTENTS

Dedicated to:
Cheryl White—the first black woman jockey
to ride on a U.S. commercial track at
Thistledown Race Track in Cleveland, Ohio,
on June 15, 1971, and Isaac Murphy—the first jockey
of any race to win the Kentucky Derby three times.

Sons, listen to what your father teaches you.
Pay attention, and you will have understanding.
—*Proverbs* 4:1

Dear Reader,

You have asked and I have attempted to give you what you want—another family series.

Whenever I sit down to brainstorm to create a new family, the question is always "what if?" The Blackstone Legacy's "what if" was the result of an article I'd read about Isaac Murphy, who was the first jockey of any race to win the Kentucky Derby three times.

My interests in horse racing spawned the Blackstones of Virginia: Ryan, Jeremy and Sheldon, a prominent African-American horseracing family. *The Long Hot Summer* and *Very Private Duty* are the first two books. *Beyond Business* concludes the trilogy, but look for another Blackstone to take center stage next year in the first of a Hideaway summer wedding trilogy, scheduled for the summer of 2012.

Sit back, put your feet up with a cool drink and make certain you have a fan handy when you read about the incredibly sexy men in the Blackstone Legacy.

Don't forget to *read*, *love* and *live* romance.

Rochelle Alers

www.rochellealers.org

ralersbooks@aol.com

THE LONG HOT SUMMER

Chapter One

"**W**ho the hell are you?"

Startled by the voice below where she stood on a stepladder hanging a colorful border of zoo animals above a corkboard—a booming voice sounding as if it had come from the bowels of the earth—Kelly Andrews lost her balance and fell backward. Her fall was halted as she found herself cushioned against the solid chest of the man who had silently entered the schoolhouse.

A swooshing rush of breath escaped her parted lips at the same time her eyes widened in surprise. Glaring down at her under lowered lids was the man who was her tormentor and rescuer.

There was no doubt he was a Blackstone. The angular, raw-boned face was the same as Sheldon Blackstone's. His eyes were gray, not the silvery sparkling shade of his father's, but a dark gray that reminded Kelly of a wintry sky before a snowstorm.

She wondered which Blackstone son he was—Jeremy the DEA agent or Ryan the veterinarian. Whoever he was, the black stubble on his jaw made him look formidable. Her startled gaze settled on his sensual full lower lip, wondering if it ever softened in a spontaneous smile.

Ryan Blackstone's expression mirrored that of the woman in his arms: shock. He'd just returned to Virginia and Blackstone Farms from the Tuskegee University of Veterinary Medicine where he'd taught several courses as a visiting professor for two semesters.

Minutes after he'd parked his car in the garage near the main house he had noted the sly grins and muted whispers from long-time employees, but chose to ignore them because he had been anxious to reunite with his father. His four-year-old son had spent the drive from Alabama to Virginia chattering incessantly about returning to the horse farm and seeing Grandpa.

Sheldon had warmly welcomed his son and grandson home, then told Ryan that he wanted him to meet the teacher for the new child care center, at the same time extolling the woman's credentials and experience. This news pleased Ryan because now the young children who lived at Blackstone Farms would have a structured daily environment. For years they had become free spirits, wood sprites with the horse farm's property as their backyard. They ran barefoot in the grass, climbed trees, swam in one of the two in-ground pools and raced in and out of the dining hall several times a day for snacks. Establishing the Blackstone Day School was an ideal situation, but only if the woman in his arms wasn't its new teacher.

Kelly placed a palm on his chest, pushing against solid muscle. "Please, put me down, Mr. Blackstone."

The sound of her husky voice jolted Ryan. The soft, perfumed body pressed against his was so pleasurable that he'd almost forgotten how good it felt to hold a woman—especially one who was certain *not* to share his bed.

Dark gray eyes narrowed slightly under raven eyebrows. He held his breath before letting it out slowly. "Who's asking?" He had tightened his grip under her knees.

"Kelly Andrews, Blackstone Farms Day School's new teacher. And I hope you don't make it a habit of using profanity around children."

Ryan glared at Kelly. Who did she think she was? "What did you say?"

"Mr. Blackstone, if you're hearing impaired I can sign for you. I'm certified in American Sign

Language as well as certified to teach nursery through sixth grade. Now, I'm going to ask you again to put me down or I'll be forced to show you what other certifications I have."

Ryan decided he liked holding Kelly. He liked the husky timbre of her voice and the way her curvy body melded with his; he also liked the smell of her hair and skin.

"Are you warning me that you're trained in martial arts?"

Smiling, Kelly admired the masculine face inches from her own. Slanting cheekbones, a strong nose with slightly flaring nostrils, and a square-cut chin made for an arresting visage. His eyes were beautiful. They were a striking contrast to his brown skin.

Slowly, as if in a trance, Ryan lowered Kelly until her sandaled feet touched the newly installed oak flooring.

So, he thought, she *was* the one everyone had been whispering about. She was the teacher who would assume the responsibility for socializing the farm's young children. Studying her upturned face, Ryan stared down into eyes the color of newly minted pennies with glints of gold. They were framed by long, thick black lashes, which seemed to enhance their vibrancy. Her delicate copper-brown face was exquisite: sculpted cheekbones and a delicate chin with a hint of a dimple. A slight smile tugged at the corners of his mouth. Kelly Andrews was lovely; no, he mused, she was stunning!

When Ryan had walked into the schoolhouse, he'd stood there mutely, staring at a pair of incredibly long legs under a pair of cutoffs, a narrow waist and slim hips. The hem of her sleeveless white blouse was tied at her midriff, offering a glimpse of velvety flesh at a waist small enough for him to span with both hands. Her dark chemically relaxed hair, cut to graze the back of her long neck, was secured off her face by a wide red headband.

"How old are you, Miss Andrews?"

Kelly took a quick breath of utter astonishment. Counting slowly to herself, she bit down on her lower lip. She had to choose her words wisely or she would walk away from this position.

Staring up at the tall man looming over her, she forced a smile she did not feel. "In case you aren't aware of it, Mr. Blackstone, there are laws against age discrimination in the workplace." A spark of satisfaction lit her eyes when a rush of deep color darkened his tanned gold-brown face.

Ryan's right hand tightened at his side. "I'm very much aware of the law, Miss Andrews," he said. "And you can call me Ryan. My father is Mr. Blackstone."

Even though Sheldon Blackstone was legally listed as owner of the horse farm, it was Ryan who had eventually assumed responsibility for its day-to-day operation. His father had resumed the role this past year only because Ryan had been teaching as a visiting professor at his alma mater. In Ryan's absence Sheldon had advertised, interviewed and had hired Kelly to teach the children of Blackstone Farms.

And given Sheldon's penchant for beautiful women, it was obvious why he had hired Kelly Andrews.

Pulling herself up to her full five-foot-eight-inch height, Kelly flashed a confident grin. "If you're that versed in the law, then why did you inquire about my age?"

Aware that he'd been caught in a trap of his own making, Ryan struggled to extricate himself from a terminal case of foot-in-mouth.

"You look so young that I…I," he stammered, unable to complete his statement. There was something in her gaze that tightened the muscles in his stomach. It had been a long time since a woman had excited him with just a glance. Not since the first time his gaze met the woman's who had eventually become his wife and the mother of his son.

Kelly lifted an eyebrow and decided to let Ryan squirm a bit longer. It would serve him right if she turned her back on him and went back to decorating her classroom. She had wanted to finish by the end of what had become a very long day.

But there was so much to do. She still had to unpack and catalog books, games, art supplies and videos before she'd be ready. She had hoped to open the school on Monday—exactly one month since her arrival at Blackstone Farms.

"I can assure you, *Ryan,*" she said, stressing his name, "I'm old enough *and* qualified to teach."

"That may be so, Miss Andrews, but I intend to monitor you closely during your probationary period."

Gazing up at him, Kelly noticed a sprinkling of silver in the thick, close-cropped wavy black hair. There was something rakish and sophisticated in Ryan. His dark skin and light colored eyes reminded her of lightning in a bottle.

"Ryan?" Her voice was soft and layered with a sensuality that jerked his head up like a marionette manipulated by a puppeteer.

His eyes darkened until they were nearly black with an indefinable emotion. "Yes, Kelly." It was the first time he'd called her by her given name.

Tilting her chin, she gave him a captivating smile. "I don't have a probationary clause in my contract."

Ryan closed his eyes, silently cursing his father for being taken in by her pretty face. It was Sheldon who had vehemently insisted that everyone employed at Blackstone Farms sign a contract—one that always included a clause detailing a probationary period.

He opened his eyes to find Kelly staring at him, while at the same time the curvy pout of her sexy mouth taunted and challenged him. "What did you promise my father?"

Her smooth forehead furrowed. "Excuse me?"

Ryan leaned closer. "You heard me the first time, Kelly. Don't make me have to sign for *you*." His gaze roamed leisurely over her body. "I hope when you begin teaching you'll be wearing more clothes."

Without giving her an opportunity to come back at him, he turned on his heel, walked out of the schoolhouse, and closed the door softly, leaving her to stare at a pair of broad shoulders that seemed almost too wide for the doorway.

She sat on the stepladder, her shoulders slumping in resignation as the enthusiasm she had felt earlier that morning dissipated. It did not take the intelligence of a rocket scientist to know that Ryan Blackstone did not like women. And apparently it wasn't all women—just the younger ones.

At thirty, she had experienced what most women her age hadn't: widowhood. Several months before she'd celebrated her twenty-eighth birthday Simeon Randall had been killed by a hit-and-run driver when he'd pulled off the parkway to fix a flat tire. Simeon, mercifully, had died instantly from massive head trauma.

The appearance of two police officers at her door, asking that she come to a local hospital because her husband had been killed in a traffic accident had changed her and her life forever. She'd lost her first love, soul mate and life partner. Even after she had buried her husband she refused to accept that he would not walk through the door each night to share dinner with her. She'd continued to set the table for two. When her mother, who had come to see her without calling first, asked about the extra place setting, Kelly broke down and sobbed in her arms the way she'd done as a child. Camille Andrews stayed the night, holding her daughter in her arms while they slept in the bed her son-in-law had shared with Kelly.

The following day Kelly walked into the principal's office at the school where she'd taught third grade, and resigned her position. Two days later she got into her car and headed for Washington, D.C. to spend time with her sister and brother-in-law. A month's stay became two, and eventually twenty-three.

She had returned to New York City to clean out her co-op apartment, sell items she did not want, place heirloom pieces in storage and list the property with a real estate agent. The apartment was sold six months later, and Kelly deposited the proceeds into a Washington, D.C., bank account. She continued to pay to store her furniture until she received official documentation of her hire as a teacher for Blackstone Farms Day School. The antique mahogany sleigh bed, armoire, heirloom linens, quilts and the wrought-iron table and chairs that had once sat on her grandmother's patio now graced the charming bungalow she would call home for the next year.

She sat on the stool until the door opened again, and this time it was Sheldon Blackstone who had come to see her. "Don't bother to get up," he said, as he came closer. Leaning against the wall, he crossed his legs at the ankles. "It looks nice, Miss Kelly."

She nodded. "I should finish decorating tonight."

A slight frown marred Sheldon's lined forehead. "Why don't you put that off until tomorrow?"

Kelly studied the older man's profile, finding him quite handsome. Tall, solidly built, with brilliant light-gray eyes in a face the color of toasted pecans, she knew the widowed horse breeder could easily attract a woman from thirty to eighty.

"Why?"

"Everyone's gathering in the dining hall tonight at six to welcome my son and grandson home." Since coming to Blackstone Farms Sheldon noticed that Kelly rarely took her meals in the dining hall with the other employees.

She nodded. "I'll be there, Mr. Blackstone."

Straightening, he wagged a finger at her. "I told you before that we're pretty informal here. Please call me Sheldon."

"If that's the case, please call me Kelly."

"No," he said, shaking his head. "I'll call you *Miss* Kelly in front of the children. There's an unwritten rule here. The children aren't allowed to address adults by their given name, especially women. I know it may sound outdated and quite Southern to a Northerner, but it is a Blackstone tradition."

Kelly smiled. "I may be from New York, but I do claim some Southern roots. I have some Virginia blood on my daddy's side and South Carolina on my mama's."

Sheldon flashed a rare smile. "Where in Virginia?"

"Newport News."

"The best seafood I've ever eaten was in Newport News."

"I have relatives there who are fishermen."

Sheldon took a quick glance at his watch. "I expect to see you later."

"You will."

Kelly had to smile. *I expect to see you later.* It was Sheldon's way of ordering her to eat with the other employees. Since she had come to live on the farm, she had eaten at the dining hall twice, both times for breakfast. Sheldon had informed her that breakfast and lunch were served buffet-style, while dinner was a sit-down affair where everyone who lived or worked on the property shared in this meal—all except for her.

She usually prepared a light dinner, cleaned up the kitchen in the bungalow before throwing all of her energies into her craft projects. She'd worked practically nonstop to ready her classroom for the projected first day of school, which was now only three days away.

Curbing the urge to salute her boss, she watched as he walked across the floor of the spacious outbuilding that had been converted into a schoolhouse. She wanted to say *like father, like son,* but decided to reserve judgment on the Blackstones. After all, they were responsible for an enterprise that included thousands of acres of land, millions of dollars in horseflesh and a payroll for more than thirty employees.

After seeing an ad in *The Washington Post* for an experienced teacher certified in early childhood education to teach on a horse farm in the western part of Virginia, Kelly had searched the Internet for information on Blackstone Farms. She had learned that Blackstone Farms was one of a few owned and operated African American horse farms in the state.

She liked this part of Virginia. It was so different from New York City and Washington, D.C. Although it was early summer, the heat and humidity were noticeably lower. The property, west of the Blue Ridge and east of the Shenandoah Mountain ranges, lay in a valley like a shimmering emerald on blue-black velvet, was to become her home for the next year.

She glanced at her watch. It was almost four-thirty. She would finish putting up the banner, then go home to prepare for dinner.

Twenty minutes later, the border in place, Kelly walked out of the schoolhouse, closing the door behind her. Sheldon had introduced her to some of the other employees, but tonight would be the first time she would interact with all of them socially. It would also be the first time she would meet the parents of the children who would become her responsibility.

Attending the dinner would also bring her face-to-face with Ryan Blackstone again. He'd caught her off guard when he'd entered the schoolhouse undetected, but she made a solemn promise it would be the last time he would catch her off guard.

Chapter Two

Kelly parked her Honda between two late-model pickup trucks and stepped out into an area set aside for parking. It was fifteen minutes before six, yet the lot was almost filled to capacity. She hadn't taken more than a few steps when she saw him.

Ryan was dressed in black: linen shirt, slacks and low-heeled boots. The color made him appear taller, more imposing. Although he'd slowed his stride to accommodate the pace of the young child clinging to his hand, Kelly still admired the fluidity of his beautifully proportioned physique. There was something about Ryan that reminded her of her Simeon even though the two men looked nothing alike.

"It's a beautiful evening, isn't it, Miss Kelly?" Cooling mountain breezes ruffled the leaves of trees, bringing with it the cloying sweetness of wildflowers blooming throughout the valley.

Kelly stopped in midstride, her breathing halting momentarily before starting up again. Ryan had also stopped and turned around to face her. He stood several feet away, flashing a wide, white-tooth smile.

Recovering quickly, she returned his smile. "Yes, it is, Dr. Blackstone." Her gaze shifted to the boy staring up at her. Kelly knew the child was a Blackstone. He had inherited his father's features. His eyes were a mirror image of Ryan's. She extended her hand. She knew from the records Sheldon had given her that Sean Blackstone had recently celebrated his fourth birthday.

Bending at the knees, she said, "Hi."

Ryan placed a hand on his son's head. "Sean, this is Miss Kelly. She's going to be your teacher. Miss Kelly, this is my son, Sean."

Sean stared at her hand and inched closer to his father's leg. Vertical lines appeared between his large eyes. "I don't want to go to school."

Ryan hadn't registered his son's protest because all of his attention was directed at the woman dressed in a sheer white silk blouse, slim black linen wrap skirt and black heels.

He hadn't known Kelly was behind him until he'd detected the scent of her perfume. Her exposed arms and legs shimmered with a dewy glow from a scented cream that sent a jolt of electricity through his body. Biting down on his lower lip, he struggled for control.

Sean tugged at his father's hand. "Do I have to go to school, Daddy?"

"Yes, you do."

Sean pushed out his lower lip. "But I don't want to."

"We've talked about this, Sean." Ryan's voice held a thread of hardness.

"No! I'm not going. I hate school!"

Kelly stared at Sean for several seconds. It was apparent the child was as stubborn and opinionated as his father. "School's not so bad," Kelly said, trying to calm the little boy down. "How about coming by the schoolhouse after dinner to check it out?"

Tears filled the boy's eyes. "No!"

Ryan opened his mouth to reprimand his son for being rude, but Kelly shook her head. Threatening or bullying the child was not the solution. She'd discovered gentle persuasion usually worked well with young ones.

She met Ryan's gaze. "I'm going to hold an open house for all of the children tomorrow morning at ten to show them their new school." She stared at Sean. "You are more than welcome to come."

She hadn't planned to show the children their new

classroom until Monday morning, but she would make an exception if it meant winning Sean over.

Tightening his grip on Kelly's elbow, Ryan led her and Sean toward the entrance to the dining hall. Leaning closer, his moist breath sweeping over her ear, he whispered, "Thank you."

Holding the door open, Ryan permitted Kelly and Sean to precede him into a large, one-story brick building that had been referred to over the years as the dining hall. The entryway was crowded with people, some he had known for most of his life. The tantalizing aromas coming from the kitchen reminded him that he had come home.

He reached for Sean's hand while his free hand rested at the small of Kelly's back as if it were a gesture he'd done many times before. She stiffened slightly before relaxing her back beneath his splayed fingers.

Closing her eyes briefly, Kelly endured Ryan's touch and his closeness. It reminded her of what she had missed. There was never a time when she went out with Simeon that he hadn't silently announced she was his. Whether it was cradling her hand in the bend of his elbow, or circling her waist with an arm, he'd communicated possession and protection. She opened her eyes to find Ryan staring at her, his expression impassive.

"Have you met everyone?"

Kelly shook her head, thick dark strands moving fluidly with the slight motion.

"I haven't had the time," she explained in a soft voice. "It took me a week to settle into my bungalow, and all of my free time has been spent readying the classroom for Monday."

He frowned. "Why didn't you get someone to help you?"

"I did. Your father made Dennis available for me whenever I needed to move or lift something heavy."

Kelly, Sean and Ryan walked into the central dining hall amid a rousing round of applause and whistles. Sheldon stood under a colorful hand painted banner reading: Welcome To Blackstone Farms. Red and black helium-filled balloons—the colors of the farms' silks—tied with contrasting ribbons served as centerpieces for each white cloth-covered table. A dozen tables, each with seating for four, were filling up with employees who lived on the property.

Sheldon motioned Ryan closer. "You, Sean and Miss Kelly will sit with me."

Ryan pulled out a chair for Kelly, seating her while Sheldon performed the same motion for his grandson. He ruffled the child's curly black hair.

Kelly removed the strap to the tiny black purse she'd slung over her chest, placing the crocheted bag on her lap. Her gaze swept around the large room.

The exterior of the dining hall, as with most of the buildings on the farm, was deceiving. Simply constructed of brick or wood, the interior was extraordinary. The dining hall's furnishings rivaled those of any upscale restaurant in any major city. Dark paneled walls with decorative moldings, wide windows with stained-glass insets, plush carpeting, cloth-covered mahogany tables, Tiffany-style table lamps, fine china, crystal stemware, sterling silver and softly played taped classical selections set the stage for exquisite meals prepared by a resident chef.

Blackstone Farms was a thriving, profitable working horse farm and Sheldon had made certain it maintained a certain image given the numerous purses won by Blackstone champion Thoroughbreds over the years.

Still on his feet, Sheldon held a goblet filled with sparkling water. Raising a hand, he signaled for silence. "This isn't going to take long." A ripple of laughter followed his announcement.

"Yeah, right," Kevin Manning, the head trainer called out.

Sheldon put down his glass and crossed his arms over his chest, glaring at his lifelong friend. "You keep running off at the mouth and I'll pull out my prepared speech."

"No!" came a collected groan from everyone in the room.

Kelly glanced at Ryan when he threw back his head and laughed. Her gaze was fixed on his strong throat. So, she thought, he can laugh. The gesture changed his face, softening it.

Sheldon inclined his head. "May I continue?"

"Please," Kevin said, raising a hand in supplication.

"Tonight is very special not only to me," Sheldon continued, "but to everyone at Blackstone Farms. I get to have my son and grandson back for what I hope is more than a few months, and I want all of us to welcome the newest member of our farm family, Miss Kelly Andrews, the new teacher and director of Blackstone Farms Day School."

All gazes were fixed on Kelly. She felt a wave of heat sweep up her chest and settle in her cheeks as everyone applauded. She was grateful for her darker coloring otherwise they would have been able to see the blush burning her face. She jumped noticeably when Ryan placed a hand over hers.

"You're expected to say a few words," he whispered, his mouth pressed to her ear. She jumped again, this time from the moist breath flowing into her ear. Rising, he pulled back her chair, assisting her as she stood up. He stood beside her, his left hand resting against her spine.

Composing herself, Kelly flashed a smile, eliciting gasps of appreciation from several men seated at a nearby table. "I'd like to thank Sheldon and everyone for their kindness and assistance in helping me set up the school." Her beautifully modulated husky voice was hypnotic. Her gaze swept around the room and settled on Sean. "I'm hosting an open house at the schoolhouse tomorrow morning at ten for everyone, especially the children, to give you an idea of what I've planned for the coming year. School begins officially Monday morning at eight o'clock, but for parents who want to drop their children off earlier, please let me know tomorrow." She smiled again. "Thank you."

Ryan seated Kelly, flashing a smile that signaled his approval. Listening to her speak, it was easy to tell she wasn't a Southerner. It was also obvious that she wasn't married, and in that instant he knew he wanted to know more about Miss Kelly Andrews. He knew he could go through her personnel file to glean her vital statistics, but it was the personal information he wanted. Did she have an ex-husband or a lover?

His musings were interrupted when a young woman approached the table to take their orders. Kelly studied the printout of the dinner choices. Appetizers included curried corn-crab cakes, sesame shrimp with a miso dipping sauce, and skewered spiced pork and red pepper with a spicy mango sauce. Entrées included grilled steak, broiled salmon, and roast chicken along with an assortment of steamed and grilled vegetables.

Leaning to her right, her breast brushed Ryan's shoulder and he turned and stared at her, the dark pupils in his eyes dilating. Their gazes caught and fused as their breathing found a common rhythm. Within a matter of seconds Kelly registered the overt virility Ryan exuded just by breathing. His warmth, the clean masculine scent of his body, the sensual fragrance of his cologne, and the penetrating gray eyes that appeared to see everything, miss nothing.

"What do you recommend?"

"Everything," he said in a soft voice as he continued to stare at her under lowered lids.

"How's the salmon?"

A slight frown marred his smooth forehead. "You've never eaten Cook's salmon?" Salmon had become a regular Friday night selection.

"I've never eaten dinner here."

His frown deepened. "Where have you been eating?"

"I cook for myself."

"Why would you cook for yourself when we have a resident chef?"

Kelly heard the censure in his question. "I've been working long hours, and by the time I leave the schoolhouse the dining hall is closed."

"You can always put in a request to have your dinner delivered to you."

She lifted a shoulder. "No one ever told me I could do that."

"Well, I'm telling you."

Kelly studied his grim expression, willing he

smile again. Raising her dimpled chin slightly, a smile trembled over her full lips, drawing one from him. "Thank you for the information, Ryan." His name had become a whispered caress on her lips.

Sheldon sat across the table from his son and Kelly, watching a subtle game of seduction being played out in front of him. He doubted whether Ryan or Kelly were aware of their entrancement with the other.

Less than an hour ago he and Ryan had had a short and pointed discussion about his decision to hire Kelly Andrews. And it was the first time in years that he had used his status as majority owner in Blackstone Farms to counter Ryan's opinion. Ryan thought they should've hired a teacher with more experience. Sheldon had ended the conversation, stating that Ryan should find a woman to release his sexual frustration, and then walked out of the room leaving his firstborn with his mouth gaping.

It was never Sheldon's intent to become a matchmaker, and he knew Ryan had never been involved with any woman who lived or worked at the farm. But, watching Kelly the past three weeks he suspected she would be able to handle herself when it came to his son just fine.

She had proven that once Dennis Poole had tried to come on to her when she'd asked him to move several boxes that had been delivered to the schoolhouse.

Dennis had confided to one of the grooms that Kelly told him that if he ever tried to touch her again she would change his gender in a New York minute. Dennis wasn't certain what she meant by the statement, but had decided it wasn't worth the risk to find out.

Sheldon gave his dinner selection to the waitress, thinking it would be nice to have another grandchild before he turned sixty. Ryan had made him a grandfather once already, but he looked forward to spoiling more than one of the next generation of Blackstones.

Kelly thoroughly enjoyed her dinner. The salmon was exquisite. The freshly caught fish, packed in ice the day before, had been flown from the Northwest. Dinner conversation was light and entertaining as she listened to Sheldon and Ryan talk about horses while Sean politely interrupted his father several times to ask a question. Kelly found the boy quiet and somewhat withdrawn, and she wondered how much contact he'd had with his mother.

Two hours after dinner began, people began drifting over to the table to introduce themselves to Kelly and to welcome Ryan and Sean back home. Young children hid shyly behind their parents when Kelly told them she expected to see them the following morning at the schoolhouse.

Touching her napkin to the corners of her mouth, she pushed back her chair. Smiling at Ryan and

Sheldon, she said, "Thank you, gentlemen, for your company. Dinner was wonderful." Both Blackstone men came to their feet, Ryan helping her to stand. She smiled at Sean, who wouldn't look at her. "I hope to see you tomorrow morning, Sean." Frowning, he pushed out his lower lip.

Sheldon winked at Kelly. "I'll take care of everything."

Picking up her crocheted purse, she opened it, and took out her keys. "Good evening."

Ryan reached for her hand, tucking it into the curve of his elbow. "I'll walk you to your car."

Her eyes widened. "That's all right. I believe I can find my way to the parking lot." There was a hint of laughter in her voice.

"I want to apologize to you."

"For what?"

He leaned closer. "I'll tell you later."

Sean rounded the table and tugged at Ryan's arm. "Daddy, can I stay with Grandpa tonight?"

Ryan glanced down at his son before looking at his father. Sheldon nodded. "Of course. You have to listen to Grandpa or it will be a long time before you'll be permitted to sleep over again. Do you understand?"

Sean flashed a wide smile, showing a mouth filled with tiny white teeth. "Yes, Daddy." Turning, he launched himself against Sheldon's body.

Ryan escorted Kelly to the parking lot. "My father will bring Sean to your open house tomorrow."

"Are you sure he'll be able to get him to come?"

"My father can get Sean to do anything. The child worships him because Sheldon spoils him."

Standing next to her car, Kelly smiled at Ryan in the waning daylight. "That's what grandparents are suppose to do—spoil their grandchildren."

He nodded, extending his hand. "Please give me your keys."

She tightened her grip. "Why?"

"I'll drive you back to your place."

"Don't be ridiculous, Ryan. I live less than a quarter of a mile from here."

Reaching for her hand, he gently pried her fingers apart. "I know where you live."

"But Ryan—"

"But nothing," he said softly, cutting her off.

"How will you get back?"

"I'll walk."

Opening the passenger-side door, he held it open for her. His gaze lingered on the expanse of her bare legs and feet in the high heels as her skirt shifted upward when she sat down. Rounding the car, he slipped in behind the wheel, adjusted the seat, and put the key in the ignition in one, smooth motion. The engine turned over and he backed out of the lot. Three minutes later he parked her compact sedan alongside Kelly's bungalow. The sun had set, leaving the sky with feathery streaks of orange crisscrossing a backdrop of navy-blue. Pinpoints of light from millions of twinkling stars emerged in the encroaching darkness.

Within minutes the landscape was completely black, except for an occasional light coming from windows in buildings spread out over the seventy-two hundred acres making up Blackstone Farms. The farm was laid out in a quadrangle: the main house, dining hall, and school in one quad; the barn, stables, paddocks and grazing area in the second; the cottages for resident employees in the third, and the last quadrant left for future expansion.

The farm was secure and protected by closed-circuit cameras strategically placed throughout the property, and at no time could anyone arrive or leave undetected.

Kelly waited for Ryan to come around and assist her. He opened the door and she placed her hand on his as he tightened his grip and pulled her gently to her feet. He was standing close, too close, but she did not attempt to pull away.

Holding out her hand, she said, "My keys, please."

Ignoring her request, he led her up the porch and to the door. He unlocked it, pushed it open, and then dropped the keys in her palm. The glow from a table lamp in the parlor spilled a ribbon of light out into the night.

"Thank you for seeing me to my door."

The sultry sound of Kelly's voice swept over Ryan like an invisible caress. "Thank you for a lovely evening. Sharing dinner with you helped make my homecoming even more special."

Kelly stared at the highly polished toes on Ryan's low-heeled boots rather than look into his eyes. "Good night."

Reaching out, his right hand cupped her chin, forcing her to meet his gaze. "I'm sorry."

"For what?" Her voice had dropped to a whisper.

"For using profanity, for being rude and for acting like a complete ass."

"Ryan!"

He flashed a wide grin. "I could've said ass…"

"No," she screamed, covering her ears with her hands.

Releasing her chin, he curved his arms around her waist. "Don't tell me you're a prude, Miss Kelly."

She placed her hands over his chest. "I'm not a prude. It's just that I've heard enough profanity to last two lifetimes. You can't imagine the words I've heard from kids as young as five or six. A lot of them can't string a sentence together using the correct verb, yet they can cuss you out using words that can make the most jaded adult cringe."

Ryan lifted an eyebrow. "Whenever I cursed as a kid my mother used to wash my mouth out with lye soap. After a while I learned never to curse in front of her. She refused to accept my rationale that if Pop said it, then it had to be all right."

"I hope you don't use those words around your son."

He shook his head. "Never."

"Good." She eased out of his loose embrace. "I have to go in now."

He did not want her to go in. He wanted to sit out under the stars and talk—talk about…

"Good night, Kelly."

She stared at him for several seconds. "Good night, Ryan."

Kelly stood on the porch, watching Ryan as he turned and walked away. Within minutes he disappeared and was swallowed up by the warm early summer night.

Chapter Three

Ryan walked back to his house, his mind filled with images of Kelly. During the evening meal he had watched her, admiring her natural beauty and the ease in which she seemed to accept her femininity.

She had sat upright, spine pressed against her chair, shoulders pulled back and her full breasts thrusting forward. He had felt like a voyeur whenever he watched her breasts rising and falling in an even rhythm. She had worn a lacy camisole under her blouse, and he had fantasized unbuttoning the blouse to run his fingertips over her skin.

Although he had been divorced for three years he had not lived a monkish existence. The day he signed his divorce papers he'd driven to Waynesboro, gone to a local bar and drank himself into oblivion. He woke up hours later in a woman's bedroom with a hangover that had him retching for hours. It was the first and last time he had gotten drunk.

Once he cleansed his mind and body of the alcohol, he'd called his father to let him know he was still alive. He spent the next day baring his soul to a stranger. Lisa—she wouldn't tell him her last name—was eight years his senior, but she had become his confidante and eventually his lover. Their on-and-off-again relationship ended abruptly last Christmas when she called him to say him she had decided to remarry her ex-husband. He wished her well, and mailed her a generous check as a wedding gift.

In light of his casual attitude toward women, he simply couldn't understand the intensity of his initial attraction to Kelly. There was something so deeply alluring about her that he wanted to lie with her, damn the consequences.

He arrived at his house and opened the door. The moment he walked inside he felt the emptiness. Whenever Sean spent the night with Sheldon or overnight with one of his little pals, the emptiness was magnified. He thought he would get used to the loneliness, but it never seemed to dissipate completely.

It had begun several months after he'd married Caroline Harding, a young woman he'd met in college. She had begun to withdraw from him the day she found out she was pregnant. As her pregnancy progressed she confessed to feeling trapped, that she hated living on the farm, and pleaded with Ryan to let her out of their marriage. He'd granted her wish, and she got into her car, drove away from Blackstone Farms two months after she had given birth to a baby boy—alone.

Climbing the staircase to the second story, he walked into his bedroom and prepared to go to bed— alone.

Even though Kelly had been in bed for eight hours, she woke up fatigued. She'd spent the night dreaming and tossing restlessly. She'd dreamed of making love with Simeon, but when she'd opened her eyes it wasn't her late husband's face staring down at her but Ryan Blackstone's.

She'd jumped out of bed, shaking uncontrollably as guilt assailed her. She'd been unfaithful to her husband's memory. It had taken half an hour before she fell asleep again only to be awakened by the same dream. This time she lay, savoring the pleasurable pulsing aftermath of her traitorous body. Within minutes she succumbed to a sated sleep and woke at sunrise.

Leaving her bed, Kelly padded to the bathroom. Peering into the face in the mirror over the sink, she searched for a sign of shame or guilt, but found none. She had to face the realization that she was attracted to Ryan because she was a normal woman with normal sexual urges. At thirty she was much too young to permanently forgo sexual gratification with a man. That was what her sister Pamela had tried to tell her. *I'm certain if you'd died instead of Simeon he wouldn't stop seeing other women,* Pamela had said repeatedly. *So why have you set yourself up as the martyred widow?*

I don't know, she had told Pamela over and over. And she hadn't known—not until now. What Pamela and Leo Porter and even she hadn't known at the time was that she had not met the right man.

But, was Dr. Ryan Blackstone the right man? "No," she said to her reflection.

She reached for a facial cloth in a small plastic container and wet it. Using a circular motion, she washed her face, then splashed cold water over her tingling skin before patting it dry with a fluffy towel. She filled the tub with water, adding a capful of perfumed oil, and brushed her teeth and tried to dismiss the erotic musing about a certain veterinarian from her mind.

Ryan raised his head to peer at the clock on the bedside table, groaning under his breath. It was minutes before three, and he hadn't had more than two hours of sleep since retiring for bed at ten-thirty. He knew the reason for his insomnia was Kelly Andrews.

It was as if he still could see the play of sunlight on her warm brown skin, the contrast of her white blouse against her velvety throat, and the lush curves of her hips in the slim skirt. What had surprised him was that she hadn't worn any makeup other than a soft shade of orange-brown lipstick, and still she was stunning.

Everything about her, from the way she'd dressed, her poise and the way she spoke screamed big-city sophistication. A wry smile curved his mouth, and Ryan wondered how long would it take before she tired of smelling hay, horse urine and manure. And when the weekends came would she be content to stay on the farm or would she head to the nearest big city for some *real fun?*

Throwing back the sheet, he sat up and left the bed, knowing he wasn't going back to sleep. Twenty minutes later, dressed in a plaid cotton shirt, jeans and a pair of old boots, he walked to the stables.

Sensors lit up the area where the prize horses were stabled for the night. Placing his right hand on a panel, he waited until a flashing red signal switched to a steady green before he punched in a code. The lock to the stable was deactivated. Sliding back a door, Ryan walked into the dimly lit space, and closed the door behind him.

He stopped at the stall of an exquisite foal, smiling at the potential Triple Crown winner. The colt, Shah Jahan, was the product of Blackstone Farms's winningest mare and a former Preakness winner. He had the bloodlines of a potential Thoroughbred champion.

Ryan lingered in the stable, checking on each horse, and when he walked out the workers were arriving with the rising sun. The build-up of heat had begun to burn away the haze covering the valley as he had made his way to his house, a weighted fatigue settling over him. His eyelids were drooping but he managed to shower before falling across his bed and into the comforting arms of Morpheus.

He slept deeply, not waking until late afternoon— well after the Blackstone Farms Day School's open house ended.

Kelly stood in the doorway to the brick structure, noting the curious expression on the face of a little girl. She was expecting a total of five children, ranging in ages from three to five. Two were brothers— identical twins Trent and Travis Smith. One glance at the redheaded, freckled, green-eyed twins signaled trouble—double trouble. Sean Blackstone, Allison Cunningham and Heather Whitfield had also come to the open house. Delicate Heather had arrived first, her large brown eyes widening when she spied the area Kelly had set up as the housekeeping corner, followed by the twins, then Allison.

"You may go look at it," she urged in a gentle

voice. Heather raced over to the play stove, turning knobs and stirring a pot with a wooden spoon.

Sheldon walked in with Sean clinging to his hand as if he feared his grandfather would disappear if he didn't hold on to him.

"Good morning, Sean." He stared up at Kelly, eyes wide.

"Miss Kelly spoke to you, Sean," Sheldon admonished.

"Good morning, Miss Kelly," he mumbled under his breath.

"Come in and join the others. We're going to have juice and cookies." Sean gave Sheldon a lingering look before he walked over to the other children gathering in the housekeeping corner.

Kelly smiled. "Please wait while I get the children settled."

Three women sat on a sofa and two of the four club chairs covered in supple black leather, talking quietly. A glass-topped black lacquered coffee table set on an area rug with a distinctive Asian motif in black and red mirrored the farm's silks. Solid brass floor lamps with pale linen shades completed the inviting sitting area. Kelly planned to use this area to meet with parents to discuss their children's progress or her concerns.

Sheldon sat down. His penetrating gaze swept around the large space, cataloguing everything. Flowering plants lined empty bookcases under a wide window with southern exposure. A color-ful plush area rug with large letters of the alphabet covered the gleaming wood floor. An entertainment center contained a wall-mounted, flat-screen televi-sion, VCR and DVD player. Oversized throw pillows were positioned on the floor in front of the screen.

The science corner held a tank of colorful tropi-cal fish. Posters of farm animals, flowers, birds and fish graced another wall. Cubbies with hooks and the names of each child stood ready for sweaters, coats and boots with the change of seasons. Half a dozen portable cots were stacked against another wall. He was amazed that it had taken Kelly only a month to order the supplies and furnishings she needed to set up her classroom.

He watched her firmly, yet gently, steer the five children to a sink in a far corner. They washed their hands and dried them on paper towels before racing to a round table with half a dozen chairs. Each one claimed a seat, waiting patiently as Kelly filled plas-tic cups with apple juice and placed a large oatmeal raisin cookie on the plate at each setting.

"After you finish your cookie and juice, you can watch a movie while I talk to your parents. Take your time, Travis," she admonished softly when he stuffed a large piece into his mouth.

Ten minutes later, cups and plates stacked on a tray for a return to the dining hall, the five children settled down on the large pillows to watch their movie.

Kelly walked over to the sitting area, joining the parents. Smiling, she said, "The Blackstone Farms Day School will open officially Monday morning, and I want to reassure you that your children will be exposed to a safe and positive environment while in my care...."

It was noon when the parents pulled their reluctant children away from the blank television screen, promising them they would come back in two days.

"Are you going to be here on Monday, Miss Kelly?" Sean asked.

She smiled at the expectant look on his face. "Of course I am, Sean. I'm going to be here for a very long time." She knew a year was a long time to a four-year-old. He smiled at her, his expression so much like his father's, and then skipped away to catch up with Sheldon.

Once everyone left, Kelly sat down on one of the club chairs, rested her feet on a corner of the coffee table, and closed her eyes. The open house had gone well. She waited half an hour, then began the task of unpacking and cataloguing books into a database of the personal computer Sheldon had given her for the school's use. It was later, well after the dinner hour when she slipped behind the wheel of her car and drove back to her house.

* * *

Kelly showered, changed into a pair of shorts and top, and then went into the kitchen to prepare her dinner, a small salad, which she devoured hungrily. She had just dried and put away her dishes when the doorbell rang. The sound startled her. It was the first time anyone had rung her bell. Drying her hands on a terry-cloth towel, she made her way out of the kitchen, through the parlor and to the door.

"Yes?" She had lived too many years in New York City to open the door before identifying who was behind it.

"Ryan."

The sound of his voice made her heart skip a beat before it settled back to a normal rhythm. "What do you want?"

"Open the door, Kelly," he said after a pregnant silence. "Please."

Her hand was steady as she unlocked the door, opened it and looked at Ryan staring at her as if he had never seen her before. It was only when she noticed the direction of his gaze that she realized her state of half-dress—a pair of too-tight, low-riding shorts and a revealing midriff top. The narrow waistband on her black lace bikini panties and the outline of her nipples under the white top were ardently displayed for his viewing.

Tilting her chin, she repeated, "What do you want?" The question was filled with fatigue.

Ryan closed his eyes, but he still could see the soft curves of Kelly's body. Why was it whenever he met her one-on-one she was half-dressed?

He opened his eyes, forcing himself to look at her face and not below her neck. "I missed you at dinner. I just came by to check whether you'd eaten."

She nodded. "I had a salad."

He lifted a raven eyebrow. "Just a salad."

"I was too tired to fix anything else. I've had a long day."

"I thought I told you that you could order from the kitchen."

Kelly gave him a smile. "I know you did, but—"

"You're working too hard, Kelly."

"I'm not working too hard, Ryan," she countered. "I had a deadline to meet, and I met it."

He smiled, tiny lines fanning out around his eyes. "Congratulations. Do you want to celebrate?"

Vertical lines appeared between her eyes. "Celebrate?"

His smile vanished. "I'm certain you're familiar with the word."

"Celebrate how?"

He shrugged a shoulder. "Go into town."

Her gaze narrowed. "And do what?"

"Talk. If you want we could share a drink."

Kelly recalled her erotic dream earlier that morning and she fought the dynamic vitality Ryan exuded. She knew she wasn't immune to him, but she had no intention of permitting herself to fall under his sensual spell. She had come to this part of Virginia to teach, not become involved with a student's father or have an affair with her boss.

She offered him a conciliatory smile. "I'm flattered that you asked, but I'm afraid I have to decline. First of all, I'm tired. It's been a very exhausting week for me."

Ryan noticed the puffiness under her eyes for the first time. "And the second reason is?"

Her expression changed, hardening. "I've made it a rule not to *date* my boss." Much to Kelly's surprise, he threw back his head and let out a great peal of laughter. She frowned. "What's so funny?"

He sobered enough to say, "You."

"Me?"

"Yes, you, Kelly. Let me remind you that I'm not your boss. I didn't interview you, hire you or sign your contract. And that translates into my not being able to fire you. Only my father can do that." Crossing his arms over his chest, he angled his head. "Now, you're going to have to come up with another reason for rejecting my offer."

Bracing her hand on the door, she smiled. "That's an easy one." Without warning she closed the door and locked it. "Good night, Ryan," she said loud enough for him to hear.

Ryan stood motionless, staring at the door. She'd

closed it in his face. "Well, I'll be damned," he whispered.

Kelly had called his offer to take her out a date while he thought of it as a meeting. Sean had come home that afternoon bubbling with excitement when he'd talked about his new school. It had been the most spontaneity he had seen in the child in over a year. He wanted to talk to Kelly about his son, but was he using Sean as an excuse to spend time with Kelly? In any case, meeting at her place was out of the question. The last thing he wanted was to generate gossip about the boss's son coming on to the new schoolteacher. As it was, there was enough gossip circulating around Blackstone Farms to fill a supermarket tabloid.

He chuckled in spite of his predicament. In that instant he realized he liked Kelly Andrews. He'd found her poised and beautiful. But he also knew she had a lot of fire under what she'd projected as a dignified demeanor.

Unknowingly she had issued a challenge when she closed the door in his face. And Ryan Blackstone had never walked away from a challenge.

Chapter Four

Kelly hadn't realized her hands were shaking until she picked up the telephone on the table beside her bed. At that moment she wanted to curse. She was pissed! And it wasn't Ryan she was angry at. She had become what she detested most: discourteous and ill-mannered.

Ryan had come to her, asking they go somewhere and talk. She hadn't even asked him what he had wanted to talk about before she slammed the door in his face.

Was she losing it because of an erotic dream?

Dialing the area code for Washington, D.C., she waited for the connection. She smiled upon hearing her sister's cheery greeting.

"Hi, Pam."

"Hey, Kelly. I hope you're calling to tell me that you have a date tonight."

She ignored the reference to a date. Even if she had gone out with Ryan she still would not have considered it a date. "I called to say hello to my big sister."

A groan came through the earpiece. "You called me last Saturday to say hello. What are you doing, Kelly? You've moved across the state and your social life hasn't changed. I think it would've been better if you had stayed in New York where you at least had a circle of friends."

"Married friends, Pamela."

"I know that, Kelly. But there's always the possibility that they could've hooked you up with a single friend or relative."

"I can always stop calling you—"

"I'm sorry," Pamela said, interrupting her. "I just got off the phone with Mama and Daddy. They've begun an intense campaign to try to make me feel guilty because I finally came out and told them that Leo and I decided not to have children. I don't know how much more of it I can take."

"Tell them that you don't want to discuss it."

"You try and tell Camille Kelly Andrews not to say what's on her mind."

Kelly smiled. Pamela was right. Camille may have

been outspoken and opinionated, but she was also fiercely supportive of her daughters.

"If she mentions it to me the next time we talk I'll be diplomatic when I tell her that you and Leo have a right to determine your own lives. That you're still a family even if you decide not to have children."

"Thank you, Kel," Pamela said, using her pet name for her younger sister.

The two sisters talked for another ten minutes, Pamela giving Kelly an update on her new position as an assistant curator at the National Gallery of Art. Leo, her husband, had taken over as curator at the National Museum of African Art two years before.

The first star had made its appearance in the sky when she stripped off her clothes and pulled a sheet over her nude body. This time when she went to sleep there were no erotic dreams to disturb her slumber.

Ryan's footfall was heavy as he made his way up the porch steps to his father's house and sat down on a rocker across from the older man. Sean sat on his grandfather's lap, asleep.

"That was quick."

"It was quick because she wouldn't talk to me."

Sheldon leaned forward. "Why not?"

"Why?" Ryan repeated. "I don't know why, Pop."

"What do you do to her?"

Stretching long legs out in front of him, Ryan crossed his feet at the ankles. "Nothing. I told her I wanted to talk to her and she closed the door in my face."

"Is that all?"

Ryan threw up a hand. "Is what all?"

"Why are you repeating everything I say?"

"Because I don't believe you're asking me these questions," Ryan shot back.

Recessed porch lights came on automatically in the waning light, flooding the space with beams of gold. It provided enough illumination for Sheldon to see a quivering muscle in Ryan's jaw.

"How did you look at her?"

Ryan struggled to contain his temper. "How does my looking at her have to do with anything?"

"Last night you looked at her as if she were dessert." He held up a hand when Ryan opened his mouth to refute his accusation. "You need to be gentle with her, son," Sheldon continued. There was a wistful quality to his voice.

Ryan decided to ignore his father's assessment of his reaction to Kelly as he stared at Sheldon, seeing what he unsuccessfully tried to conceal—pain. The last time he had seen pain in his father's eyes was the day Sheldon had buried his wife and the mother of his two sons.

"What happened to her, Pop?" he asked softly.

There was a noticeable pause and emerging nocturnal sounds were magnified in the silence. Sheldon sighed audibly. "She lost her husband a couple of years ago in a hit-and-run accident."

Ryan's eyes widened. He had no idea she was carrying that much emotional baggage. "How old is she?"

"Thirty."

A mysterious smile lifted the corners of Ryan's mouth when he recalled asking Kelly how old she was. He still thought she looked much younger than her age.

Sheldon glanced down at the small child sleeping on his lap. There were three generations of Blackstone men sitting on the porch and not one woman.

"Have you thought about remarrying and giving Sean a mother?"

"No more than you have when it came to giving Jeremy and me one."

Sheldon shook his head, smiling. "Touché, son."

"You've been widowed for twenty years, Pop. Don't you think it's time to let go?"

"I could say the same to you."

"No, you can't. Mom died. That's very different from dissolving a marriage."

"Do you ever think of remarrying?"

Ryan's eyes darkened until they appeared near black. "Yes and no. Yes, because I miss being part of an intact family unit, and no, because I have to think about Sean."

"Are you really thinking of him, Ryan? Both of

you need a woman in your lives. How else will he learn to respect a woman if not from his father?"

"I'm thinking only of him, Pop."

"The boy needs a *mother,* Ryan."

"People said the same to you when Mom died."

"That's true," Sheldon agreed. "The difference was you and Jeremy were fourteen and ten when Julia passed away. That's very different from a little boy who has no memories of his mother."

Ryan stared out into the night. He was so still he could have been carved out of granite. He knew his father was right, but knew he also was right. From the day he was born Sean had become the most important person in his life, and he made a pledge to never sacrifice the emotional well-being of his son for any woman.

Ryan stood at the window in his second-story bedroom early Monday morning, watching Kelly as she made her way to the stables. The last time he saw her had been Saturday night at her house. He had waited in the dining hall on Sunday, hoping to catch a glimpse of her, but she did not put in an appearance.

His eyes narrowed as he watched her knock on the door. It opened, and she disappeared behind it. Three grooms worked on a rotating basis once the stables were opened at sunrise to groom the eighteen horses before they were turned out to graze. The trainer and his assistants exercised the Thoroughbreds during the morning and early-afternoon hours.

What was she doing in the stable? Who was she meeting?

Turning away from the window, Ryan descended the staircase in a few long strides. He hadn't realized he was practically running until he felt his heart pumping rapidly in his chest. Taking a deep breath, he opened the stable door and walked inside.

An emotion he could only identify as relief swept over him when he saw Kelly rubbing Jahan's nose. She hadn't come to meet a man, but to see the horses.

"Beautiful."

Kelly jumped, turning to find Ryan standing behind her. It was the second time he had caught her off guard. She hadn't heard his approach over the sounds of a worker sweeping out a stall.

Turning back to the horse, she nodded. "That he is."

Ryan wanted to tell Kelly that he wasn't talking about Jahan. She looked scrumptious, casually dressed in a tank top and pair of jeans that showed every dip and curve of her tall, slender body. He stared at her feet.

"You should be wearing boots in here instead of running shoes."

"I don't have boots."

"Why not?"

"Because I haven't had the time to go buy a pair."

She had spent Sunday restocking her pantry and refrigerator and putting up several loads of wash.

He moved closer. "Look at me, Kelly."

She went completely still. It had been only three days since she'd met Ryan for the first time, but the magnetism was definitely there. Something about him jolted her nervous system each time she met his gaze.

She wanted him even though she did not want to desire him, because in her head she wasn't quite ready to let go of the memory of her late husband. She had purposely avoided going to the dining hall, knowing Ryan would be there, so she continued to prepare her own meals at home.

"Why, Ryan?"

Resting his hands on her bare shoulders, he turned her to face him. "Because I want to look at you." He dropped his hands.

Her lashes fluttered before sweeping up to reveal what she so valiantly tried to conceal: her loneliness and a longing to be held and loved. Her gaze moved slowly over his face, lingering on his mouth. He wasn't wearing a hat, and his damp coal-black hair lay against his scalp in layered precision. His coloring, hair and features were a blending of races so evident in people in this region of the country.

"What do you see, Ryan?"

His dark gray eyes widened as they dropped from her steady gaze to her shoulders and chest. "I see an incredibly beautiful woman who in a few hours has worked wonders with my son." Sean had spent Saturday afternoon and all day Sunday asking when he was going back to school so that he could see Miss Kelly.

Kelly closed her eyes. It was not about her, but Sean. "He's a charming child."

Ryan wanted to tell his son's teacher that she had charmed him, too. He inclined his head. She tried stepping around him but he blocked her path.

"Why did you follow me in here? What is it you want from me?"

"I saw you from my bedroom window and I was curious as to why you'd come here so early. What is it I want from you?" He lifted a broad shoulder under a stark white T-shirt at the same time he shook his head. "I don't know, Kelly. That's something I haven't quite figured out."

Rising on tiptoe, she thrust her face close to his, close enough for him to feel her breath feather over his mouth. "Your homework assignment is to figure out what you want."

She pushed past him, heading for the door, but Ryan was quicker. He caught her arm, pulling her into an empty stall. "I want this," he whispered, seconds before his mouth covered hers in a hungry kiss that sucked the breath from her lungs.

His hands slipped up her arms, bringing her flush against him, and he deepened the kiss. Kelly put her arms around his neck to keep her balance, her soft curves melding with his lean length.

Her mouth burned with the pressure of his mouth moving over hers. The harsh, uneven rhythm of her breathing matched his; she was lost, drowning in the passion and the moment. It was only when she felt the probing of his searching tongue parting her lips that she pulled out of his embrace, gasping. The smoldering flame she saw in his eyes startled her. The lightning was out of the bottle.

Crossing his arms over his chest, Ryan angled his head. "I think that assignment deserves an A. What do you think, Miss Kelly?"

She placed her hands on her hips, ignoring the tingling sensations tightening her nipples. "I think you're disgustingly arrogant, Dr. Blackstone." She'd meant to insult him, but the breathlessness of the retort sounded like a compliment.

He smiled. "I've been called worse."

This time as she turned to walk out of the stables, he did not try to stop her. He followed, watching her straight back and the seductive sway of her hips.

"You owe me an apology, Miss Kelly."

She stopped, not turning around. "For what, Dr. Blackstone?"

"For closing your door in my face."

Kelly pulled her lower lip between her teeth. It was obvious she was attracted to Ryan, and despite her verbal protests she wanted to see him. "Share

dinner with me tonight and I'll apologize properly."
She glanced over her shoulder, seeing his shocked
expression. A satisfied grin curved her mouth as she
continued walking in the direction of her house.

Ryan knew he had shocked Kelly when he'd kissed
her, but she had also surprised him when she'd held
on to his neck.

There was a banked fire under Kelly Andrews's
cool exterior. All he had to do was wait for the right
time to re-ignite it. And something told him it would
be good—not just for Kelly but also for him.

Kelly sat in the library corner with her students.
All had eaten breakfast, cleaned up their table and
were eagerly awaiting the first activity for their first
day of school. Sitting on a stool, she smiled at their
expectant expressions.

"Does anyone know what a calendar is?" Five
hands went up. "Heather?"

"It tells days."

Kelly nodded. "Very good, Heather. What else
can a calendar tell us?" She nodded to Sean, who
hadn't lowered his hand.

"It tells weeks and months."

"We are going to use our calendar not only to tell
us the date, but also for holidays, historic events,
birthdays and special days, weeks and months. Today
is May 23—World Turtle Day."

"I found a turtle," Travis announced proudly.

"Yeah, but Mama wouldn't let him keep it. She said it belonged outside," Trent countered before he stuck his tongue out at his twin.

Reaching for a picture book, Kelly opened it to an illustration of a turtle. "Your mother is right. Animals need to live in what it is called their natural habitat. The turtle is the only reptile that has a shell."

Allison pointed to the picture. "His shell is his house."

Sean raised his hand. "Miss Kelly, my daddy said a turtle can put his head, tail and legs inside his house when other animals want to eat him."

"Your dad's correct." Kelly was certain Sean knew more about animals than most children his age because Ryan was a veterinarian. She handed Trent a green felt cutout of a turtle with a Velcro backing. "Please put this on today's date under the heading of World Turtle Day. Can anyone tell what kind of weather we're having today?"

"Sunny!" They all had called out in unison.

Kelly picked up another cutout of a yellow oval shape with points circling it. "Heather, can you put up the sun?"

She jumped up. "Yes, Miss Kelly."

The morning hours passed quickly wherein Kelly showed the children how to hold paste scissors and cut animal shapes from a stencil. They put on smocks, painted their animals, placing them on a table to dry.

Lunch was delivered from the dining hall at exactly at noon, and an hour later three boys and two girls lay on cots in the darkened room, lying quietly until they all fell asleep.

The children were awakened at two-thirty and taken outside where they played an energetic game of tag and hide-and-seek. They stopped long enough for an afternoon snack of juice and nuts with raisins; they returned to the playground area, playing on the swings and teeter-totter. Their moods and interests changed quickly when they retrieved a jump rope from a large plastic bin.

Allison's mother came to pick her up, and Kelly enlisted her aid in helping to turn the rope as the children jumped while reciting the letters of the alphabet. None of them got past M before their feet got tangled in the rope's length.

Allison took the rope from Kelly. "Let me turn with Mommy while you jump, Miss Kelly."

Before Kelly could refuse all of the kids were chanting, "Jump, Miss Kelly. Jump, jump, jump!"

She remembered her childhood days when she'd jumped Double Dutch with her girlfriends during the summer months. The life span for a pair of her sneakers was usually two weeks.

Measuring the speed of the turning rope, Kelly jumped in. "A, B, C, D..." The children recited the alphabet as she jumped up and down as if she were ten instead of thirty. She heard Sean call Daddy and she faltered.

Standing less than five feet away was Ryan, grinning from ear to ear. He, not Sheldon, had come to pick up Sean.

"You win, Miss Kelly!" Heather shouted. "You got to *S*."

"My name starts with S," Sean crowed proudly, pumping his little fist in the air. He wrapped his arms around Ryan's waist. "We had lots of fun today, Daddy."

Ryan smiled at Kelly. "I think Miss Kelly had lots of fun, too."

"She did. We all did."

"Yeah!" chorused five young voices.

Allison hugged Kelly around her knees. "I will see you tomorrow, Miss Kelly."

She pulled one of the girl's curly dark braids. "You bet I will."

Allison left with her mother and Kelly stared at Ryan staring back at her. Something intense flared through his entrancement, sending waves of heat throughout her body. His stormy gray eyes stoked a banked fire.

Ryan reached for Sean's hand, his gaze fixed on Kelly's face. A hint of a smile softened his strong mouth, and he was not disappointed when she returned it with a mysterious one of her own.

"Daddy?"

"Yes, Sean."

"Do I have to go home now?"

Ryan tore his gaze away from Kelly to glance down at his son for the first time since arriving at the schoolhouse. "Yes. Miss Kelly is tired. She has to go home and get some rest so she can be ready for school tomorrow."

"Can't she come home with us? She can rest in my room."

"No, she can't."

"Why not?"

"Because…because…"

"Because Miss Kelly lives in her own house," Kelly said when Ryan did not complete his statement.

"Why can't she live with us, Daddy?"

"Let's go, Champ. We have to wash up before dinner." Even though he had spoken to Sean, he continued to stare at Kelly. "I'll see you later," he said in a quiet voice.

Kelly nodded. "Okay."

Ryan smiled the sensual smile she had come to look for. His smile was still in place when he led Sean toward a pickup truck. Kelly turned her attention to the remaining children, her pulse quickening when she thought of her promise to meet with Ryan later that night.

There was no doubt she was drawn to his sexual attractiveness, but was that enough? Was it enough to lessen the pain of loving and losing a man she'd loved all of her life? She had met Simeon Randall when both were assigned to the same first-grade class, and he had become her hero, protector. As they grew older she discovered and experienced passion in his arms and bed. A passion she did not know she had.

Simeon had offered her all the emotional and physical gratification and fulfillment she needed. And for the first time since she had come to Blackstone Farms she had to question whether she might be lucky enough to capture both again.

Chapter Five

Ryan hadn't realized he had been figuratively holding his breath until Kelly opened her door.

He knew he was staring at her like a star-struck adolescent, but he couldn't help himself. "You look very nice, Kelly."

Kelly smiled, opening the door wider. "Thank you, and please come in."

She knew she looked very different from the woman he'd seen jumping rope earlier that afternoon. Her hair, brushed off her face, was swept up in a twist on her nape. The sleek style was the perfect complement for a black cap-sleeved off-the-shoulder dress ending at her knees. A pair of sling back animal print leather sandals covered her bare feet.

She admitted to herself that he also looked very nice. A chocolate-brown jacket and matching slacks complemented a finely woven beige, banded-collar linen shirt.

His right hand concealed behind his back, Ryan walked into Kelly's home. The miniature Tiffany-style lamp on a round table cast a warm glow on exquisite antique pieces from another era. An apple-green armchair covered in a watered-silk fabric with a matching footstool was the perfect complement for a lavender-hued sofa dotted with light green sprigs. Classical music played softly from a stereo system hidden from view.

He followed her into the dining area, staring mutely at a table set for two. The crystal, china and silver patterns were exquisite. A multifaceted crystal vase held a bouquet of wispy sweet pea.

Kelly moved closer to Ryan, measuring his stunned expression. "What are you hiding behind your back?"

He blinked several times before handing her a decorative shopping bag. "This is for you."

Kelly took the bag, peering inside. She walked over to a countertop and removed two bottles of chilled red and white wine and a cellophane-wrapped plant. Nestled in a hand-painted pot was a delicate orchid plant.

"It's beautiful, Ryan." Turning, she smiled at him. "Thank you so much."

Angling his head, he returned her smile. "You're welcome."

"We'll have the white wine because I'm making chicken." Grasping his hand, she steered him toward the sofa. "Please make yourself comfortable. Everything should be ready in about ten minutes."

He stopped suddenly, and she lost her balance and bumped into him. They stood motionless, her chest pressed against his arm. Ryan stared down at her under lowered lids. "May I help you with anything?"

Kelly wanted to tell him that he could help assuage the emptiness and loneliness that plagued her whenever she opened the door to the bungalow, or readied herself for bed. Everything that was Ryan Blackstone seeped into her at that moment: his height, the breadth of his shoulders, his penetrating eyes that saw everything, his haunting scent, his deep, drawling baritone voice and the virility that made him so confidently male.

"No, thank you," she said instead.

He held her gaze. "Are you sure, Kelly?"

She felt as if she were being sucked into a sensual vortex from which there was no escape. Kelly knew at that instant she had made a mistake. She never should've invited Ryan to dinner.

She wanted him! It was an awakening realization

that left her insides pulsing like the sensations from her erotic dream. And the harder she tried to ignore the truth the more it persisted. She was a normal woman with normal sexual urges.

She had cut herself off from people for two years. At Blackstone Farms she prepared her own meals instead of eating with the other employees in the dining hall. How long, she had to ask herself, was she going to continue to mourn for what was…what would never be again?

It was apparent Ryan was attracted to her—or why else would he have kissed her? And she could honestly admit to herself that she was very attracted to him. Why else would she have invited him to her home?

"Open the wine," she said as she turned and made her way to the kitchen.

A half-smile curved Ryan's mouth as he slipped out of his jacket and laid it over the armchair. Kelly wasn't as composed as she appeared. He had counted the fast beats of her pulse in her delicate throat. He had accepted her invitation because he wanted to spend time alone with her, not frighten her. He had never been one to come on heavy with any woman. If a woman rejected his advances then he retreated honorably.

The only exception was when he'd kissed Kelly in the stable. He'd told himself it was because she had challenged him, but he knew the instant his mouth had covered hers that it was what he'd wanted to do the first time he saw her lush mouth.

Ryan picked up a corkscrew off the countertop while Kelly removed a roasting pan from the oven. The mouthwatering aroma of baked chicken filled the kitchen. "No wonder you don't eat in the dining hall," he said, his gaze fixed on a golden-brown chicken surrounded by little cubes of roast potatoes.

He removed the cork from the wine bottle with a minimum of effort, watching as Kelly transferred the chicken to a platter, surrounding it with the potatoes and rosemary sprigs for a garnish. He washed his hands in the stainless steel sink, and dried them on a terry-cloth towel.

"I'll put that on the table," he said, taking the platter from her grasp.

Kelly emptied the juices from the chicken into a gravy boat, then removed a bowl of tossed greens, chopped celery, radishes and chives from the refrigerator. Reaching for a bottle of vinaigrette dressing she shook it over the salad.

Ryan took the salad bowl and gravy boat, placing them on the table before he pulled back a chair and seated Kelly. He lingered over her head longer than was necessary, inhaling the fragrance of her perfume. The scent claimed a subtle clean freshness bursting with a warm feminine sensuality.

His mother died after a long illness the year he'd turned fourteen, and although he could recall a lot of things about Julia Blackstone, it was her perfume that he remembered most. There was never a time when she hadn't smelled wonderful. She would say that just because she lived on a horse farm it didn't mean she had to smell like a horse. His mother loved the farm while his ex-wife had hated it. Sitting down across from Kelly he wondered whether she would be like Julia or Caroline.

Kelly smiled at Ryan. "Will you please carve the chicken?"

Picking up the carving knife and fork, he cut up the fowl with the skill he demonstrated in surgical procedures. He served her, then himself before filling their glasses with the wine.

Lifting his glass in a toast, he stared at the softness of his dining partner's lush mouth. "I offer you a very *special* welcome to Blackstone Farms."

Kelly lifted her glass, smiling at him over the rim. "And I accept your special welcome." Putting the glass to her lips, she took a sip. It was excellent. "The wine is wonderful."

Ryan nodded. After a bit of cajoling, he had gotten Cook to give him a bottle from his private stock. "Now that I've seen your home I see why you eat here instead of at the dining hall." He'd found her bungalow warm, inviting, and intimate.

"I eat here because once I come home and shower I'm usually too relaxed to get up and go out again."

"Are you tired now?"

She shook her head. "Not the exhausted kind of tired."

"I know I would be if I spent all day with five energetic kids."

Blushing, Kelly speared a portion of her salad. "How was your day?"

"Uneventful. And I can assure you that I did not have as much fun as you did."

After chewing and swallowing a portion of her salad, she said, "Uneventful as in boring?"

Ryan stared at Kelly, his expression impassive. He shook his head. "Do you find living on a horse farm boring?"

"It certainly hasn't been for me. I found setting up the schoolhouse a challenge, but after meeting the children I'd willingly do it all over again."

"You like teaching?"

"I love it."

"How about the children?"

"What about them?"

"Do you like children?"

Vertical lines appeared between her dark eyes. "Of course I like children. I love them."

"Why is it you haven't had any of your own?"

"I was waiting until I was thirty."

"How old are you now?" he asked, even though he knew.

"Thirty." She and Simeon had decided to wait until

they'd celebrated their fifth wedding anniversary before starting a family.

Ryan's hands stilled as his gaze fused with hers. "Have you selected the man who will father your child?"

"Not yet."

"Are you looking?"

"I wasn't."

"And now?"

Kelly took another sip of wine, choosing her words carefully. "Now that I've set up the school I'll have more time for a social life."

"You expect to find a baby's daddy at Blackstone Farms?"

"No, Ryan," she countered in a quiet voice. "If a man fathers my child, whether it is someone here or elsewhere, he will not be my baby's daddy but my husband."

He measured her with a cool appraising look, finding everything about her perfect. "Are you looking for candidates?"

Kelly laughed, the sound low, husky, and sensual. "Why, Ryan? Are you applying?"

His gray eyes darkened at the same time he lifted a shoulder. "Maybe."

She was shocked by the smoldering invitation in the gray pools. There was no doubt he was as physically attracted to her as she was to him. But it had to be more than sex. That she could get from any man. What Kelly wanted was love *and* passion. She concentrated on the food on the plate in front of her, feeling the heat from Ryan's gaze monitor her every motion.

"Well, Kelly?"

Her head came up. "Well what, Ryan?"

"Will you consider me as a candidate?"

"Why?" she asked, answering his question with one of her own.

He placed his hands, palms down, on the lace tablecloth. "Why? Because I like you—"

"But you don't know me," she said, interrupting him.

"And you don't know me. I only know what my father has told me about you. I know you're a widow and a teacher, while I'm a divorced father of a four-year-old son who wouldn't know his mother if she sat down next to him.

"I've never brought a woman around Sean because I know how much he wants a mother like the other kids. I don't want to give him false hopes that the woman his father is dating will become his new mother."

"And you're saying it would be different with us?"

Ryan nodded. "Yes. I could court you without Sean becoming confused about our relationship."

Kelly held up a hand. "Who said anything about a relationship?"

His eyes crinkled as he smiled. "There will never be a relationship if you won't let me court you."

"Why me and not some other woman, Ryan?"

"I don't know."

"We may see each other a few times, then decide it's not going to work," she argued softly.

"If that's the case then we'll remain friends."

Kelly wanted to tell Ryan that women did not have male friends who looked like him. Either he would be a lover or nothing. What he was proposing sounded like a sterile business arrangement, but then wasn't that was what marriage was? It was an agreement between two people to love each other forever.

But she and Ryan did not love each other. They hardly knew each other. What she did have was a year in which to get to know him. And if it didn't work then she would leave Blackstone Farms Day School to teach somewhere else.

"Okay, Ryan. I'm willing to try it."

Pushing back his chair, he stood up and rounded the table. Curving a hand under Kelly's elbow, he pulled her gently to her feet. His large hand spanned her waist as he pulled her close.

He studied her upturned face, seeing indecision in her brown eyes. He hadn't lied to her. He did like her. Unknowingly she had shattered the barrier he had erected after Caroline rejected the child they'd created. Kelly had loved and lost like he had loved and lost. The difference was her loss had been final.

"I promise not to hurt you, Kelly."

She placed her fingertips over his mouth, while shaking her head. "No promises, Ryan."

"No promises," he whispered, repeating her plea. Lowering his head, he brushed his mouth over hers, sealing their agreement.

Kelly felt her breasts grow heavy against the hardness of his chest. If she had been in her right mind she would've questioned why she had just agreed to become involved with a man who was a stranger, a man on whose property she would live for the next year, and a man whose son was a student of hers.

All of her common sense dissipated like a puff of smoke as he staked his claim on her mouth and heart. She snuggled closer, leaving an imprint of her body on his. Ryan's hands moved from her waist to her hips, his splayed fingers pulling her against the solid bulge between his powerful thighs.

Pleasure, pure and explosive shook Kelly, leaving her trembling like a withered leaf in an icy blizzard when his tongue slipped between her lips. Her arms tightened around his neck, making him her willing prisoner.

Returning his kiss with reckless abandon, she moaned softly when he left her mouth to leave a series of light kisses down the column of her neck and over her shoulders. Eyes closed, head thrown back, she moaned again. The pulsing between her legs grew stronger and stronger, and she knew if she did not stop she would beg him to take her to her bed where she would play out her dream in the real world.

Somewhere, somehow she found the strength to pull out of Ryan's embrace. Her breasts were rising and falling heavily, bringing his gaze to linger on her chest. His head came up, and she bit down on her lower lip to keep from gasping aloud. The passion radiating from Ryan's eyes caused her knees to weaken. Reaching for her chair, she managed to sit without collapsing to the floor. He did not know her and she did not know him, yet the passion between them was strong and frightening.

Ryan sat down and picked up his wineglass, emptying it with one swallow. The cool liquid bathed his throat and body temporarily. He looked down at the delicious meal Kelly had prepared, unable to finish eating because she had lit a fire in him, a fire only she would be able to extinguish.

He wanted her in his bed, but he was willing to wait for her to come to him. After all, they had time, a lot of time....

Chapter Six

Kelly lay on a cushioned wicker love seat on the porch, her head resting on Ryan's chest. Raising her right leg, she wiggled her toes. She had left her sandals in the kitchen. She and Ryan had barely touched their dinner after the kiss. He'd helped her clear the table and wash and dry the dishes, and she'd suggested they sit out on the porch where it was safer than remaining indoors.

"What made you decide to become a veterinarian?"

Ryan rested his chin on the top of her head. "I've always loved horses and science, and becoming a vet was the logical choice. Also, I knew one day I would inherit the horse farm from my father, as it was with him and his father."

"You'll be the third generation Blackstone to run the farm?"

"Yes. And hopefully Sean will become the fourth."

"What about your brother?"

"Jeremy has no interest in horses. Pop refers to Jeremy as his vagabond progeny. My younger brother would lose his mind if he had to stay here more than a month."

"How did the Blackstones become horse breeders?"

"My granddaddy was a white tobacco farmer who fell in love with a young black woman who had come to work for him as his cook. They couldn't marry or live openly as husband and wife because of Virginia's miscegenation laws. But she did give him a son. When James Blackstone died he left everything to Sheldon. Grandpa had grown tobacco for about twenty years, but after my grandmother died from lung cancer from a two-pack-a-day cigarette habit, he harvested his last tobacco crop and decided to raise horses."

"Did he breed them to race?"

"No. He raised working breeds like the Welsh Cob, horses known for their hardiness and strength. He sold them to farmers and for riding. My father brought his first Thoroughbred several years after he'd married my mother. Within ten years he was racing competitively."

What he did not tell Kelly was that his mother was an only child of a wealthy Charleston, South Carolina black family, and that his parents had used her inheritance to establish the largest and most successful African-American-owned horse farm in the state of Virginia.

"I know nothing about horses or racing," Kelly admitted. "In fact, I've never been to a racetrack."

Ryan's forehead furrowed. "You've never watched our trainers exercising the horses?"

"No."

"If you don't have anything planned for Saturday, then I'll have Kevin Manning show you how he trains horses for races."

"Do you go to the races?"

Ryan hesitated. During his short marriage, the only time Caroline had deigned to grace him with her presence was at a horse race. "Yes."

Shifting slightly, Kelly gazed up at him. A shaft of sunlight hit his face, turning him into a statue of molten gold. Turning his head quickly, he glanced at her and she shuddered noticeably from the intensity of his stare. The large gray eyes glowed with an inner fire that ignited a spark of longing that left her gasping.

Ryan returned his gaze to the sprawling landscape in front of Kelly's bungalow. The homes for resident employees were constructed far enough apart to allow absolute privacy.

The fingers of his right hand traced the outline of Kelly's ear. "If I'd come back earlier I would've taken you to the Virginia Gold Cup. It's held the first Saturday in May at Great Meadow near The Plains. The Great Meadow also hosts the International Gold Cup the third Saturday in October."

"Isn't the Kentucky Derby run the first Saturday in May?"

He chuckled. "I thought you knew nothing about horseracing?"

"I do know the date for the Kentucky Derby," she said defensively. "How many winners has Blackstone Farms produced?"

Kelly listened intently as Ryan listed the races, the names of the horses and their jockeys who'd worn the black and red silks of Blackstone Farms into the winner circle. He explained domestic horses were bred in many different races and were grouped as ponies, heavy draft horses, lightweight draft and riding horses.

"Barbs and Arabs, the two most popular riding horses, originated from North African stock. Thoroughbreds are descended from Arabians."

She thought of the colt she went to see most mornings. "Jahan is the most exquisite horse I've ever seen."

"We call him our black diamond. Everyone

connected with the farm believes he's going to become a champion."

"What do you believe, Ryan?"

He wanted to tell Kelly that he liked her, liked her more than he dared admit. He wanted to tell her that something about her kept him a little off center. That he found himself thinking about her when he least expected. That he thought about her when he retired for bed and when he woke up.

"I believe if he stays healthy, he will stand in many a winner circle," he said instead. "Have you ever ridden?"

"No." She laughed. "Remember, I'm a city girl."

"Do you want to learn?"

"Yes," she said, refusing to think of the consequences if she fell off a horse.

"Don't worry, we have a few Thoroughbreds with Irish Draught and native pony blood. They're less high-strung and more suitable for a novice rider like you."

"Do the children ride?"

"Most of them sit a horse by the time they're walking. One of the boys who was born on the farm is now a jockey."

"How old is he?"

"Nineteen.

Staring up at him, she gave him a saucy grin. "By the way, how old are you?"

"Thirty-four."

"I suppose you're not too old to court me."

"How old did you think I was?"

"At least forty."

"No!"

"Well, you do have gray hair."

"Come on, Kelly, cut me some slack."

"That's hard when my first impression of you was that of a *doof* ball.

"Doof ball," he murmured under his breath. "Is that anything like a doofus?"

She nodded, clapping her hands. "Bravo! You just scored another A."

He glared down at her. "You've got a real smart mouth." Grasping her shoulders, he shifted her to sit on his lap. "If you play, then you have to pay. Are you prepared to pay, Kelly?"

She stared at him through her lashes. "That all depends on the game, Ryan."

He lowered his head. "Have you ever played *for keeps?*"

"No."

"Then I'm going to have to teach you," he whispered seconds before his mouth covered hers.

His kiss was slow, deliberate and methodical. It was gentle and persuasive. Healing. Exploratory. Drugging. Desire sang in Kelly's veins as she parted her lips, sampling and tasting the texture of the tongue exploring her mouth. His left hand moved up between her thighs, burning her bared flesh as her breathing deepened.

As quickly as it had begun it ended when he pulled back. And what she saw would be imprinted on her brain until she ceased breathing. The color in Ryan's eyes shimmered like a newly minted silver dollar. His eyes changed color with his moods, and instead of darkening with desire, his eyes turned into pools of liquid lightning.

Kelly tried to slow the runaway beating of her heart. "I think you'd better go *now* before we do something we may regret later." Her husky voice had lowered an octave.

Ryan slowly shook his head. "No, Kelly. I never do things I later regret."

Her senses were reeling as if her nervous system had been short-circuited by a powerful jolt of electricity. She hadn't known Ryan a week, yet he had lit a fire of desire she thought long dead.

Sitting upright, she pushed off his lap and stood up. Hands on her hips, she watched him stand. His body language was measured, precise. It was as if Ryan was in control of his life and everything in it.

Rising on tiptoe, she kissed his cheek. "I forgot something."

"What's that?"

"I forgot to apologize for closing the door in your face."

He lifted an eyebrow. "There's no need to apologize."

"But you told me you expected an apology."

"That was before you agreed to date me."

She nodded. "Good night, Ryan."

Bending over, he pressed a kiss under her ear. "Good night, princess."

He walked off the porch to where he had parked his car. He knew he had to slow down, not frighten Kelly. After all, they had a year to get to know each other.

I'm crazy. I've lost my mind, Kelly told herself over and over on the short drive to the schoolhouse. She had spent a restless night replaying her conversation with Ryan the night before.

She had also thought of herself as sensible and practical. When all of the girls she had grown up with were experimenting with alcohol, drugs and sex, it was Kelly Andrews who did not succumb to peer pressure. Why had she permitted Ryan to talk her into a situation in which she was not certain of the outcome?

She might be frustrated—after all, she was undergoing a sexual drought—but that did not mean she should contemplate sleeping with her boss's son. Kelly was certain she was certifiably *C-R-A-Z-Y!*

She parked her car and walked toward the entrance to the schoolhouse. Her step slowed when she saw a man at the door, waiting for her. Her car was the only one in the lot, which meant he had walked. She recognized his face, but not his name.

Smiling, Kelly said, "Good morning."

Snatching a battered straw hat from his head, he held it to his chest. "Good morning, Miss Kelly." He extended a hand. "I don't know if you remember me. Mark Charlesworth, ma'am."

She shook his hand. Although his clothes, his hands and clothes were clean, he smelled of the stables. "What can I do for you, Mark?"

He lowered his head, and a profusion of dreadlocks swept over his broad shoulders. "Can we talk, Miss Kelly? Inside?"

"Sure." She unlocked the door and pushed it open. A blast of hot air assaulted her as soon as she walked in. She had neglected to adjust the thermostat. Moving quickly, she pressed several buttons on a wall. Within seconds, the fan for the cooling system was activated.

"We can sit over there." Kelly gestured to the sitting area.

Mark followed Kelly, waiting until she sat down before he took a chair opposite her. Rolling the brim of his battered hat between long, brown fingers, he stared down at the floor.

Kelly waited for him to speak. The seconds ticked by. "Yes, Mark?"

His head came up and he stared at her with large, soulful dark eyes. "I need your help, Miss Kelly."

Leaning forward on her chair, she nodded. "How can I help you?"

"I want to go to college, but I don't know if I can pass the test the college says I need to get in."

She smiled. "You want me to tutor you?"

He smiled for the first time, showing a mouth filled with large white teeth. "Yes, ma'am."

"How old are you, Mark?"

"Twenty-two."

"Do you have a high school diploma?"

"Yes, ma'am. I dropped out at sixteen, but I went back and finished up last year. My dad said if I passed the test to get into a college he would pay for me to go."

"What do you want to be?"

He dropped his head again. "I'm not sure. I know I don't want to muck out stables for the rest of my life."

"Good for you." Kelly paused. "I'll help you."

Mark leaned forward and grasped her hands. "Thank you, Miss Kelly."

She winced as he increased the pressure on her fingers. "You can let go of my hand now." He released her hand, mumbling an apology. "If I'm going to tutor you, then it will have to be in the evenings."

He bobbed his head. "Yes, ma'am."

"Do you have any SAT practice books?"

"No, ma'am," he said quickly. "If you want I can pick up some."

"No, Mark. I'll buy them. I have an account with a company in Richmond that specializes in educational materials and equipment. I'll call and have the books sent to me at the school."

"But I'll still pay for it."

Shaking her head, Kelly said in a quiet voice, "Save your money, Mark. I'm certain Blackstone Farms will not be forced to file for bankruptcy because I charged a few review manuals to their account. As soon as they arrive I'll get in touch with you so we can arrange a schedule that will be conducive to both of us. Do you live here on the farm?"

"Yes, ma'am."

Kelly stood up, Mark rising with her. "I'll meet you in the dining hall, and we'll talk."

He closed his eyes, inhaled, and then let out his breath slowly. When he opened his eyes they were glistening with moisture. "I'd like to ask another favor, Miss Kelly."

She arched an eyebrow. "Ask."

He managed a sheepish grin. "I don't want anyone to know you're tutoring me."

Nodding, Kelly said, "It will remain our secret."

"Thank you, Miss Kelly."

"Thank me after you get an acceptance letter from a college."

"Thank you," he repeated before he turned on his heels and walked quickly out of the building.

Kelly felt a warm glow flow through her. She had come to Blackstone Farms to teach the preschool children of its employees, but there was nothing in her contract that precluded her extending her teaching skills to the farm's employees.

All of the children arrived by eight o'clock. They babbled excitedly about going swimming. Kelly had promised them the day before that if the morning temperature rose above seventy degrees, they could go swimming before lunch.

Sheldon motioned to Kelly. "I'll be bringing Sean for the next few days. Ryan had to take a mare to Richmond late last night for surgery."

"What happened?"

"He had to repair a bone spavin." Sheldon noted Kelly's puzzled expression, reminding himself she hadn't lived on the horse farm long enough to become familiar with equine terminology. "That's when there is an indefinite hind-lameness that shortens a horse's stride."

"Will she be all right?"

"Ryan says her chances of recovery are at least ninety percent."

"Ryan told me that all of the children ride." Sheldon nodded. "But do they know exactly what everyone who works at the farm does?"

Sheldon's silver-colored eyes narrowed as he angled his head. "I don't know."

Kelly lifted her dimpled chin and smiled up at Sheldon, unaware of how attractive she was. "I'd like to set up a field trip. I'd like to take the children on a tour of the property to see firsthand what makes up a working horse farm. I want them to talk to the grooms, trainers, the people who put up and repair fences, cut the grass, muck out the stables and bale hay. I'd even like to give them a tour of the kitchen. It will help them to appreciate where they live and the importance of their parents' jobs."

Sheldon flashed one of his rare smiles. "Let me know when you want to do it, and I'll set it up."

"How about next week?"

"Monday is a holiday, so that's out. By the way, we always have big outdoor doings to celebrate Memorial Day, Fourth of July and Labor Day."

Kelly mentally filed this information. "What if we do it over four days? An hour for each presentation should be enough. Any more time than that will challenge their attention span, especially since they know everyone."

"You're right about that. Kids growing up on a farm tend to know a lot more than city kids when it comes to things like birth and reproduction, but we have strict rules about keeping kids away from the mares in heat. Seeing a stallion mount a mare can be an awesome sight for a child, especially if they believe he's hurting her."

Waves of heat warmed Kelly's cheeks. She'd seen dogs and cats mate, but not horses. "Thanks for your cooperation."

"Don't mention it," Sheldon said as he left.

One of the kitchen personnel walked in with breakfast, and the children raced over to the sink to wash their hands as Kelly smiled at her charges. They were so eager to learn and to please. She had bonded quickly with them, refusing to think of the time when she would be forced to let them go.

The wall telephone rang, and she rushed over to answer it. "Blackstone Day School, Miss Kelly speaking."

"Good morning, Miss Kelly."

Her heart leapt, turning over when she heard the deep, drawling voice. "Hi, Ryan."

"How are you?"

"Good." She wanted to tell him she was very good now that she'd heard his voice. "Sheldon told me about the mare."

"Peachy Keen is still in recovery, but I expect her to come through okay. She stopped racing several years ago, so we've used her exclusively for breeding purposes. Thankfully she has already foaled two colts, both of which could be potential winners."

Kelly smiled. "That's good for Blackstone Farms."

"You've got that right. I'll probably be here until

the end of the week. I want to wait to bring her back."
There was a noticeable pause. "If you're not busy on
Friday, I'd like to take you out for dinner."

Kelly wrinkled her nose. Ryan was asking her out.
Finally her sister could stop haranguing her about
not dating. "I have to check my calendar, but I believe I should be able to put aside a few hours for
you Friday evening, Dr. Blackstone."

His sensual laugh came through the wire. "Still
with the quick tongue? I believe I have the perfect
remedy to take care of your tongue."

"Really?" she teased.

"Yes, *really,* Kelly."

"Hang up, Ryan."

"You first."

"Bye." Depressing the hook, she ended the call.
A dreamy smile settled into her features, one that
lingered throughout the day.

Chapter Seven

Sean sat on the padded bench at the foot of his father's bed, watching Ryan loop the length of a dark brown tie into a knot under the collar of a white shirt. "Do I have to sleep at Grandpa's tonight?"

Ryan caught his son's reflection in the mirror over a triple dresser. He tightened the tie, then turned to stare at Sean. "Yes, Sean."

The young boy stuck out his lower lip. "But, Daddy," he wailed.

"No whining, Sean. What is it you want?"

"I want to sleep over with Travis and Trent. They are having a Spider-Man party tonight."

"They may be having a party, but were you invited?"

"Yes, Daddy. They invited everybody from school. Even Miss Kelly."

Ryan studied his son's deeply tanned face and smiled. Sean had talked nonstop about what he did with Miss Kelly and the other kids at school during the time Ryan was in Richmond. He said he could read a lot of words, could count up to one hundred and match shapes and colors.

"Go get your sleeping bag while I call Miss Millie."

Sean jumped off the bench and raced out of the bedroom. Ryan picked up the telephone and dialed the number to the twins' house. Millicent Smith answered the call after the first ring.

"Hi, Millie. This is Ryan. I'm calling about the Spider-Man sleepover at your place tonight."

"Doc, I really need to have my head examined for agreeing to this," Millie drawled.

He smiled. "So, it's on?"

"Yeah. Drop Sean off at the dining hall and we'll bring him back with us."

"What time do you want me to pick him up in the morning?"

"Don't bother to pick him up. The kids don't have school tomorrow, and if the hot weather holds we'll probably hang out at the pool most of the day."

"You know if he gets to be too much for you just bring him back to Sheldon."

"Dr. Blackstone, you have the most well-behaved child on the farm. If my boys were half as good as Sean I'd consider myself blessed."

Ryan wanted to tell Millie that she *was* blessed. She had two bright, healthy sons. A parent couldn't ask for more than that. "They're boys, Millie."

"That's what Jim says. Thanks for letting Sean come."

"No problem, Millie."

"Bye, Doc."

Ryan rang off, then picked up the jacket to his suit, slipping his arms into the sleeves. He walked out of his bedroom and into Sean's across the hall. The boy was busy putting out changes of clothes on his bed. He watched as Sean took out socks, briefs, T-shirts and shorts.

Sean glanced up at his father. "Is that enough?"

Nodding, Ryan smiled. "Yes."

Sean picked up a backpack and put the clothes inside. After zipping the colorful bag, he hoisted it over one shoulder, then picked up a small duffel bag containing his sleeping bag.

"Are you ready, Champ?"

The little boy puffed out his narrow chest. "Yes, Daddy."

Ryan had taught Sean independence early. He had learned to select the clothes he would wear for the next day, laying them out the night before. He had to keep his room clean by picking up his toys and books. He knew he had to brush his teeth twice a day, wash his hands before and after meals, and say his prayers before he went to sleep.

Ryan cupped the back of his son's head, leading him down the staircase and out of the house. "I'm going to drop you off at Grandpa's."

Sean looked up at Ryan. "You're not going to eat with us?"

"No, Sean. I'm going out to eat."

"Who you eating with, Daddy?"

"Miss Kelly." He'd never lied to his son, and he did not want to begin now.

"She's pretty, Daddy. She's pretty like a princess."

"You're right about that, son."

"You like her, Daddy?"

"Yes, Sean, I like her."

"I like her, too. Isn't it good we both like her?"

"Yes it is."

Ryan wanted to tell Sean that what he felt for Kelly went beyond a simple liking. What he wanted was to see her—every day. He wanted to hold her close and feel her feminine heat, inhale her feminine fragrance. He wanted that and so much more.

He led Sean up the steps of the porch to the house where he'd grown up. The inner door stood open, as it did every day until Sheldon closed it to retire for the night. He held the screen door open for Sean.

"Grandpa!" Sean's strident voice echoed in the large living room.

Sheldon came from the direction of his study. It once had been called the family room. A network of lines fanned out around his eyes. He saw Sean's backpack and sleeping bag.

"Where are you going tonight?"

"I'm going to eat with you, then I'm sleeping over with Travis and Trent. We are going to have a Spider-Man party."

Sheldon's head came up and he stared at Ryan, who nodded. "Good for you."

Sean turned and stared at his father. "But Daddy's eating with Miss Kelly."

Sheldon angled his head, grinning. "Boo-yaw!"

"Boo-yaw to you, too," Ryan mumbled, while trying not to laugh. "I'll see you guys tomorrow."

"Have fun," Sheldon called out.

"Yeah, Daddy. Have fun with Miss Kelly."

Ryan walked out of his father's house head high, and his step lighter than it had been in years. And it had been years since he really looked forward to sharing time with a woman, especially one as sexy as Kelly Andrews.

The week had passed quickly for Kelly and her students. They'd frolicked and splashed in the in-ground kiddie pool before they were served a picnic lunch under a large tent. Everyone napped, then swam again. When the parents came to pick up their sons and daughters later that afternoon all remarked how tanned and healthy they looked.

On Thursday Heather brought a kitten to school to show off her new pet. Miss Buttons had caused a stir when she jumped on the table to press her tiny nose against the fish tank. Kelly had to issue her first mandate: no pets in school.

It was now late Friday afternoon and she lay in the bathtub, eyes closed, and her hair wrapped in a silk scarf. A soft sponge pillow cradled her head. She had just completed her first full week teaching, and had almost forgotten how much energy it took to keep up with preschoolers. The only time they were still and quiet was at naptime.

The doorbell rang and she jumped, opening her eyes. "He can't be here!" she gasped. Ryan had called her earlier that afternoon to inform her he would come by to pick her up at six. Rising quickly, she stepped out of the tub, splashing water onto the tiled floor. She reached for a bath sheet, wrapped it around her wet body, and walked out of the bathroom.

She hadn't taken half a dozen steps when she saw him. Kelly sucked in her breath. Ryan stood in the middle of her parlor, dressed in an ecru-colored suit that made him look like a *GQ* cover model. His black hair was neatly brushed off his forehead and his deeply tanned gold-brown skin radiated good health. But it was his eyes—a smoky-gray that pulled her in and refused to let her go.

"Did you know that you left your door open?"

Her eyelids fluttered as she shook her head. She couldn't remember whether she had closed or locked the door. "I must be slipping. That never would've happened back in New York. By the way, what are you doing here so early?" Her voice had dropped to a whisper.

"I told you I'd be here at six."

"But…but it's not six."

Extending his left arm, the face on his timepiece showed beneath the starched cuff of his stark-white shirt. The hands indicated that it was exactly six o'clock.

Clutching the towel over her breasts, Kelly wrinkled her nose. "I'm sorry, Ryan. I must have lost track of time." She backpedaled, unable to believe she had fallen asleep in the bathtub. "Please excuse me while I put some clothes on."

A mysterious smiled curved Ryan's mouth. "Please…don't," he said in a quiet voice. "I happen to like what you're wearing."

Kelly stared at him. "I'm not wearing anything."

His eyes widened until she saw their sooty centers. "Exactly."

Her heart pounded an erratic rhythm as she turned on her heel and rushed into her bedroom, slamming the door behind her. The clothes she had selected to wear lay across the bed.

Trying not to think of the man waiting in her parlor, she patted her body dry, moisturized her skin with a perfumed cream, dotted a matching scent at her pulse points, then slipped into her underwear and dress. It took another fifteen minutes to apply a powdered bronzer to the face, feather her eyebrows, apply a coat of mascara to her lashes and outline her mouth with a shimmering red lipstick.

She removed the scarf and pins holding her hairdo. Lowering her head, she brushed her hair forward off the nape of her neck and flipped it back until it settled into layered precision around her face and neck. Taking one last glance at her reflection in the mirror on the door inside the armoire, she slipped into her heels and picked up her evening purse. She walked into the parlor to find Ryan standing where she had left him.

It had taken only three days away from Kelly— only seventy-two hours for Ryan to realize how much he'd missed her. He knew nothing about her other than what he saw, but that was enough for him want her with an emotion that bordered on craving.

There was so much he wanted to share with her, yet he knew it was too soon in their relationship to make his desires known. He wasn't a boy, hadn't been one in twenty years, yet his need to share her bed exceeded any he had ever known in his life.

He watched her move closer, unable to take his gaze off her face and slender body that was show-cased in a slim black tank dress. He measured each step she took in a pair of black, three-inch, sling strap sandals.

Moving closer, he placed his hand on her bared back. Peering over her shoulder he went suddenly still. He wasn't certain whether the back of the dress—what there was of it, began or ended just inches below the small of her back.

He grimaced at the same time he gritted his teeth. "Aren't you going to need a shawl or something for your shoulders?"

A smile trembled over her lips. "Nope."

"It might get cold."

She cut her eyes at him. "The temperature hit ninety today." Curving an arm through his, she smiled sweetly at him. "I'm sorry I made us late. Let's go."

"If any man looks sideways at you he's going to get a serious beat-down," Ryan mumbled under his breath.

Kelly frowned at him. "What did you say about a beat-down?"

"Nothing," he mumbled again, leading her to the door. Taking her keys from her hand, he closed and locked the door. He slipped the keys into the pocket of his trousers.

Ryan caught a glimpse of Kelly's bared back, admiring the silkiness of her dark brown skin. A lighter band of color showed beneath the narrow straps on her velvety shoulders. He smiled. It was obvious she had gone swimming with her students.

He opened the door to a low-slung two-seater black convertible sports car, waiting until Kelly was seated and belted in before he removed his jacket and placed it on the narrow space behind the seats. He sat down, put the key in the ignition, and the engine purred to life. Pressing a button he raised the top, adjusted the flow of cooling air coming through the vents, and pulled away from Kelly's home with a burst of speed.

Resting her head against the leather headrest, Kelly closed her eyes, enjoying the surge of power propelling the car forward. "Where are we going?"

"To an inn in West Virginia."

She opened her eyes and stared at Ryan's profile. "West Virginia?"

"It's not that far. It's a quaint little place in the mountains."

"Mountains as in Appalachian?"

"Yes, ma'am."

Those were the last two words they exchanged until more than an hour later Ryan maneuvered into a parking lot of a hotel and restaurant that had been built into the side of a mountain.

A valet opened the driver side door for Ryan, handing him a ticket while Ryan reached for his jacket, putting it on as he came around to assist Kelly. His right arm curved around her waist and he led her to the entrance of the restaurant.

Kelly felt as if she had stepped back into the nineteenth century when she surveyed the Victorian furnishings. The maître d' directed them to a table in a corner where a quartet of large painted urns provided a modicum of privacy.

Ryan ignored the menu and wine listing on the table; he stared at Kelly's face in the golden glow of flickering candlelight. The nostrils of his aquiline nose flared slightly. "Did I tell you how beautiful you look tonight?" Her lids lowered, the demure gesture enchanting him.

"No." She glanced up, meeting his heated gaze. "But you could've told me that back at the house."

"No, I couldn't, Kelly."

"Why not?"

"Because I don't think we would've left the house."

Unconsciously her brow furrowed. "What are you talking about?"

"I would've asked if you would let me make love to you."

She gasped softly. "Is that what you want to do, Ryan? Make love to me?"

Reaching across the table, he captured her hands. "Yes."

Kelly felt her stomach muscles contract. There was so much passion in the single word that she found it hard to swallow. Her breasts rose and fell heavily, bringing his gaze to linger there.

Could she tell him? Did she dare reveal what lay in her heart? That she also wanted him. Had wanted him the first time he'd held her in his arms after she had fallen off the stepladder.

"I do, too," she admitted in a voice so soft Ryan found it difficult to believe what he was hearing. "However, there is a part of me that says becoming physically involved with you will change me, change everything."

He tightened his grip on her fingers. "How, Kelly?"

"I…I don't want to forget Simeon. And I know once I sleep with you he will no longer exist for me."

"Simeon is your late husband?" She nodded. "Do you still love him?"

She smiled a sad smile. "I'll always love him."

"There's nothing wrong in loving him. But he's gone. And if he loved you as much as you loved him, then I believe he would want you to be happy."

Moisture shimmered in her eyes. "Do you think you can you make me happy, Ryan?"

He made love to her with his eyes. "Only you can make that possible."

Kelly shook her head. "I don't understand."

"Not only do you have to love with your head, but also with your heart. Loving has to be both, not one or the other."

She sniffled, and Ryan reached into a pocket and produced a snow-white handkerchief. Moving his chair closer to hers, he held her chin and dabbed her eyes. Resting his forehead against hers, he kissed the end of her nose.

"You're not the only one hurting, princess. I've been there, too. I fell in love with a girl I'd met in college. After graduating we went our separate ways, then one day out of the blue she called me. I invited her to the farm and she was caught up in the prerace excitement and parties. Blackstone Farms had entered a horse in the Virginia Gold Cup. Miss Fancy Pants was a twenty-to-one long shot, but we still had a lot of faith in her because she had heart. Our horse won, and that night Pop threw a party to end all parties. Caroline and I celebrated in our own special way, and the next day we announced our engagement.

"We had a September wedding, and by December she discovered she was pregnant. That's when everything changed. She became depressed and talked about aborting the baby." Ryan ignored Kelly's audible inhalation. "I was forced to watch her around the clock because I thought she was going to…" His words trailed off.

"Take her own life," Kelly said softly, completing his statement.

He nodded. "She said she hated me and hated living on the farm. She cried that she was being smothered to death and wanted to go back to Los Angeles. Caroline carried to term, but when she went into labor she made me promise to either give her a divorce or she would kill herself. I know I probably could've had her committed, but I agreed on one condition. She could leave, but she could not take my son. I refused to jeopardize his life with a woman who had proven herself to be emotionally unstable.

"I had my lawyer draw up the agreement before she left the hospital. Sean was two months old when she got into her car and drove away. I loved her, Kelly. Loved her enough to let her go so that she could find her happiness."

Kelly laid her head on Ryan's shoulder. "You've had your share of pain."

Curving an arm around her bare shoulder, he pulled her closer. "That's true, but I've learned not to wallow in it. There comes a time for healing."

Kelly knew he was talking about her. She had been wallowing in her pain for two years, accepting it as readily as breathing and sleeping.

"You want me, Ryan, knowing I'm still carrying baggage? Knowing that I'm not ready to offer you what you feel you deserve from a woman?" She sucked in her breath. "I haven't slept with a man in two years, and what I miss most is the intimacy." There was a sob in her voice. "Are you willing to accept me giving you my body without offering my heart?"

Ryan eased back, his gaze meeting her tortured one. He did want her, more than any other woman in his past. "You fascinate me, Kelly," he confessed. "I don't know whether it is your beauty, spunk or your intelligence. And I have no right to demand or expect you to offer me anything. What I will accept is anything you're willing to give me."

Her lids slipped down over her eyes as her lips parted. Ryan angled his head and slanted a kiss on her mouth, silently acknowledging the terms of their agreement. The kiss ended and they exchanged a knowing smile.

Ryan blew out his breath. "I don't know about you, but I could use a drink right about now."

Closing her eyes, Kelly sighed softly. "I could use one, too."

Chapter Eight

"An apple martini?"

Kelly rested her chin on the heel of her hand. "Yes, Ryan, an apple martini. It's the rage in New York City."

He stared at her animated features, smiling. The tears that had filled her eyes when she had spoken about her late husband had vanished. They had reached the point where their relationship had to be resolved. Kelly wanted him to make love to her, and he would but only when the time was right. What he did not want was anything planned or staged. He wanted spontaneity.

Curving a hand around her neck, he wound his

fingers through her hair. "It must be a girlie girl con-coction. A real martini is vodka or gin, not some sissy-tasting apple liqueur."

Smiling up at him through her lashes, Kelly shook her head. "Girlie girl?"

"Yes," he whispered against her lips. "You are the ultimate girlie girl."

"I stopped being a girl a long time ago," she crooned.

Ryan's hand went from her neck to her back. His fingers trailed down her spine, eliciting a shudder from her. "Wrong, princess. You're a woman-girl." He lowered his head and kissed the nape of her scented neck.

His mouth longed to follow the direction of his hand down the length of her spine. He wanted to taste Kelly—all over—until he gorged on her lush flesh.

Kelly felt the heat from Ryan's body seep into hers, it igniting an inferno between her legs. Her body began to vibrate with liquid fire, and she gasped softly as her flesh pulsed with a need that bordered on insanity.

Ryan's sensitive nostrils caught the scent of her rising passion, and he stared at the sensuality part-ing her full lips and dilating her pupils. Their waiter approached the table, carrying their drink order.

Kelly barely noticed the waiter placing her drink in front of her because of the hardness of the thigh brushing against hers. Her whole being was flooded with a desire she hadn't known she possessed. *It's been a long time,* she mused. It had been a long time since the mere presence of a man had her quaking with desire.

Reaching for the icy glass with the pale green liquid, Ryan took a sip of Kelly's drink. It slid down his throat, cooling it before a warming spread in his chest. "Nice."

She picked up his tumbler filled with the concoctions for a Rob Roy, taking furtive sips. She grimaced. "Now, that's strong."

Handing Kelly her martini, he said, "It's definitely not Kool-Aid." He put the tumbler to his lips and drank deeply.

"Ryan?" Her voice was a mere whisper.

"Yes."

"Do we have to eat here?"

His sweeping eyebrows lifted. "Where do you want to eat?"

"Upstairs."

"You want to check into a room?"

She gave him a long, penetrating stare. "Yes."

Long, black lashes concealed the intensity in his gunmetal-gray eyes as he nodded. "Wait here while I register at the desk."

Kelly nodded, then slumped back to the cushioned softness of her chair. It was about to begin. She was ready to move forward, turn a corner and leave her past behind her. She would always love Simeon, but she knew she had to take a chance at finding love again, and that would only become possible if she looked forward. She had finished her drink when Ryan returned.

He helped her to her feet, cradling her against his side as he led her toward the elevator. His large hand covered the small of her back, fingers splayed over the roundness of her hips.

A tall, flaxen-haired man who looked as if he'd just left an Icelandic ski slope joined them at the elevator. Rocking back on his heels, he stared at Kelly's bared back. *"D-a-a-m-n-n!"* he gasped, drawing out the word.

Ryan's head snapped around, and he glared at the blond giant. "What's up?"

The man put up his hands at the same time he shook his head. "Nothing, man."

Dropping his arm, Ryan took off his jacket and draped it over Kelly's shoulders. The doors to the elevator opened and he escorted her into the car. He gave the man a narrow stare. "Aren't you coming?"

Kelly's admirer shook his head. "No. I'll wait for it to come down."

Ryan punched a button for the fourth floor. "Suit yourself."

Waiting until the doors closed, Kelly stared at Ryan as if he were a stranger. "What was that all about?"

Staring straight ahead, he said, "Nothing."

"Were you calling that man out?"

"Nope."

Shrugging off his jacket she handed it to him. "I'm not cold, thank you very much."

The doors opened with a soft swooshing sound, and Ryan reached for Kelly's hand. They walked the length of the carpeted hallway to a room at the end of the hall. A brass plate on the door read Skyline. He inserted the magnetic card in a slot and seconds later he opened a door to reveal an opulent suite of rooms.

This suite was designed with walls made entirely of glass. The view through the glass of the Appalachian Mountains and forested areas was breathtaking. Ryan dropped his jacket over the back of chair in the entryway.

Leaning against Ryan, Kelly bent down and slipped off her heels. Her toes disappeared in the deep pile of the plush gold carpeting. She turned into his embrace, sighing as he pulled her to his chest. Tilting her head, she smiled up at him. "It's beautiful."

The corners of his mouth curved in a half smile. "You are beautiful, Kelly."

Rising on tiptoe, she pressed her mouth to his, tasting the liquor on his lips. He deepened the kiss, his tongue slipping into her mouth.

Ryan's hands moved to cradle her round face between his palms; he willed himself to go slow. It had been a while since he had shared his bed with a woman, but nowhere as long as it had been for Kelly and a man. He left nibbling, teasing kisses at the corners of her mouth, over her eyes, along the length of her neck. His lips feather-touched her throat.

"I want you so much," he moaned against her ear.

Kelly clung to Ryan's neck like a drowning swimmer. "Then take me," she whispered hoarsely.

Bending slightly, Ryan scooped Kelly up into his arms, carrying her through the sitting room and into a bedroom with a king-size bed. The shimmering glow of the setting sun coming through the wall of glass threw shadows across the bed. Outside the shadows covering the mountains and valleys were reminiscent of the landscape pictures painted by the artists from the Hudson River School.

Cradling Kelly with one arm, Ryan pulled back a duvet and lightweight blanket to reveal a pale-yellow sheet. He lowered her gently to the mattress, his body following hers down. Gazing deeply into her clear-brown eyes, he smiled. Glints of gold sparkled as she gave him a shy smile.

He returned her smile. "I want it to be good between us." He needed it to be good because…he was falling in love with Kelly.

"Being here with you, having you hold me is good."

His fingers traced the outline of her delicate jaw.

"Don't worry about anything. I'll protect and take care of you."

She wasn't certain what he meant by the cryptic statement, but mentally dismissed it as he slipped his hands under the straps on her shoulders, easing them down and off her arms and gasping softly when he stared at her naked breasts rising and falling above her rib cage.

Her breasts were perfect. Not too large or small, they were tipped with dark chocolate-brown nipples. He undressed her slowly, his gaze burning her flesh everywhere it touched. Sitting back on his heels, he removed her dress and black lace bikini panties. Everything about her body was alluring. From her flat belly, curvy hips and long shapely legs to her flawless brown skin that gave the appearance of whipped mousse.

Kelly forced herself not to cover her body with her hands, because there was something about the way Ryan was staring at her nakedness that made her uncomfortable. Rising off the mattress, she went to her knees. "Now, it's my turn," she whispered, her mouth touching his.

Ryan did not move, not even his eyes, as he permitted Kelly to undress him. His breathing quickened as she slipped off his tie and unbuttoned his shirt. Moving closer, her breasts touching his chest, she reached up and pushed the shirt off his shoulders. He did close his eyes once she unbuckled the belt

around his waist. By the time she undid the waistband and unzipped his trousers, he felt the constric-
tion in his chest.

Kelly felt the rising heat from Ryan's body like
the steam in a sauna. It intensified the natural masculine scent and the sensual fragrance of his cologne.
He pushed her hands away, slipped off the bed and
finished undressing.

She stared at the broad expanse of his chest covered with a profusion of black hair. Seeing Ryan
like this reminded her of how different he was from
Simeon. Wherein Simeon was only several inches
taller than she was, Ryan exceeded her five-foot,
eight-inch height by at least six inches. Simeon's coloring was dark, while Ryan's was golden-brown.
Simeon's body was smooth, unlike the crisp black
hair covering Ryan's chest, arms and legs.

She would not let her gaze venture below his
waist after she'd glimpsed the thick, heavy organ
nestled between his powerful thighs. Ryan wasn't
fully aroused, yet he was huge! The mattress dipped
when he joined her on the bed. She closed her eyes.

Ryan eased her down to a pillow. "Look at me,
darling." She complied and slowly opened her eyes.
Curving his arms around her waist, he shifted her
until she lay over his chest, her legs nestled between
his. Moaning softly, Kelly buried her face between
his neck and shoulder.

"Tell me what you me want to do," he said in her

hair. "Tell me what I have to do to make you feel good."

Kelly felt tears prick the backs of her eyelids. Simeon had been the only man she had slept with, and never had he asked what she'd wanted in bed.

"I don't know." Her voice was soft and childlike.

Ryan smiled. "Do you want me to kiss your body?"

"Yes."

"All over?"

"Yes."

"Do you want to be on top or underneath me?"

It was her turn to smile. "Both."

"Front or rear?" She gasped, and he laughed, the sound coming from deep within his broad chest. "We'll save the rear position for another time."

Reversing their positions, he supported his weight on his elbows. He closed his eyes and lowered his head, brushing a kiss over her mouth and leaving it burning with heat. Kelly found his mouth warm and sweet, moving with a slow, drugging intimacy that left both trembling.

Nothing was rushed. Not the shivering kisses starting between her breasts and trailing lower to her belly. Not his teeth nipping her nipples, turning them into hard buttons. But once he placed his hands against the inside of her thighs, spreading them wider, the sensual assault began.

She arched off the mattress as he searched for the

tiny bud of flesh between her legs, and once finding it he laved it with his tongue until it hardened and swelled to twice its size.

Kelly gripped the sheets, swallowing the moans trapped in her throat. Ryan's mouth and tongue played havoc with her nerve endings as she struggled not to climax.

Cupping her buttocks in both hands, Ryan raised her hips and plunged his tongue into her quivering flesh and drank deeply. He felt Kelly trembling, heard her soft pleas for him to stop, but he ignored her.

It was his intent to brand her with his possession, to make her forget all other men ever existed. He wanted to be the last man in her bed and in her life.

Kelly felt as if she stood outside of herself, watching herself float to a place where she'd never been. The desire streaking through her body was strange and frightening.

"No," she gasped, her head thrashing from side to side. She didn't want to feel this way, unable to control what was happening to her. "Ryan, please stop."

He did stop, but only long enough to open the packet containing a condom he had taken from the pocket of his trousers. He rolled it down his tumescence, moved her over again and guided his engorged sex into her body.

Ryan kissed Kelly's taut nipples, rousing her

passion all over again. She groaned with each inch that disappeared into the folds of her pulsing flesh. Once fully engulfed in her heat, he began to move.

Slowly.

Deliberately.

Pulling out.

Pushing in.

Pulling out a little more.

Pushing in a little harder until he established a rhythm that had them both moaning in ecstasy and gasping for their next breath. She rose to meet his powerful thrusts, their bodies in exquisite harmony with one another.

Opening her mouth, Kelly gasped in sweet agony as she felt the waves sweeping over her increase. The pleasure Ryan offered her was pure and explosive. He quickened his movements, his head buried between her neck and shoulders, and it was then that she cried out as love flowed through her like liquid heat.

She climaxed once, twice, then lost count as she was hurtled to another dimension. She lay drowning in the aftermath of her sensual journey when Ryan exploded, his deep moans of ecstasy echoing in her ear.

He collapsed on her and she welcomed his weight and strength. Their shared moment of ecstasy had passed, yet she was filled with an amazing sense of fulfillment.

Wrapping his arms around Kelly's waist, Ryan reversed their positions and smiled. Her face was moist, her mouth swollen from his kisses. He lifted his eyebrows. "Did I hurt you?"

Kelly stared down into the gray eyes that reminded her of streaks of lightning across a summer sky. "No." And he hadn't hurt her. However, she was certain muscles she hadn't used in a while would be a little sore.

Resting her head on his shoulder, she snuggled closer. She could feel the heat of his large body course down the length of hers. "Thank you, Ryan."

"For what, darling?" His hand moved up and down her spine in a comforting motion.

"For reminding me what it means to feel like a woman again."

He dropped a kiss on her mussed hair. "If I make you feel womanly it's because this is the first time in a long time I'm glad that I was born a man."

Raising her head, she stared at him staring down at her under lowered lids. He was so handsome that she found herself speechless for several seconds.

"I'm glad I waited."

His arm tightened around her waist. He wanted to tell her that he was glad he had waited for her. Reaching over to his right, he picked up the watch he had left on the bedside table. It was after eight. "Are you hungry?"

"Starved."

"I'll call and have our dinner sent up."

Kelly pulled out of his embrace and sat up. "I need to take a shower first."

Grinning, he reached for her hand. "We'll save time by sharing one."

She gave him a knowing look. "No seconds before we eat."

"I don't know what you're talking about. I already ate."

Kelly slapped playfully at Ryan, missing his shoulder when he ducked. He swept her up, throwing her over his shoulder as he headed toward the bathroom.

They shared a shower, Kelly complaining because he had ruined her hairdo when he held her under the flowing water while kissing her until she pleaded with him to let her go.

Wrapping her wet hair with a towel, she dried her body from a supply of thick, thirsty towels in a closet in the spacious modern bathroom. The closet yielded bathrobes and terry-cloth slippers in varying sizes.

Two hours later, she sat on a love seat in the dining area, her bare feet resting on Ryan's thighs. They had turned off all the lights, lit several candles and turned on the radio to a station that played mostly slow love songs.

She patted her belly under the terry robe. "I ate too much."

Resting the back of his head on the love seat, Ryan said, "Nonsense. I ate more than you did."

They'd devoured a platter of marinated asparagus, artichoke, grilled peppers, steak tidbits and grilled shrimp.

"That's because you ate faster than me."

"True," he said, lifting a flute of champagne.

Kelly raised her own flute, sipping the bubbling liquid. She hadn't finished her first glass. "What time do you plan to drive back?"

"What makes you think I'm driving back tonight?"

She could not make out his expression in the shadowy darkness. Sitting up straighter, she said, "What are you talking about?"

Ryan put his flute down on the table. "Unless you have another engagement this evening, I don't see the need to leave."

"What about Sean?"

"What about him?"

"Wouldn't he..."

"Wouldn't he what?" Ryan asked when she did not finish her question. "I'm not neglecting my son, Kelly, if that's what you're concerned about. He's spending the night with the Smith twins. They're having a Spider-Man party."

Heat flared in her cheeks. "I just don't—don't want to be responsible for keeping you from your son."

He curved his fingers around her slender ankles, holding her fast. "That could never happen. I've assumed total responsibility for Sean from the first time he drew breath, and there has never been a time when I've neglected him. I may not have always made the right decisions where it concerned him, but I've done the best I could.

"Sheldon begged me not to take him with me when I went to Tuskegee, but there was no way I could leave him for almost a year even though I knew he would be well cared for at the farm. Sean sulked the entire time he was away. He acted out because he didn't want to go to the daycare center whenever I taught a class, and he refused to talk to me whenever I came to pick him up. I made a mistake because I thought I knew what was best for my son. That was one time when I was thinking only of myself, but that will never happen again."

Kelly put her flute next to Ryan's, then leaned forward to curve her arms around his neck. "No one is born a parent. We learn through trial and error. But in the end you will find that you've done a pretty good job." She kissed his chin. "Sean will grow up to be as proud of you as you are of Sheldon."

He nodded. "Pop and I sometime have our differences, but if I turn out to be half the father he is then I'll be more than grateful. It wasn't easy for him when Mom died, leaving him with two boys who thought they knew more than he did. He was still pretty young when he became a widower, but he refused to remarry because he said he did not want another woman believing she could replace his sons' mother."

"How old were you when your mother passed away?"

"Fourteen. Jeremy had just turned ten. We were so angry, unable to accept that our mother was gone. I'm ashamed to say that we gave Pop hell for a few years until he said he wouldn't treat us like men until we started acting like men."

"Did you straighten out?"

"I'm still here, aren't I?"

"Were you and your brother *that* out of control?"

"We weren't what you would call thugs or criminals, but we never walked away from a fight. I wasn't as bad as Jeremy, but I had to back him up because he was my brother."

"You haven't changed that much, Ryan."

His forehead creased in a frown. "Why would you say that?"

"You were looking to start something with that guy at the elevator." He let go of her legs, picked up his flute, and took a swallow. She peered closely at him. "And because you're not saying anything lets me know that you're still a brawler."

He lifted an eyebrow. "It wouldn't have come to anything, Kelly."

"Why?"

"I'd never let you see me act like that."

"But are you still capable of brawling?"

"Sure. But I'd rather make love." He put aside his flute and reached for her. He untied the belt holding her robe together, running a hand up her inner thigh.

A moan slipped past her lips. "Ryan."

"Yes, baby," he whispered in her ear.

She moaned again. "That's not fair."

"What's not fair, princess?"

"You're taking advantage of me."

He chuckled. "You can always take advantage of me."

Kelly reciprocated as her hand searched under his robe to find him hard and ready. "What are you waiting for? Let's go back to bed."

This time there was no prolonged foreplay as Ryan paused long enough to slip on a condom, then entered Kelly's pulsing body and sent shivers of delight through her.

Their lovemaking was strong and passionate, each striving to delay fulfillment until the last possible moment. But they were not to be denied as they used every inch of the large bed in their quest to touch heaven. They exploded together, incinerating in flames of passion that burned long after they fell asleep entwined in each other's embrace.

Chapter Nine

Kelly returned to Blackstone Farms Saturday morning with Ryan, wrapped in a cocoon of contentment. She woke up to find him lying on his side, his head resting on a folded arm, smiling at her. They had not made love again, but lay in bed for several hours talking. She told him how it had been to grow up in New York City and how different Virginia was from the fast pace of a city that never slept.

Ryan had revealed that he'd visited New York twice, both times for professional conferences. He said he'd been shocked by the number of people crowding into a single subway car, but admitted that while he loved the pulsing excitement he knew he could never survive living in a big city. After a wonderfully long night, they'd finally left the bed, showered and eaten breakfast in their suite before checking out.

Kelly stood on the porch to her house, a hand resting in the middle of Ryan's chest. "Pick me up at one." He'd promised to take her into Staunton where she could buy a pair of riding boots.

Lowering his head, he kissed her tenderly. "I'll see you later." He smiled, turned and walked back to his car.

She unlocked the door and was met with the shrill ringing of the telephone. Rushing into the bedroom, she picked up the receiver before the answering machine switched on. A blinking number indicated two calls had been recorded.

"Hello."

"Where have you been? I've been trying to reach you since last night. I left two messages on your machine. Leo had to talk me out of driving across the state to find out what happened to you."

Kelly smiled as she kicked off her shoes. "I didn't know I was on work-release this weekend."

"Very funny, Kel."

"You bitch and moan when I call you every Friday or Saturday night, and when I don't you overreact."

There was a pulse beat of silence before Pamela's voice came through the wire again. "You had a date?"

"Yes, I had a date." Kelly held the receiver away from her ear as her sister let out an ear-piercing shriek.

"Who is he? Where did you go? What did you do?"

"Dang, Pamela."

"You can say damn, Kelly."

"All right. Damn, Pamela."

"You don't have to tell me what you did," she said. "But you have to tell me who he is."

"His name is Ryan Blackstone."

"He's one of the Blackstones?"

"He's the eldest son."

"Hot damn! My little sister struck the mother lode."

"Back it up, Pamela. It was just one date."

"One, two, three, four. It doesn't matter. The fact that you went out with him, and apparently spent more than a few hours together, says a lot."

Kelly wanted to argue with her sister, but decided against it. Pamela Andrews-Porter refused to accept that she was exactly like their mother, Camille Andrews. She just could not resist meddling.

"I'm going to ring off because I have to go into town to do some shopping."

"Don't hang up yet, Kel. I was calling to let you know that Leo and I are hosting a Fourth of July cookout. Mama and Daddy are driving down for the weekend, and cousins Bill, Flora, Verna and her kids said they're coming up. It's going to be somewhat of a mini family reunion."

"I'll be there."

"Are you bringing your man?"

"No! And he's not my man."

"You said that a little too quickly, little sis."

"Goodbye, big sis."

"Goodbye, Kelly," Pamela crooned, chuckling softly.

Kelly hung up, mumbling to herself. Just because she had slept with Ryan that did not mean he was her man or she his woman. What they had become were lovers before they'd become friends. How different it was from her relationship with Simeon. He had been her friend since first grade, and it wasn't until she was twenty that she offered him more than friendship: her body and a promise to love him forever.

She glanced at the clock on the table next to the phone. She had an hour to blow out her hair and ready herself for an afternoon of shopping with Ryan.

Ryan found his father by the pool. A few of the employees had gathered around the Olympic-size pool to cool off from the unseasonable ninety-degree temperatures. Two hundred feet away smaller bodies frolicked in the kiddie pool like baby seals under the watchful eyes of their parents.

Sitting down at the table under one of a dozen large black and red striped umbrellas positioned around the deck, he nodded at Sheldon. "Good afternoon."

Sheldon stared at his son through a pair of sunglasses. Missing was the tailored suit from the night before. This afternoon he wore jeans, T-shirt and a pair of running shoes.

"Good afternoon. How was your date?"

"Good."

He smiled, nodding. "How's Kelly?"

Ryan bit back a grin. "She's good."

Sheldon turned to stare out at the blue-green water. "I'm glad to hear it."

Ryan patted his father's bare shoulder. The sun had darkened his caffe latte complexion skin to a rich cinnamon-brown. The muscle under his hand still hard for a middle-aged man in his prime.

"I like her, Pop." He inhaled a lungful of hot air. "I just hadn't realized how much l liked her until I was able to spend time with her. She has a quick mind and a wonderful sense of humor. She also has a sharp tongue."

Sheldon lifted his left eyebrow. "She sounds a lot like your mother."

Ryan chuckled. "It helps that she's beautiful and sexy."

Just like your mother was, Sheldon mused. "I'm

glad you found someone you enjoy being with," he said aloud.

Gaze narrowing, Ryan searched the kiddie pool for his son. "Where's Sean?"

"He's in the dining hall eating lunch."

Ryan was pleased that Sean had begun eating again. During their stay in Alabama he'd refused to eat with the other children at the child care center. "I'm going to take him with me."

"Where are you going?"

"To Staunton. If Kelly's going to learn to ride, then she's going to need boots." Pushing to his feet, he said, "I'll see you later."

"Enjoy," Sheldon said in parting.

Sean sat between Ryan and Kelly in a specialty shop that featured leather goods, talking non-stop as she tried on several pairs of riding boots.

"Cook's gonna cook the three little pigs before the wolf eats them up." Kelly smiled at Ryan, who winked and returned her smile.

"Cook plans to roast a couple of pigs for the Memorial Day cookout, Sean, but I can assure you they are not *the* three little pigs," Ryan said in a quiet voice.

"Are you sure, Daddy?"

"Ask Miss Kelly."

She cut her eyes at Ryan who gave her a *please*

help me out expression. "Your father's right, Sean. When we go back to school on Monday—"

"Monday is no school, Miss Kelly," Sean interrupted. "You said it was Me—more Day."

She made a show of hitting her forehead with the heel of her hand. "That's right. I did forget that *Memorial* Day is Monday. Thank you for reminding me."

Sean patted Ryan's shoulder to get his attention. "We made flags in school."

"You didn't show it to me."

"You can't see it until Monday."

Sean explained to Ryan how they had counted the stars and stripes while Kelly indicated to the salesperson which pair of boots she had decided to purchase. Rising from his chair, Ryan reached into his rear pocket for a wallet, removed a credit card and handed it to the clerk.

Kelly reached for the card, but Ryan caught and held her wrist. "Let's not make a scene," he warned softly.

"There won't be a scene if you let me pay for my own purchases."

Curving an arm around her waist, he pulled her closer to his side. "What if we compromise?"

"How?"

"I pay for the boots and you pay for ice cream for the rest of the summer. It's going to work out equitably because Sean and I eat a lot of ice cream."

Sean bobbed his head up and down. "That's right."

Kelly knew when she was outnumbered. "How often do you eat it?"

"Every day," they chorused.

"I think I've just been had," she murmured under her breath.

They left the store and Ryan drove Sheldon's SUV to Shorty's Diner on Richmond Road. The restaurant looked like a 1950s jukebox. All stainless steel with neon lights and glass, it was colorful and inviting. Ryan ordered a monstrous ice-cream concoction large enough for four people.

Kelly, who rarely ate sweets, could not stop eating the homemade vanilla, strawberry and pistachio ice cream topped with nuts, whipped cream and fresh berries.

"You're going to make me fat," she whispered to Ryan as he helped her up into the SUV for the ride home.

"You'd look good with a few extra pounds."

"Not in the belly and butt," she growled.

"Especially in the belly," he countered, still holding the door open.

She went completely still, her gaze fusing with his. She berated herself for telling him she wanted a baby. And did she really want Ryan to father her child?

Was she ready for motherhood?

Did she want to marry again?

The questions taunted her because she had grown up believing one fell in love, married and then had children—in that order. She had done that with Simeon, but had not completed the cycle because he had been taken from her.

Turning to look out the windshield, she stared straight ahead. She had offered Ryan her body, but not her heart. She wasn't certain when she would—if ever.

Kelly met Ryan in the stables early Sunday morning. She found him kneeling in one of the stalls, examining the right foreleg of a stallion. A large black bag filled with rolls of bandages stood open on the floor.

She watched as he wrapped at least four layers of cotton wool and a bandage tightly around the leg. He removed a pair of latex gloves, dropping them in the bag and closing it.

"What happened to him?" she asked.

Ryan stood up, his gaze taking in everything about Kelly in one sweeping glance. Her hair was pulled back into a ponytail under a baseball cap. She was dressed for riding: blouse, jeans and boots. She held a pair of leather riding gloves in one hand.

"He sustained a simple fracture a couple of months ago."

"Will he be okay?"

He smiled. "He's healing nicely." Curving an arm

around Kelly's waist, he led her to a door near the entrance. He punched several buttons on a panel, and the door opened automatically.

He ushered her into a large space where he had set up his office. It contained a large stainless-steel examining table, sinks, cabinets filled with bandages, vials of drugs, and surgical instruments.

"Do you perform surgeries here?"

He opened the bag, discarded the latex gloves, and then stored the bag on a corner shelf. "Only in an emergency. I'm a registered on-call vet with a hospital in Richmond."

He washed his hands in one of the sinks with a strong antiseptic-smelling solution, dried them on several paper towels, discarding the towels in a plastic-covered container.

Smiling at Kelly, he said, "Are you ready for your first riding lesson?"

She returned his smile. "Yes."

Taking her hand, he led her out of the stable to an area where Mark Charlesworth stood waiting with two saddled horses. Mark's expression brightened when he saw Kelly.

"Good morning, Miss Kelly."

"Good morning, Mark."

"Mark, please hold my horse while I help Miss Kelly."

Spanning her waist with both hands, Ryan swung her up effortlessly onto a horse. The horse sidestepped and he caught the reins, handing them to Kelly. "Hold them either in your right or left hand. Your fingers should close over the reins with your hand turned over so that the wrist is straight and your thumb up."

Kelly felt half a ton of muscle and raw power between her legs, refusing to acknowledge her fear as Ryan adjusted the stirrups to accommodate her legs. She'd never sat on a horse in her life, and the fact that she was at least six feet above the ground made her stomach roil.

"Put your feet in the stirrups, then lean forward in the saddle." She reacted like automaton once he showed her how to use her knees and reins to control the animal.

The horse Ryan had chosen to ride reared up, his forelegs pawing the air. Mark tightened his hold on the bridle. "He's a little flighty this morning, Doc."

"That's because he wants to run." Ryan put his left foot in the stirrup, mounting in one continuous motion. Mark handed him his wide-brim hat. Reaching over, he held on to the bridle of Kelly's horse and he led her away from the stables.

Once she became accustomed to the rocking motion, she found herself relaxing. She followed Ryan as he cantered toward the open portion of the property.

An hour later Kelly sat under a tree watching Ryan as he raced his horse across the verdant landscape.

Horse and rider became one as the Thoroughbred established a long, low, raking stride. Sinking down to the grass, she closed her eyes.

Ryan returned to Kelly, finding her reclining on the grass, asleep. He tethered his horse next to where hers grazed on the sweet tender grass. He sank down beside Kelly, resting his head on his folded arm. She had taken off her cap. Without warning she opened her eyes.

"How do you like riding?"

"I like it, but I'm sore."

"Where?"

"My behind and between my legs."

Moving from his reclining position, he sat back on his heels. He did not give Kelly time to protest as he removed her boots. Her socks followed, then he unsnapped her jeans.

She slapped at his hand. "What are you doing?"

He pushed her hand away. "I'm going to give you a massage."

"No-ooo," she wailed in protest.

"Yes," he insisted, lifting her hips and easing her jeans down her legs. Any further protest ended once Ryan turned Kelly over to lie on her belly. "Rest your head on your arms."

She moaned once as she gave herself up to the strength in his strong fingers as he kneaded her buttocks and the flesh of her inner thighs. After ten minutes he straddled her, his chest pressing against her back.

"You look as beautiful from behind as you do in front," he whispered against her ear.

Her breathing halted then started up again. "What are you doing?"

"It's not want I'm doing but what I want to do." Curving an arm around her middle, he eased her gently to her knees.

Kelly groaned inwardly when she felt the solid bulge in his groin pressing against her hips. The only shield between them was his jeans and her navy-blue thong panties.

Reaching between her legs, he cupped her feminine heat and desire shot through her like a jolt of electricity, leaving her wet and pulsing against his palm.

"Kelly," he growled deep in his throat.

"Now, Ryan," she gasped, praying she wouldn't climax before he penetrated her.

He unsnapped his jeans, pushing them and his briefs down around his knees and pulled aside the narrow strip of fabric. He entered her in one, swift, sure motion.

She felt his hot breath in her neck, raspy breathing in her ear, and the power in his thighs as he pushed into her pulsing flesh. Resting the back of her head on his shoulder, she closed her eyes, trying unsuccessfully not to explode.

Kelly had become a mare in heat as Ryan inhaled the feminine musk rising from between her legs. And like a rutting stallion, he gloried in the pleasure that came from pumping in and out of her lush body. Cupping his hands over her breasts he cradled them, measuring their weight as her nipples hardened under his fingertips.

He loved her, each deliberate thrust, joining their bodies, every gasp, groan, moan bringing them closer to the brink of a spiraling ecstasy and fulfillment. It was no longer flesh-to-flesh, man-to-woman, heart-to-heart, but soul-to-soul.

Pressing his face against the nape of her neck, Ryan caught the tender skin between his teeth, biting gently and leaving his brand. His lips left her neck and seared a path along the silken column of her neck.

Mouth open and gasping for her next breath, Kelly felt herself slipping away from reality. She writhed against Ryan, the curve of her buttocks tucked neatly against his groin. They had become a perfect fit.

Her body flamed and froze at the same time. Her world tilted and careened on its axis. She cried out for release and seconds later she exploded in a floodtide of shimmering fire that shattered the barrier she had erected around her heart to love again.

Kelly's passion spread to Ryan as her heat swept over him like a raging forest fire. His fingers tightened around her waist, holding her fast as he spewed liquid love into her still-pulsing flesh. He eased her down to the grass, gasping loudly.

Ryan pulled Kelly against his chest and buried his face in her hair. Everything that was Kelly Andrews seeped into his pores. He loved her!

He had fallen in love with her.

Easing back he stared at her staring back at him. In that instant he saw his unborn children in her eyes. The realization he had made love to her without protection squeezed his heart. Splaying a hand over her hip, he kissed her moist forehead.

"I wanted to make love to you, but not without a condom."

She offered him a tender smile. "Don't beat up on yourself, Ryan. I'm safe right now."

"Are you certain?"

She nodded. "Yes. I woke up this morning with the familiar symptoms telling me I should see my period in a few days."

He wanted to tell her that it did not matter if she was or wasn't pregnant, because he loved her enough to ask her to share his love and his future.

They waited until their passions cooled and then dressed. Ryan led Kelly to her horse, helped her mount before he mounted his. Their return to the stables was unhurried as they rode side by side in silence.

Chapter Ten

Ryan saw Kelly enter the dining hall, his gaze following her as she walked past his table and over to Mark Charlesworth's. The young stable hand rose to his feet at her approach. He went completely still when Mark cupped her elbow and led her away.

"Easy," Sheldon said softly, noting Ryan's thunderous expression. "It's not what you think."

Turning his head, Ryan stared at his father as if he were a stranger. "Just what is it I'm thinking, Pop?" The query, though spoken quietly, was ominous.

"There's nothing going on between them."

Ryan wanted to believe Sheldon. It was now the end of June, and he and Kelly continued to see each other, but only on weekends. They had established a practice of sharing dinner, movie or concert, and a bed on Fridays at hotels far enough from Staunton to ensure their privacy.

He dropped off Sean and picked him up from school during the week. Kelly related to him the same way she related to the other parents. Knowing he was in love with Kelly had increased Ryan's frustration because he wanted to spend more time with her. His need to spend more than twelve consecutive hours with her each week went beyond physical desire. One night they'd shared a bed but had been content to hold hands and talk rather than make love.

There was so much he longed to tell her but hesitated because she still withheld a small part of herself—the part that would allow her to love again. And there was nothing about Kelly that he did not love: her wit, intelligence, beauty, patience and her sensuality.

He planned to turn Blackstone Day School into a private school for grades N-6. He wanted to hire a music teacher so the children could learn to sing, read music and play musical instruments. The building would be expanded to include actual classrooms, and as the school's headmistress Kelly would hire and train the staff.

Ryan knew Kelly loved teaching as much as her students loved her. Every day Sean came home singing her praises. He proudly displayed his art projects and showed Ryan his notebook filled with the letters of the alphabet and corresponding words for the letter of the day. Instead of playing with computer games or watching television, Sean now preferred reading picture books.

Kelly Andrews had become a positive role model for the children at Blackstone Farms, while at the same time she had taught the resident veterinarian that it was possible not to love once, but twice in a lifetime.

Floor lamps burned in the school's sitting area. Kelly sat with Mark, listening intently as he explained his answer to one of her questions. She had given him several practice PSAT examinations, and out of the possible sixteen hundred points, he averaged seven fifty-five on the math segment, but less than four hundred on the verbal.

Although his combined scores topped one thousand, she wanted him to increase his score on the verbal portion. It had taken two weeks for her to assess Mark's weak reading comprehension.

"You must train your eye to recognize key words within the paragraph." She circled half a dozen words with a pencil.

Mark studied the circled words. "Is it B?"

Kelly shook her head. "You're guessing, Mark. Take your time."

He stared at the paragraph, exhaling audibly. "I can't, Miss Kelly."

"Yes, you can. If you can ace the math there's no reason why you can't ace the verbal as well."

He ran his hand over his dreaded hair. "Math has always been easy for me, but I've always had a problem with reading."

Kelly saw the frustration on his face. "Do you like reading?"

He shrugged a shoulder. "Not much."

"Do you read the newspaper?"

"No."

"Well, you should. There are three newspapers delivered to the farm—*USA Today, The Washington Post* and the *Virginian-Pilot.* I want you to read one every day. Underline the words you don't understand and look them up in the dictionary I gave you."

He grimaced. "Do I have to?"

Kelly wanted to laugh. He sounded so much like her younger students when they sought to get out of performing a task. "Yes, you do. I'm volunteering my time to help you, Mark. The least you can do is complete your homework assignments."

What Mark did not know was that she had sacrificed seeing Ryan during the week because she was committed to tutoring him. She wanted to see Ryan more than just Friday nights. Waking up beside him on Saturday mornings in a strange hotel was not what she had envisioned for their relationship.

If she had been employed at the farm in any position other than a teacher, she would have eagerly dated Ryan openly. But she was his son's teacher, and for her this presented a personal conflict. She did not want Sean to know she had fallen in love with his father because she and Ryan talked about everything except a future together. He had not confessed to loving her, or she him.

And she was mature enough to know that falling in love with Ryan had nothing to do with sharing his bed. Ryan was intelligent, patient, generous and gentle despite his admission that he was once known as a brawler. He was a devoted father. He praised and encouraged Sean while setting limits for the child. Ryan took her to charming restaurants and even more charming hotels and inns for their overnight liaisons.

"I'll read the newspapers," Mark said, breaking into her musings.

She smiled at him. "Good. I'm going to make a list of vocabulary words for you to study. Come by tomorrow afternoon to pick it up."

Mark smiled, his deep-set dark eyes sparkling like polished onyx. "Thanks, Miss Kelly." Mark pushed his study manuals into a leather saddlebag, murmured a soft good night then turned and walked out of the schoolhouse.

The door closed and seconds later it opened again.

Ryan stood in the doorway, staring at her. "Isn't he a little young for you?"

Kelly felt her pulse quicken. Could it be Ryan was jealous? And for him to display jealousy, then that meant his feelings went deeper than a mere liking?

"Yes, he is. So is your son. And don't forget the Smith twins."

Ryan didn't know whether to laugh in relief or kiss Kelly until she begged him to stop. It was apparent her relationship with Mark was that of teacher-student. He'd left the dining hall and was heading home when he saw the light coming from the schoolhouse. He'd told Sean to go back to Grandpa while he turned and walked to the school. He was less than twenty feet away when he saw Mark Charlesworth leaving. Maturity and his responsibility for Sean had stopped him when he thought about confronting Mark about Kelly. It was in that instant he knew he was still capable of brawling.

Walking over to the wall-mounted bulletin board, he stared at the photographs and drawings depicting Blackstone Farms. "Exploring Our World" had become an enlightening experience for the five children who had lived on the farm since birth.

They'd taken photographs of the numbers tattooed under the upper lip of each horse that was used for identification purposes. They photographed Kevin Manning as he trained a horse, stable hands mucking out stalls, grooms brushing the hides of the horses to keep the coats free of eggs left by flies, men hauling bales of hay from the barn to the stables, more working to repair a fence to keep the horses from running away, and Carl Burton and his kitchen personnel.

His contribution was demonstrating preventive measures for keeping the horses healthy. They'd watched, transfixed, as he held a horse's mouth open and checked its teeth.

He read the penciled compositions of the children who wrote about the work their parents did at the horse farm. He smiled when he read: *My daddy is very strong, my mommy works hard.*

Kelly walked over to Ryan. "You were not supposed to see this until Parents' Night."

He stared at her under lowered lids. "And I'm not supposed to be alone with you until Friday."

She gasped. She had forgotten to tell Ryan. "I can't see you Friday."

"Why not?"

"I'm going to visit my sister in D.C. We're having a small family gathering for the Fourth of July holiday weekend."

Ryan's jaw tightened. The plans he had made to take her and Sean to Williamsburg would have to be cancelled. "I wish you would've told me sooner."

"Why?"

"I'd planned to take you and Sean to Williamsburg for the weekend."

"You made plans without telling me?"

"I wanted it to be a surprise for you and Sean." He hadn't told anyone about the trip. Not even Sheldon.

"Well, it's more than a surprise. It's a shock."

"What's the problem, Kelly?" There was an edge to his voice she had never heard before.

She moved closer. "What signals are you sending to Sean when he sees his father and his teacher shack up together in a hotel room?"

Ryan struggled to contain his temper. "I reserved a suite with adjoining bedrooms. Sean and I would occupy one and you the other."

"Okay, so you have an answer for the sleeping arrangements. What about the three of us going away together? What are we telling Sean? That we're a couple and a family?"

His gray eyes bore into her. "We could be, Kelly."

She shook her head. "No, we can't, Ryan. Not without love. And if there's no love then you, me and Sean will never become a family."

The seconds ticked off in silence before Kelly turned and walked out of the schoolhouse, leaving Ryan staring at where she had been. Reaching into the pocket of her jeans, she pulled out her keys. The lights were still on in the building when she drove away, tears blurring her vision.

She loved Ryan. Loved him so much it pained her to be in the same room with him. And she was realistic enough to know that he was drawn to her because of Sean. She'd confessed to wanting to become a mother, and he needed a mother for his son.

What was so ironic was that she and Ryan could both get wanted they wanted if only he told her that he loved her.

Kelly maneuvered her car into the winding driveway to her sister's home, parking behind a late-model sedan bearing New York plates. Her parents had arrived before she had.

She retrieved a bag from the trunk, leaving it open, then made her way up the steps to the wraparound porch. The inner door stood open, and she peered through the screen door. She tried the door, finding it locked. Ringing the bell, she waited for someone to answer it.

A smile crinkled the skin around her eyes as she spied her brother-in-law striding toward her with a coal-black ball of fur at his heels. "Hey, Leo."

He unlocked the door and held it open. "Hey, yourself." He kissed her cheek. "You look good, Kelly." He sniffed her neck. "And you smell nice for someone hanging out with horses."

She returned the kiss, his neatly barbered beard grazing her lips. "Not only am I hanging with horses, but I'm learning to ride."

"I'd willingly bet a week's salary to see you clinging to the back of a horse."

"Hold on to your wallet, because you'll lose. I sit a horse, not cling to it."

"Ouch," he teased. "Let me take your bag up to your room."

Kelly tightened her grip on the leather handles. "I can carry it. You can get the carton in my car. I left the trunk open."

Tall, handsome and with a smooth-shaven head, Leo Porter wagged a finger. "You know you're not supposed to bring anything." Because of their careers and active social life the Porters had made it a practice to cater their parties.

"Oh, well," she crooned. "Then I'll just take the wine back to Blackstone Farms with me."

Leo hugged her. "Where did you find it?"

"In a quaint little store not too far from Lexington." Kelly smiled down at the puppy licking her toes. "Who is this?"

"That's Miss Porter. Pam and I call her Poe-Poe. We got her a week ago."

"Is she paper trained?"

"Yes. Pam wouldn't have a dog in her house unless it was trained."

Bending, Kelly scooped the puppy up. "Hello, Miss Porter." The poodle pup yipped and wiggled. "Okay, I'll put you down." She placed the dog on the floor and she took off, her feet slipping out from under her on the highly waxed wood floor. She rolled several feet before regaining her footing.

"I'll meet you in the back," Kelly said as she walked through the entryway of the spacious Colonial.

It took less than fifteen minutes to unpack, wash her face and brush her hair. As she secured it in a ponytail, she made a mental note to call the salon she had visited when living in D.C. to make an appointment.

She skipped down the carpeted staircase and made her way through the modern kitchen to a door leading to the Porters' expansive backyard.

Camille sat on a chair, her silver-haired head covered by a wide straw hat, laughing at something her first cousin had said to her. Her clear-brown eyes widened as she spied Kelly. Holding out her arms, she stood up.

Kelly walked over to her mother and sank into her comforting embrace. "Hi, Mama."

Pulling back and holding Kelly at arm's length, Camille nodded. "You look wonderful Kelly. Look at your baby, Horace," she called to her husband who was engrossed in a chess game.

Pushing back his chair, he pointed a finger at his brother-in-law. "Don't you breathe until I get back," he warned. Turning, Horace Andrews turned the brilliance of his smile on his youngest daughter.

"Hello, Daddy," Kelly said before she kissed his rounded cheek. Resting a hand over his belly, she whispered, "You need to go on a diet."

Horace grimaced. "Not only do you look like your mother, but now you're beginning to sound like her."

"But you're sixty, Daddy—"

"I happen to know how old I am," he countered, cutting her off. "Your mother haunts and nags me constantly about losing weight. And I will."

"When, Daddy?"

"When I get to be a *grandfather*," he countered with a wide grin.

"Stop it, Daddy! You and Mama have to stop this insanity about becoming grandparents or it will never happen."

"Pamela and Leo would rather get a *dog* than have a baby." He'd spat out the word.

"That's their choice and their business." She had enunciated each word. Horace Andrews mumbled under his breath about what his children could do with their choices. Patting his arm, she said softly, "Go back to your game. I want to speak to Cousin Flora."

Pamela lay on the pillow next to Kelly the way they'd done when they were growing up together. "How are you and your Blackstone?"

Turning on the side and facing Pamela, Kelly rested her head on her folded arm. People would never take her and Pamela for sisters, because they looked nothing alike. Her older sister was the image of their paternal grandmother: petite, delicate features, black curly hair and sable coloring.

"His name is Ryan. We're doing all right."

"Just all right?"

Kelly lifted her left shoulder. "We see each other on Fridays and spend the night together. We usually get back to the farm before noon on Saturday."

Pamela's waxed eyebrows wrinkled. "You're sleeping together off the property?"

"He has a four-year-old son who just happens to be my student."

Pamela's mouth formed a perfect *O*. "I see where you're coming from." She gave Kelly a long, penetrating stare. "You're in love with him, aren't you?"

"Am I that transparent?"

"No. It's just that you seem so calm—at peace with yourself."

Kelly wanted to tell Pamela she was wrong. What she was feeling wasn't serenity, but turmoil. She wanted to tell Ryan that she loved him, but balked each time she lay in his arms. And she did love him enough to marry him and bear his children. All he had to do was open his mouth and ask her.

Chapter Eleven

Ryan's hand flailed out as he tried brushing away whatever it was crawling over his cheek. He moaned and turned over onto his belly. Seconds later a sliver of ice trickled down his spine and he sprang off the bed, his hands bunched into fists, but was rendered immobile by an arm around his throat, cutting off his breath.

"You still have good reflexes for an old man," a familiar voice whispered in his ear.

"Dammit, Jeremy!"

Jeremy Blackstone released Ryan's throat and stepped back quickly as his older brother swung at him. Grinning, he winked. He had anticipated his reaction.

Ryan stood in the middle of his bedroom, muscular arms crossed over his bare chest. It had been more than a year since he'd seen Jeremy. He didn't look any older, but there was something about him that communicated danger. As an undercover agent for the Drug Enforcement Administration it was obvious that he had become as hardened and dangerous as the criminals he sought to bring to justice.

"How did you get in?" He was certain he had locked the door before he retired for the night.

Jeremy lifted a thick black eyebrow. "I picked the lock."

"You're nothing more than a legal thug."

"You should try it. Thug life ain't too bad."

"No thanks. Do you mind if I put some clothes on?"

Shrugging his broad shoulders, Jeremy moved over and sat in an armchair. "It doesn't bother me what you wear. You happen not to be my type."

Crossing the bedroom, Ryan opened a drawer and took out a pair of boxers. He slipped into them and walked over and sat down on a matching chair opposite his brother. Jeremy's pitch-black hair was longer than he had seen it in years. Pulled back off his forehead and secured in a ponytail on his nape, the style provided an unfettered view of his striking olive-brown face with a pair of high cheekbones, aquiline nose, firm mouth, short dark beard and dove-gray eyes. Diamond studs glittered in each ear.

Ryan knew Jeremy had had his ears pierced when on an undercover assignment in South America, but this was the first time he could recall him wearing earrings at Blackstone Farms.

"How long are you staying?"

"I'm out of here tomorrow night."

"That only gives you one day. Why do you bother to come if you can't stay for more than a day?"

Jeremy frowned. "Now, you sound like Pop."

"That's because he's right, Jeremy. Once you become a father you'll understand how he feels when he doesn't hear from you for months. And he has no way of knowing whether you're dead or alive."

"That's because he refuses to accept what I've chosen to do with my life."

"He doesn't have to accept your career. All he has to do is accept you as his son. A son he loves, a son he worries about. And maybe even a son who may one day claim his rightful place at Blackstone Farms."

Jeremy leaned over, resting his elbows on his knees. "Read my lips, Ryan. I don't do horses. I don't know what has Pop all bent out of shape. You're a brilliant veterinarian rumored to be able to raise horses from the dead."

Ryan's eyebrows lowered as he glared at Jeremy. "This is not a joke." Jeremy sobered quickly. "I might know horses, but you're the one with the business background. Pop has been running this farm for a long time, and even though he's not complaining I know he's tired. Before I left to teach at Tuskegee I picked up some of the slack, but since I've been back I realize that it takes more than one person to run a farm this size."

Jeremy swore under his breath. "Please don't pressure me, Ryan. I'm not ready to stop doing what I'm doing."

"I'm not asking you to stop. I'm just asking you to consider your options."

"Okay. I'll think about it."

"Good." Ryan stood up and extended his hand. He wasn't disappointed when Jeremy grasped it. "Why don't you bed down in the room next to Sean's?"

Jeremy shook his head. "I'd rather sleep in my own place."

"It hasn't been aired out."

"That's all right." He stood up, stretching his six-foot-three height. "I've slept in worse conditions." And he had. "If I'm not up by eight, then come and get me. Other than missing you, Pop and Sean, the thing I miss the most is Cook's pancakes."

"Okay." Ryan glanced at the clock on his bedside table. It was a few minutes past four. It was too early to get up, but he knew he wouldn't be able to go back to sleep.

Walking over to the window, he peered out through the screen. The odor of spent fireworks lingered in the early-morning air. Sheldon had hired a professional fireworks company to put on a dazzling display of brilliant color for the children who lay on blankets with their parents, staring up at the sky while cheering and applauding each explosion. Sean kept asking him whether Miss Kelly could see the color from where she was. Ryan told him he didn't believe she could, but his son mentioning her name made their separation even more acute.

Turning on his heel, he made his way into an adjoining bathroom to shave and shower.

Kelly felt as if she had truly come home once she crossed the property line leading to Blackstone Farms. She spied the flagpole with the American flag flying atop the black and red one that represented the farm's silks. The flags hung limply in the falling rain.

She had had a fun-filled relaxing weekend with her family. She went to bed late, slept in even later and generally did not do anything more strenuous than shift a lounger to a shaded area whenever the sun burned her exposed skin.

Sighing audibly, Kelly maneuvered under the

carport beside her bungalow. Recurring thunderstorms with torrential downpours had slowed her return trip. She switched off the wipers, lights and the engine. Pushing open the door, she inhaled the smell of wet earth.

Walking the short distance to the porch, she mounted the stairs. She caught movement out of the corner of her eye and froze. Rising from the love seat in the shadows was the outline of a man. The scent of a familiar cologne wafted in her nostrils. It was Ryan. He had waited for her to come home.

"Ryan?"

"Yes, princess."

"What are you doing here?" He hadn't moved out of the shadows.

"I was waiting to welcome you back to *our* home."

"This is *your* home, Ryan."

"It could be yours if you want it to be."

Her breath caught in her lungs. What did he mean? What was he trying to tell her? Shifting, she tried making out his expression but failed. It was too dark.

"I don't understand."

"What is there to understand?" he asked instead of answering her question. He took two long strides, bringing him inches from her. "I want you to stay here—forever."

She shook her head. "That's not possible, Ryan."

His hand touched the side of her face. The smell

of his cologne mingled with that of his laundered shirt. "Yes, it is, princess. It's possible if you marry me."

She couldn't move or speak. The word she longed to tell him was lodged in the back of her throat, refusing to come out. She wanted so much to tell him yes; yes she would marry him; yes she would become the mother Sean never had; yes she would be honored to have his babies. She would say yes to everything, but not without his declaration of love.

"I can't," she whispered instead.

"Is he still in your heart?" Ryan snapped. "Is a dead man still standing between us? I'm not asking you to forget Simeon, darling." His voice was softer, calm. "All I want is for you to let me in."

"You're in, Ryan. How I feel about you has nothing to do with Simeon."

"Then what is it?"

Looping her arms around his waist, she laid her head against his chest, and listened to the strong pumping of his heart under her ear. "Love."

"Love?" he repeated.

"Yes."

"You think I don't love you?"

"I don't know what to think, Ryan, because you've never told me that you loved me."

He swung her up in his arms. "Of course I love

you, Kelly. Do you think I would ask you to marry me if I didn't love you?"

She buried her face against his warm throat. "I was waiting for you to tell me you loved me before I told you how I felt about you."

"Well, I'm waiting."

Tightening her hold around his neck, she pressed her mouth to his. "I love you, Ryan Blackstone."

His smile was dazzling. "Thank you, my darling. Now, isn't there something else you want to say to me?"

"Nope," she said sassily.

"Give me your keys, Kelly."

"What's the magic word?"

"Please." The word was forced out between his teeth.

She placed her keys in his outstretched palm, holding onto his neck while he unlocked the door. Shifting her body, he flipped a wall switch, turning on the table lamp in the parlor. Ryan looked at Kelly, his eyes widening in surprise. She had cut her hair. Soft curls were brushed off her forehead and over her ears.

"You look incredible."

A blush burned her cheeks. "Thank you."

He dropped a kiss on the top of her head. "You're welcome."

She met his gaze, smiling. The love she saw

radiating from the sooty orbs made her want to cry. He loved her! He loved her and she loved him.

Kelly closed her eyes and inhaled deeply. "Yes, Ryan. Yes, I will marry you and become mother to *our* children."

Ryan carried her across the parlor and he walked into Kelly's bedroom for the first time. The time for hiding his love for her ended the moment she'd accepted his marriage proposal.

He had loved and lost and so had she, but it was time for new beginnings. He knew he could not replace the memory of her first husband and did not want to. What they would create would be new memories to reminiscence about whenever they watched a future generation of Blackstones lie on the grass and gasp in awe at Fourth of July fireworks.

Bending slightly, he lowered Kelly until her feet touched the coolness of the wood floor. She walked over to a bedside table and turned on a lamp. The space was flooded with soft golden light that illuminated an exquisite sleigh bed and towering armoire. The soft colors of lemon yellow and lime-green were predominant. The bedroom was romantic and feminine—just like the woman he had fallen in love with.

"It ends tonight, princess. No more making love in hideaway places. No more pretending that my only contact with you is because you're Sean's teacher."

Raising her hand, Kelly beckoned Ryan closer.

She stared up at him as he walked over to her. She placed her hands in the middle of his chest. "I want this night to be special, so special that I will remember it for the rest of my life."

Ryan wanted to tell her that what was to occur between them would be only one of many more special nights to come. There would be their wedding night, the night they'd celebrate their first wedding anniversary, the tenth, twentieth, thirtieth, fiftieth, the birth of their first child and the others he hoped they would have.

His hands covered her back, burning her flesh through her cotton blouse. Pulling her closer, he lowered his head and tasted her mouth. Her lips parted and his tongue mated with hers, plunging and pulling back, as he simulated making love to her.

Kelly writhed against Ryan in an attempt to get even closer. It had taken only three days away from him to make her crave him. How had she existed every Sunday through Thursday not having him touch her?

His hands moved lower, cupping her hips and allowing her to feel the solid bulge in his jeans. His hardness electrified her as she moaned and exhaled into his open mouth.

Ryan forced himself to go slow. He wanted to prolong their coming together as long as possible. He caught the tip of her tongue between his teeth and sucked gently while pulling it into his mouth. Kelly moaned in protest, but he refused to let her go. He sucked a little harder and suddenly she went pliant in his arms. He had to release her tongue when he swept her up in his arms and placed her on the bed.

Moving over her body, his lips seared a hot path down her neck and under her ears. His hands went to the buttons on her blouse. Suddenly fingers that were trained to perform the most delicate surgical procedures were heavy and clumsy. Placing both hands at the neckline, he pulled at the fabric. It parted, buttons flying in every direction.

The sight of her dark nipples showing through the sheer fabric of her white bra was his undoing. Ryan did not remember undressing Kelly or himself. What he did remember was sliding down the length of her body and drinking deeply from between her legs. He remembered turning her over and running his tongue down the length of her spine and over the curve of her hips. He remembered tasting and sampling every inch of her fragrant body as her moans of pleasure echoed his labored breathing.

It was when he guided his swollen flesh into her hot, wet pulsing flesh that he forgot everything. Slipping his hands under her hips, he held her as he pushed into her again and again.

Kelly gloried in the hard body atop hers. Her breasts tingled against his hair-roughened chest, whenever she arched to meet his downward thrusts. She trailed her fingernails up and down Ryan's back, eliciting deep groans from him. Without warning, he reversed position. She almost toppled off the bed with the sudden motion, but he caught her around the waist, holding her protectively.

A smile curved her mouth. He knew it was a position she favored because it allowed for deeper penetration and for her to set the pace for their coming together. Leaning back, she closed her eyes and established a slow rocking motion that mimicked her riding a horse. Ryan's hardness touched the walls of her womb, and she screamed out her climax, shaking uncontrollably as her screams became soft moans of satisfaction. Spent, she collapsed to his damp chest.

The muscles in Ryan's neck strained; he struggled not to pour out his passions into her hot body. Waves of ecstasy throbbed through him like blood rushing through veins, carrying precious oxygen to the heart. He tried holding back but the rush of desire seized him and sent him hurtling into a dimension where he experienced free-fall for the first time in his life.

They lay together, still joined, and waited until their respiration slowed enough for them to breathe without gasping. Their coming together was special; the night was special.

Kelly moved, shifting until her legs were sandwiched between Ryan's. The odor of their lovemaking blended with the perfume and cologne on their bodies. Resting her check on his breastbone, she sighed softly, knowing she would never forget a single detail of this joining.

Ryan ran his fingers through her short hair. "When do you want to marry, darling?"

Raising her head, she met his gaze. "How about a month from now?"

"You want to wait that long?"

"That's not long, Ryan."

"For me it is."

"Aren't you forgetting about Sean?"

Ryan's forehead furrowed. "What about him?"

"He needs time to get used to me sharing his father with him."

"Sean is crazy about you."

"That may be true, but we'll still need a period of adjustment. Right now he sees me as his teacher, not his mother."

"What do you want him to call you?"

"That will be up to him."

Holding hands, they planned their upcoming nuptials. Kelly told Ryan she wanted to be married at Blackstone Farms. She expressed a desire have her sister as her matron of honor, while Ryan said he would ask Sheldon to stand in as his best man.

"I have someone I want you to meet," he said cryptically.

"Who?"

"My brother."

Kelly sat up. "He's here now?"

Ryan nodded. "He's leaving tomorrow night."

She wanted to meet the other Blackstone son—the one who had partnered Ryan during their adolescent mishaps. "Is it possible to meet him now, because I've made plans to take the children into town for a puppet show tomorrow."

Sitting up, Ryan swung his legs over the side of the bed. "Sure."

Kelly moved off the bed, smiling. "Race you to the shower." She hadn't taken more than two steps when Ryan caught her around her waist, swept her off her feet and carried her over his shoulder into the bathroom.

Kelly felt a shiver of apprehension as she walked up the porch steps to Sheldon's home. It was only the second time she had entered the spacious structure. The first time had been for her interview.

What had caught her attention during that visit was a quartet of curio cabinets filled with trophies, mementoes and faded photographs of black jockeys dating back to the mid-nineteenth century. Sheldon had proudly revealed that of the fifteen jockeys at the first Kentucky Derby at Churchill Downs in Louisiana in 1875, fourteen were black. Oliver

Lewis, riding Aristides, became the first black to win the Derby. However, it was Isaac Murphy who was considered to be one of the greatest jockeys in U.S. racing history.

She followed Ryan through a formal dining room into a smaller room where she had sat while Sheldon had questioned her about her credentials and experience.

Her gaze met and fused with a pair of gray eyes that reminded her of Sheldon and Ryan's. Whereas Ryan's eyes reminded her of lightning, Jeremy's made her think of a cloaking fog. He stood up, his gaze narrowing. Seconds later, Sheldon also stood up.

Ryan curved an arm around Kelly's waist, the action communicating protection and possession. The gesture was not lost on Sheldon.

"Ah, Miss Kelly."

She nodded. "Good evening, Sheldon."

A mysterious smile curved Ryan's mouth. "Jeremy, this is Miss Kelly Andrews, my fiancée." He ignored his father's gasp. "Kelly, my brother and former partner in crime, Jeremy."

"When…when did you two decide this?" Sheldon sputtered.

Jeremy leaned over and kissed Kelly's cheek. "Welcome to the family. Don't say I didn't warn you, but you're about to have the ride of your life," he added, whispering in her ear.

She smiled at Jeremy, deciding she liked him. There was no doubt he and Ryan were brothers because they looked so much alike. But that's where the similarity ended. There was something about Jeremy that was overtly dangerous. A sixth sense told her he was a magnet for trouble.

Sheldon pursed his lips, whistling loudly. Everyone went completely still. Three pairs of eyes were fixed on him. "Will someone please tell me if there's going to be a wedding?"

Ryan smiled. "Yes, Pop, there's going to be a wedding. Kelly and I plan to marry sometime next month."

Sheldon crossed his arms over his chest in a gesture Kelly had seen Ryan affect so many times. "I'll say it again. When did you decide this?"

"Tonight," Kelly said in a quiet voice.

Sheldon's expression was impassive. "Are you sure you want to marry my son and spend the rest of your life on a horse farm?"

"Pop!" Ryan's voice bounced off the walls.

Kelly caught his arm, feeling tension tightening the muscles. "It's all right, darling." Jeremy and Sheldon exchanged glances at the endearment. Giving Sheldon a direct stare, she said, "The answer is yes to both questions. I will marry Ryan, and I plan to

spend the rest of my life living on a horse farm raising our children to love this land and honor the heri-
tage left them by their ancestors."

"Boo-yaw!" Sheldon yelled, pumping his fist in
the air.

Ryan and Jeremy howled, slapping each other's
back while shouting, "Boo-yaw!"

"This calls for a celebratory drink," Sheldon
said as he made his way over to a liquor cabinet. He
took out a bottle of aged bourbon. "I've been saving
this for a long time. The last time this old girl and
I danced together was the day I became a grandfather." He gave Kelly a level stare. "You are able to
imbibe, aren't you?"

At first she did not understand his question, but
realization dawned. He probably thought the reason
she and Ryan had planned to marry so quickly was
because she was pregnant.

"Yes, I am."

"Daddy? Are you having a party?"

Everyone turned to find Sean standing in the
doorway, rubbing his eyes. He was dressed in a pair
of lightweight cotton pajamas. It was apparent the
loud voices had awakened him.

Ryan smiled at Sean. "Yes. Come in." Sean
padded barefoot into the den, and found himself
cradled in his father's arms. "We're celebrating because Miss Kelly and I are going to be married."

Sean's eyes widened with this disclosure. "She… she's going to be my mama?"

Pressing a kiss to his son's forehead, Ryan said, "Yes, she is."

His eyes sparkled. "She's going to be my mama and my teacher?"

Ryan nodded. "Yes."

Pumping his fist like he'd seen his grandfather do, he crowed, "Boo-yaw!"

Kelly doubled over in laughter, unable to stop until tears rolled down her cheeks. Jeremy was right. She was in for a wild ride—one she looked forward to taking over and over again.

Chapter Twelve

Sheldon and Jeremy raised snifters filled with an ounce of premium bourbon and toasted Ryan and Kelly. Sean, standing between his grandfather and uncle, lifted his glass of apple juice.

"To Daddy and my new Mama," he said, giggling.

Kelly felt her eyes fill. Blinking, she smiled through her tears. "Thank you, Sean." She touched her glass to Sean's, Ryan's, Jeremy's and finally Sheldon's. She took a sip, holding the liquor in her mouth for several seconds before letting it slide down the back of her throat. It detonated on impact.

"Whoa!" she gasped.

Sheldon nodded his approval. "See why this old girl only comes to the dance every few years?"

Jeremy also gasped, holding his throat. "Boo-ahhh!" he whispered.

"Ditto," Ryan added after swallowing. He placed his glass on a sideboard. "That's enough of that."

Reaching for the bottle, Jeremy studied the label. "I've never heard of this brand. Pop, are you certain this stuff isn't moonshine?"

Sheldon shook his head. "I never thought my boys would grow up to be such sissies." He drained his glass, reached for Sean, and swung him up in his arms. Cradling his grandson's head to his shoulder, he whispered loudly, "It's time for the men of the house to turn in for the night." He blew a kiss at Kelly as he strode out of the room.

Jeremy walked over to Kelly and hugged her. "Congratulations again. I'm with Pop and Sean. I'm going to bed." He patted Ryan's shoulder. "All the best, brother."

Waiting until they were alone, Ryan curved his arms around Kelly's waist. "I want you to come back to my place with me. I'd like to show you something."

"What?"

He flashed a mysterious smile. "You'll see."

Kelly found herself in the middle of the living room of a house that was soon to become her home. The two-story, three-bedroom structure was the equivalent of one city block away from the ones occupied by Sheldon and Jeremy. Ryan had informed her that his father had first taken up residence in the house after he'd returned from a tour of duty in Vietnam.

The furnishings were formal and elegant. Every chair, table and lamp was meticulously positioned as if for a magazine layout. It was perfect, a little too perfect. A slight frown appeared between her eyes. There was something wrong with the room. Suddenly it hit her! It didn't look lived in. Staring at a sofa and matching love seat, Kelly mentally catalogued what she would rearrange. Firstly she would take down the drapes and replace them with a lighter weight fabric to let in the natural light.

Walking over to the fireplace, she studied the framed photographs lining the mantel. Smiling, she recognized a younger Sheldon in a United States Army uniform with his young smiling bride. Peering closely at the picture, she noted Julia Blackstone's natural beauty. Ryan had inherited her smile.

There were photographs of Ryan and Jeremy as children, and more of Sean at different ages. Nowhere was there a photograph of Sean's mother. It was if she'd been completely erased from his life. She heard footfalls, and turned around. Ryan had returned, holding a small wooden box.

He cupped her elbow, leading her over to sit on the sofa. He placed the box on her lap. "Open it."

She sprang a latch, the lid opening. Staring back at her on a bed of black velvet was a solitaire ring with a large square-cut blue-white diamond; along with the ring was a pair of drop South Sea pearl earrings dangling from a diamond cluster, and a bangle of diamond baguettes.

"They are beautiful, Ryan."

"They belonged to my great-grandmother. My mother gave them to me a month before she died. She wanted me to give them to my wife."

She gave him an incredulous look. "Why didn't you give them to Sean's mother?"

His expression was impassive. "I'd offered them to her, but she said she didn't want someone else's hand-me-downs. The pieces in that box were purchased from Cartier between 1917 and 1919."

She picked up the bangle. "It's heavy."

"That's because all of the pieces are set in platinum."

"What about Jeremy?"

"Don't worry, princess. Jeremy was given his share."

Reaching around her, Ryan picked up the box with the jewelry. He took the ring and slipped it on the third finger of Kelly's left hand. It was a perfect fit.

She extended her hand. The light from a floor lamp caught the diamond, prisms of light catching and radiating from the flawless gem.

Ryan curved an arm around Kelly's shoulders when she rested her head on his shoulder. "We're going to have to choose a date."

"What about the last weekend in August."

"How about the first weekend?" he countered.

Easing back, she stared at him. "That's only three weeks away."

"I know. We can go up to Saratoga Springs, New York before the summer racing season ends. I know it's not much of a honeymoon, but I'd like to take you away, even if it's only for a weekend. We can take a real honeymoon during the Christmas break."

"How long is the racing season?"

"Six weeks."

Kelly wondered if she could pull everything together in three weeks. She had to send out invitations, get a dress and select a ring for Ryan.

"Okay," she agreed, kissing his cheek. "I'm going back to D.C. at the end of the week to get my sister to help me with invitations. And while I'm there I'll do some shopping."

Ryan pulled her across his lap. "If you need help with anything, just let me know."

She nuzzled his neck, breathing a kiss under his ear. "You need to take me back to my place."

"Why?" he crooned.

"Because I have to go to sleep, Ryan. I'm going need all of my energy for my students tomorrow."

"Sleep here tonight."

"No. Not until we're married."

Pulling back he stared at her. "Don't tell me I'm marrying an old-fashioned girl?"

"I'm more conservative than old-fashioned. That comes from working with young children. After all, they learn from example."

Kelly had no way of knowing that when she answered an ad for a teaching position on a horse farm she would find a love that promised forever.

Kelly slept restlessly throughout the night, and when she left her bed at six she felt as if she had been up all night. She brewed a small carafe of coffee, drank several cups, then dialed the area code for D.C.

Pamela answered the phone with a cheery, "Good morning."

"Pamela, this is Kelly."

There came a pause. "What's with the Pamela?"

"I have good news to tell you."

"When are you due?"

"I'm not pregnant!" she practically shouted. Well, she didn't think she was pregnant. When she and Ryan had made love the night before he hadn't used a condom. Squinting she calculated when she'd last had her period. Sighing, she realized she was safe.

"I'm getting married in three weeks here at the farm, and I'm going to need your help with addressing invitations and shopping for a dress."

Pamela screamed at the top of her lungs, eliciting a frantic barking from Miss Porter. "I can't believe it," she said over and over. A loud sniffle came through the earpiece. "Dang, Kel. I can't believe I'm crying and souping snot at the same time. Wait until I blow my nose."

"Pamela?" Kelly said into the receiver when a full minute elapsed without her sister coming back to the phone.

"I'm back. I had to tell Leo the good news."

"I'm coming in this weekend."

"Is there anything you want me to do on this end in the meantime?

"Yes. I need you to use your artistic talents and design an invitation for me. I have to get Ryan's full name and the directions to Blackstone Farms. And you and I have to do some serious shopping in Chevy Chase."

"Where are you going?"

"Ryan and I are going up to Saratoga Springs next month for a weekend."

"Now, Miss Clotheshorse, you're singing my song."

Kelly laughed. She and Pamela had gotten their love of shopping from their mother. For Camille it was hats, Pamela handbags and Kelly's weakness was shoes.

"I'm going to call Mama and give her the news as soon as I hang up with you."

"Kel?"

"Yes, Pam."

"I'm so happy for you."

"Thanks, big sis."

She rang off and dialed her mother's number. The call lasted less than five minutes, and when she hung up it was Kelly's turn to shed tears of joy.

* * *

A portable stage had been set up under a tent large enough to accommodate the sixty invited guests and more than thirty of Blackstone Farms's extended family. It had rained steadily for two days, then the night before Ryan Blackstone was scheduled to exchange vows with Kelly Andrews, but after the rain had stopped, a strong wind swept the clouds across the sky to reveal an orange-yellow near-full moon.

Kelly stood beside Ryan, eyes closed, repeating her vows. She was afraid that if she looked at him she wouldn't be able to hold back her tears. Her hands were trembling as she slipped a platinum and yellow gold band on Ryan's finger.

She heard the judge telling Ryan he could kiss his bride, and her world stood still as she felt the pressure of his firm lips on hers, sealing their troth. It was over. She was now Mrs. Ryan Jackson Blackstone.

Ryan pulled Kelly closer, her soft curves melding with the hardness of his body. He'd run the race and won the ultimate prize.

"Didn't I warn you, Mrs. Blackstone?"

"About what?" she whispered against his warm mouth.

"That I play for keeps."

Her smile was as dazzling as the sun warming the earth. "So do I, Mr. Blackstone."

Turning, they faced all of the people who had come to witness another generation of Blackstones solidifying their place in Virginia's horse country's history.

Epilogue

Four months later...

Ryan sat at the desk in his office when the door opened. Glancing up he saw Mark Charlesworth holding a large vase with a bouquet of flowers wrapped in pale pink cellophane.

"These came for you, Doc."

Rising to his feet, Ryan smiled. "Who sent them?"

"Me." Kelly moved into the doorway, grinning at her husband.

Mark placed the flowers on a table and winked at Kelly as he walked out of the vet's office. Miss Kelly had asked him to carry the vase to Dr. Blackstone, because she did not want to lift anything that was too heavy. The glow in her eyes and her mysterious smile meant that the resident veterinarian was going to receive wonderful news.

Mark had received a bouquet of flowers from Miss Kelly once he received his test results from his college entrance exam. He had received a combined score of thirteen hundred sixty on the SAT. He was going to college! He would miss Blackstone Farms, but knew he would come back one day—as a veterinarian.

Kelly watched Ryan watching her. "Congratulations, Dr. Blackstone."

He moved closer, his gaze fixed on her moist lips. "For what, Mrs. Blackstone."

Reaching for his left hand, she placed it over her flat belly. "For this."

His gaze widened until she saw their black depths. "Are you sure?"

Her lids lowered. "As sure as I am that I'll love you forever."

Gathering Kelly to his chest, he picked her up and swung her around and around until she pleaded with him to stop.

Throwing back his head, he shouted, "Boo-yaw!"

Caught up in his infectious joy, Kelly whispered close to his ear, "Boo-yaw to you, too."

"Now I know you can do better than that with the Blackstone cheer."

Raising her chin, she closed her eyes and shouted "Boo-yaw!"

Ryan lowered his head and kissed her long and deep. They were still locked in a passionate embrace when some of the stable hands came to see what the shouting was all about.

Three men crowded in the doorway to find their boss cradling his wife to his chest. Their gazes shifted to the flowers and they backed away, smiling.

"Something tells me that we're going to have another celebration soon," one said quietly.

And Blackstone Farms had a lot to celebrate. Their jockeys had stood within the chalk markings of the winner's circle in the last five of the six races they had run.

But the best celebration was still to come—with the birth of another Blackstone come summer.

* * * * *

VERY PRIVATE DUTY

Prologue

Fourteen Years Ago

"I never thought I'd say it, but I'm scared, Jeremy. I'm afraid of leaving you and Blackstone Farms." Her hushed tone trembled.

Jeremy Blackstone stared at Tricia. "There's nothing to be afraid of. New York and California are only three hours apart."

Tricia Parker was scheduled to fly from Virginia for New York to enroll in a premed program in less than twenty-four hours, leaving the protective, cloistered world of the horse farm behind.

"Let's get out of here, Jeremy."

He hesitated, then said, "Okay. Let's go." Jeremy stood up, his arm curving protectively around her waist. They hadn't taken more than half a dozen steps when a familiar voice stopped them.

"Where are you going?"

Tricia turned and faced her grandfather. "We're going for a drive, Grandpa."

The lines in Augustus Parker's forehead deepened in frustration. "These people are here because of you, and you're walking out on them?"

"Grandpa, please don't start," she pleaded.

Gus gave Jeremy a level look. "I'd like to speak to my granddaughter for a few minutes. *Alone.*" He'd emphasized the last word.

Jeremy dropped his arm but not his gaze, holding the older man's direct stare. "Tricia, I'll wait for you outside."

Tricia watched Jeremy walk out of the main house's dining hall before her gaze returned to her grandfather's. "Grandpa, you don't understand—"

"What is there to understand, Tricia?" he said, interrupting her. "I have told you over and over not to get involved with the boss's son, because it's going to lead to no good."

She tilted her chin in a defiant gesture. "It's too late for that, because Jeremy and I *are* involved with each other. We plan to marry after we graduate from college."

"No, Tricia."

"Yes, Grandpa," she countered softly. "We're in love."

"Do you really think the son of the owner of one of the most profitable horse farms in the state of Virginia is going to marry the daughter of a woman who was a…" His words trailed off.

"A whore!" Tricia spat out the word. "Is that how you think of *me?*"

Lowering his head, Gus shook it slowly. "No, grandbaby girl. I know you're not a whore," he said in a quiet voice. "I just don't want you to get hurt."

She smiled. "Jeremy won't hurt me. He loves me too much for that." Rising on tiptoe, she kissed his cheek. "I've got to go. I'll see you later."

"Promise me you'll be careful."

Her smile widened. "I promise."

Tricia made her way out of the dining hall to the parking lot, coming face-to-face with the last person she wanted to see. She'd made certain to avoid him after he had once tried coming on to her. Russell Smith, three years her senior, was the head trainer's son. He was tall, dark and handsome, and he capitalized on his looks with every opportunity—especially with women.

"Leaving so soon, beautiful?"

"Yes, I am."

He smiled at her. "I wanted to give you a little something to celebrate your going off to college."

Tricia offered him a facetious smile. "Please give it to my grandfather for me."

Russell reached up, caught her chin and brushed a gentle kiss over her lips. "I'll bring it by your house later."

Tricia resisted the urge to wipe the back of her hand over her mouth. "Suit yourself," she said through clenched teeth. Stepping around him she walked over to where Jeremy leaned against the bumper of his Jeep Wrangler.

Jeremy straightened and schooled his expression not to reveal what he was feeling—a slow-rising fury threatening to explode. "What's up with you and Smith?"

She stared up at him. "What are you talking about?"

His jaw hardened. "I'm talking about Russell Smith kissing you."

Tricia looped her arm through Jeremy's. "He was kissing me goodbye. I'm certain I'll get a few more goodbye kisses before I leave tomorrow." Rising on tiptoe, she kissed his earlobe. "You're the one I love, Jeremy," she said with feeling.

The tense lines in his face relaxed with her passionate confession. "Where do you want to go?"

"Surprise me," she whispered in his ear.

Jeremy helped her up onto the passenger seat, closed the door and rounded the SUV. He got in, turned the key in the ignition and drove out of the parking lot with a burst of speed. "Hang on, kid." Reaching up, Tricia grasped the roll bar as the Jeep literally ate up the road.

He maneuvered into a section of the farm referred to as the north end and stopped under a copse of weeping willow trees next to a meandering stream. Using the headlights for illumination, he reached for a blanket in the space behind the seats and spread it on the ground. Then, he helped Tricia from the vehicle and settled her on the blanket, where they lay together holding hands.

Jeremy did not want her to leave Blackstone Farms any more than Tricia wanted to. He would follow her departure in two days. "You're so precious to me," he whispered against her parted lips.

Tricia's fingers were busy undoing the buttons on Jeremy's shirt while he deftly undid the hidden zipper down the back of her dress. "Don't talk," she whispered. "Just love me."

Mouths joined, they undressed quickly, leaving their discarded garments strewn over the blanket. Cradling her face between his palms, Jeremy eased her down to the blanket again as if she were a piece of fragile porcelain. Their own breathing drowned out the nocturnal sounds serenading the verdant valley nestled between the Blue Ridge and Shenandoah Mountain ranges.

Tricia inhaled the natural scent of Jeremy's skin mingling with his cologne. Her fingers tunneled through his rakishly long, inky-black wavy hair. She loved everything about him: his mysterious smoky-gray eyes, strong firm mouth and voice he rarely raised in anger.

His hairy chest grazed her breasts, her nipples hardening quickly. The motion heated her blood and ignited a fire that raced through her body and settled between her thighs. She knew without a doubt this coming together, the last one they would share for a long time, would not be the leisurely joining they'd experienced in the past.

Jeremy parted Tricia's legs with his knee and eased his sex into her hot, pulsing body. Both sighed as flesh melded with flesh, holding fast.

Tricia closed her eyes, savoring the hardness inside her. She was afraid to move because she did not want it to be over before it began. But her lover was not to be denied as he rolled his hips, sliding in and out, rocking back and forth. "Faster, Jeremy," she gasped, trembling as the little flutters grew stronger and stronger with each thrust.

Burying his face in the hollow between her neck and shoulder, Jeremy gritted his teeth, struggling not to release the straining passion in his loins. "No," he moaned as if in pain.

Her fingernails sank into the muscles in his firm buttocks. "Please."

He knew it was useless to fight the inevitable and quickened his motions until he did not know where he began and Tricia ended. They had become one in every sense of the word.

They climaxed at the same time, the sensations taking them higher than they had ever experienced together before, and released them in a shuddering ecstasy that seemed to go on and on. They lay motionless, their hearts beating in unison.

Jeremy wanted her again, but knew if he had seconds, then he'd want thirds and maybe fourths. It had always been that way with Tricia. She had become his drug of choice—one he did not want to ever give up.

Ten minutes after they'd washed away the evidence of their lovemaking in the shallow stream and put their clothes back on, they arrived at the two-bedroom bungalow where Tricia had grown up. Lights blazed from every window. The front door opened. Russell and Gus stepped out onto the porch and shook hands.

"Will I see you at breakfast?" Tricia's voice was barely a whisper.

Jeremy nodded. "Of course, sweetheart. I'll help you down."

She waited until he came around and swung her to the ground. "Good night, my love." Boldly, purposefully, she wound her arms around his neck, pulled his head down and kissed him.

Jeremy watched Tricia as she made her way up to

the porch and walked into the house, Gus following. Grabbing the roll bar, he pulled himself up behind the wheel and released the brake.

"Hold up a minute, Blackstone."

His hand froze on the gearshift. He looked over at Russell. "What do you want?"

"I want to thank you."

"For what?"

Russell's lips twisted into a cynical smile. "For making it an easier ride in the saddle."

"What the hell are you talking about?"

"Tricia. You broke her in just right. I'm not one for virgins because I always find them too clingy. But Tricia's different. She doesn't mind sharing her goodies with the hired help as long as she can hold on to the boss's son." Doffing an imaginary hat, he walked back to his pickup truck parked alongside the bungalow.

Jeremy did not want to believe Russell, but he had seen him kiss Tricia. And what, he mused, was he doing at her place? A silent voice in his head screamed no because Tricia had said there was nothing between her and Russell…but a voice of reason said otherwise. However, there was only one way to uncover the truth. A minute later he stood on the porch, ringing the bell. Gus came to the door.

"I thought you and Tricia said good night."

"I'd like to talk to her again, sir."

Gus shook his head. "No, Jeremy. You've done enough damage."

"Pardon me, but just what is it I've done?"

The older man smiled, the expression softening his dark-brown face. "I like you, Jeremy, and I respect your father. But, I think it's best you leave my granddaughter alone."

"I can't do that, sir. Tricia and I—"

"There is no Tricia and you," Gus countered angrily. "Open your eyes, son. It's been Tricia and that young Smith fellow. He's planning to visit her in New York next month. He came over to give her this." Reaching into his slacks, he pulled a small velvet box from his pocket and opened it.

Jeremy stared at the delicate diamond heart. It was true. Russell hadn't lied. He was sleeping with Tricia and she was sleeping with both of them. He inclined his head. "You're right, Mr. Parker. Good night."

Jeremy threw underwear, T-shirts, socks and a pair of jeans into a suede duffel bag and zipped it. Moving like an automaton, he forced himself to put one foot in front of the other as he descended the staircase. Several feet from the front door he saw his father coming from the direction of the family room.

Sheldon stared at the bag in his hand. "Going somewhere?"

Jeremy swallowed to relieve the dryness in his constricted throat. "Yes, Pop. I'm going to spend a couple of days in Richmond. I'll be back Sunday night."

Sheldon's gaze narrowed in suspicion. "Are you all right, son?"

"Sure, Pop."

"Drive carefully."

Jeremy waved to his father as he opened the door, then closed it quietly behind him.

Tricia woke up early, showered and dressed in record time. She wanted to see Jeremy at the dining hall before he left for the track to watch the trainers put the horses through their exercise regimen. Her heart racing, she walked into the dining hall. Sheldon sat alone at a table. She headed for the owner of Blackstone Farms, a bright smile in place.

"Good morning, Sheldon."

His light-gray eyes bore into her as if she were a stranger. "Good morning, Tricia. Jeremy's not here."

She felt her heart stop, then start up again in a runaway rhythm. "Where is he?"

"He's staying in Richmond for a few days."

Tricia's hands closed into tight fists to conceal their trembling. "When did he leave?"

"Last night."

She closed her eyes for several seconds and when she opened them her gaze was steady. "Thank you."

He'd lied to her. Jeremy had promised to see her off, but it was apparent he had changed his mind. Perhaps, she thought, her grandfather was right. She should not have gotten involved with the boss's son.

She left the dining hall, head held high, fighting back tears. She promised herself she would never contact Jeremy Blackstone unless he contacted her first. And that was a promise she intended to keep.

Chapter One

Present Day

Eyes wide, her heart pumping rapidly and knees buckling slightly, Tricia Parker stared at the man sprawled on the Blackstones' leather sofa.

She could barely recognize Jeremy with all those bruises on his forehead, cheek and jaw. There was also a slight swelling over his right eye. Dressed in a white T-shirt and shorts, he was unshaved, his short black hair spiked, his left leg covered with a plaster cast from toe to knee, and the third and fourth fingers of his left hand were taped to a splint.

Only her nurses' training prevented Tricia from

losing her composure when she saw the man to whom she had given her heart as an awestruck teenager. Each time she returned to Blackstone Farms a small part of her wanted to catch a glimpse of Sheldon Blackstone's youngest son, but it was as if their paths were destined not to cross again—until now.

"What happened to him?" Her voice was low, raspy, as if she had been screaming for hours.

Sheldon's light-gray eyes were fixed on Jeremy, who hadn't stirred since being placed on the sofa. "He had an accident—on the job," he added after a slight pause.

Tricia knew "on the job" for Jeremy was as a special agent with the Drug Enforcement Administration. He had graduated Stanford and instead of returning to Blackstone Farms he joined the U.S. Marine Corps. A month after he completed his military obligation he applied to the DEA as a special agent. She moved closer and placed a hand over his forehead. It was cool to the touch.

"How long has he been like this?"

"He was sedated before he was flown in from D.C.," Ryan Blackstone, Jeremy's older brother and the horse farm's resident veterinarian, said.

She withdrew her hand. "I'm talking about his injuries."

"Tomorrow will be two weeks," Sheldon said behind her. "He's going to need round-the-clock nursing care."

Tricia turned and stared at the imposing-look-ing owner of the most profitable African-American horse farm in the history of Virginia's horseracing. The years had been kind to Jeremy's father. Tall and solidly built, the middle-aged widower still had a full head of raven-black hair with a feathering of gray at the temples. He had extraordinary eyes: shimmering light gray in a golden-brown face.

"You want me to take care of him." Her question was a statement.

Sheldon inclined his head. "Yes."

"But, I'm only going to be here for a month." She had just begun her four-week vacation leave from her job as a registered nurse with a group of Baltimore pediatricians. "Don't you think it would be better to hire a permanent private-duty nurse?"

"I would if you weren't here. I'm certain Jeremy will respond much better to treatment with familiar faces around him. That's why I decided to bring him back to the farm."

A warning voice whispered in her head not to become involved with Jeremy again; however, she ignored it when she closed her eyes for several sec-onds. She wanted to decline Sheldon's request but couldn't. She had grown up on the farm, and tradi-tion was that everyone looked after one another. Her gaze lingered on Sheldon before it shifted to Ryan.

"Okay."

Both men sighed.

Ryan closed the distance between them, cupped her elbow and led her into the dining room. His dark-gray eyes studied her intently. He was undeniably a Blackstone: height, complexion, raven hair, high cheekbones, aquiline nose and mouth. As the older brother, he'd had most of the girls who had grown up on the horse farm fantasizing about marrying him, but not Tricia. Four years her senior, Ryan was too old and much too serious. Her choice had been Jeremy. They were the same age, carefree and at times very reckless.

Jeremy had earned the reputation of driving too fast, swearing and fighting too much, and he had been the one who had introduced her to a passion she had not experienced since.

"What am I dealing with, Ryan?"

"Broken ankle, dislocated fingers and a concussion. His ankle is held together with screws."

Tricia nodded. "Is there anything else I should know about your brother? Perhaps why he has been sedated, since it's not for pain?"

A sheepish grin softened the lines of tension around Ryan's mouth. "I could never fool you, Tricia. It's as if you have a sixth sense when it comes to Jeremy. The two of you must be bound by an invisible force that keeps you connected even though you've been separated for so many years."

A shiver snaked its way up her spine. There had been a time when she and Jeremy were able to complete each other's sentences. "You're wrong, Ryan," she said softly. "If that had been the case, then I would've known that something had happened to him. What aren't you telling me?"

"He has episodes—flashbacks of what happened to him and the other members of his team before he was rescued."

Her large dark eyes widened with this disclosure. It was obvious Jeremy was experiencing post-traumatic stress syndrome. "Was he tortured?"

Ryan shook his head. "I don't know. He was debriefed, but as civilians we're not privy to that information."

"What are his meds?"

Ryan told her about the prescribed medication and dosage. "I'll make certain to give you the hospital's report. My brother is scheduled to see an orthopedist and a psychiatrist in a couple of days. I know this is your vacation, but I will make it up—"

"There's nothing to make up for," Tricia said, interrupting him. "Remember, I grew up here, and I've always thought of you and Jeremy as my brothers."

Ryan smiled. He wanted to tell Tricia that *he* had always thought of her as a younger sister, but not Jeremy. There was something about the assistant trainer's granddaughter that softened his brother, made him vulnerable. She would only stay a month, but perhaps it was long enough to help Jeremy adjust to coming home.

"He can't stay on the sofa," Tricia said. "He needs a bed and easy access to a bathroom."

"We plan to move him into his house in a few minutes. Things will go easier for you if he's under his own roof. A hospital bed has been set up in the family room. There's also a wheelchair, shower equipment and a pair of crutches. Sleeping arrangements will also be set up for you at his place, so I suggest you pick up what you'll need and then come back to Jeremy's place."

Tricia nodded numbly as she walked out of the main house. Sheldon had houses built for his sons less than a quarter of a mile from the main house after they'd graduated from college.

Sleeping arrangements have been set up for you at Jeremy's place. Ryan's words echoed over and over as she drove back to the two-bedroom bungalow where she'd grown up with her grandparents.

She'd returned to Blackstone Farms to spend a month with Gus Parker, never believing she would have to share a house with the man she'd fallen in love with and continued to love even though she'd married another.

It had taken Dwight Lansing less than a year of marriage to realize his love and passion would never be reciprocated. A week before he and Tricia would have celebrated their first wedding anniversary, their marriage was annulled. She'd given her husband her body but never her heart. That she had given to Jeremy Blackstone to hold on to for eternity.

Jeremy surfaced from a drug-induced haze for the first time in hours. Long, thick black lashes framing a pair of deep-set, dove-gray eyes fluttered as he attempted to focus on the face looming over him.

The pain in his leg was forgotten as he stared up at the girl he hadn't seen in fourteen years. His eyes widened, moving slowly over her face and then lower. He stood corrected. Tricia Parker was not a girl, but a woman—all woman.

"Hi, Jeremy."

Her voice was soft and husky, the way he remembered it after they'd finished making love. She had been the one to do the talking when he couldn't, because making love had usually left him breathless and speechless.

The long, black curly hair that she'd worn in a braid was missing, in its place a short, cropped style that hugged her well-shaped head. Everything about her was ample: breasts, hips, round face, dark sparkling eyes and her mouth. Oh, how he'd loved kissing her mouth.

A white short-sleeved linen blouse and a pair of black slacks failed to camouflage or minimize her full figure. If her coloring had been a creamy magnolia instead of rich sable brown, she could have been the perfect model for baroque artist Peter Paul

Rubens. Tricia was now the epitome of Rubenesque. It was as if she wore an invisible badge that silently announced: I Am Woman.

He closed his eyes, temporarily forgetting the deceitful woman hovering over him. "Where am I?"

"You're home."

"Home where?" He'd slurred the two words.

"In your house."

His eyes darkened like storm clouds. He'd waited fourteen, long agonizing years to reunite with Tricia so he could confront her about her infidelity. And now that that had become a reality, he knew he couldn't. Not when pain throbbed throughout his body.

"Get out of my house!"

Shaking her head, Tricia thrust her face close to his, feeling his moist breath sweep over her cheek. "I'm sorry, Jeremy, I can't do that."

Gray eyes glowing from his olive-brown face, like those of a savage predator, he bared his teeth. "I don't want you here."

Straightening, she rounded the bed, gently lifting his left foot to rest on two pillows. "It's not what you want but what you need. I'm going to be around for the next month, so you'd better get used to seeing me."

He went completely still. "A month?"

"Yes. I'm on vacation. Once it's over, I'm going back to Baltimore."

"I don't know if I can tolerate seeing you for a month."

"Stuff it, Jeremy," she retorted. "It's not as if I want to be bothered with you, either. But I promised your father that I'd look after you, and I'll do that until another nurse replaces me."

She neatly folded a lightweight blanket at the foot of the bed. What had been a family room was now a temporary bedroom. A tobacco-brown leather club chair with an ottoman was positioned several feet from the bed. The chair matched the daybed in a spacious alcove, which was now her temporary sleeping space. Sheldon had chosen the room because of an adjoining full bathroom with a freestanding shower.

Jeremy stared at Tricia. She did not look any older than when he last saw her, but she had changed, and it wasn't just her fuller figure or shorter hair. He'd lost count of the number of hours, days, months and years she'd continued to haunt him despite her duplicity. How could she profess to love him while she'd slept with another man at the same time? Had she told Russell Smith that she'd loved him, too?

"You didn't finish medical school." His question was a statement.

She straightened. "No, I didn't.

"What happened?"

"Nothing happened. I decided I wasn't cut out to be a doctor."

He lifted an eyebrow. "So, you became a nurse instead."

"Yes, Jeremy."

"Any specialty?"

She nodded, saying, "Pediatrics."

"You became a pediatric nurse instead of a pediatrician?"

Tricia wanted to scream at him that it had been his fault that she hadn't realized her dream to become a doctor. What neither knew when she'd left the farm to enter college was that she hadn't left alone. She was seven weeks' pregnant with Jeremy's baby, despite being on the Pill.

She had dropped out of college, given birth to a little girl and then lost her three months later, after they were run down by a speeding car. Her daughter died instantly, but Tricia spent weeks in the hospital with internal injuries.

The intoxicated driver, a celebrated matrimonial attorney to the rich and famous had the clout and resources to delay the case for years. Against her attorney's advice, Tricia settled out of court for less than she would've received if the case had gone to trial. At that time in her life she had been too depressed to relive the ordeal in a lengthy trial.

She did not blame the drunk driver for killing her baby. Tricia blamed Jeremy. And if he hadn't deserted her she could've returned to the farm to live. He had deserted her and their infant daughter.

She married her attorney, but only after he insisted they sign a prenuptial agreement. Dwight Lansing claimed he wanted to marry her because he loved her and not for her money.

"And you became a DEA agent instead of coming back to run the horse farm," she retorted sharply.

"We're not talking about me, Tricia."

"And I don't intend to talk about *me,* Jeremy. For the next month you and I are patient and nurse and nothing else."

Despite the pain in his head surpassing the one in his leg, he affected a snappy salute with his uninjured hand. "Yes, ma'am!"

She managed to hide a smile as she made her way to the windows and closed the vertical blinds, shutting out some of the bright sunlight pouring into the room. "Someone will deliver lunch in a few minutes. After that I'm going to help you get out of bed, even if it's just for half an hour."

"I'm not ready to get out of bed."

"Your doctor wants you out of bed."

"He's not here, so what he says doesn't mean spit!"

Tricia struggled to control her temper. As a pediatric nurse she had encountered children with a variety of illnesses and deformities, but invariably she was always able to coax a smile from them. Jeremy wasn't a child, but a thirty-two-year-old man who had chosen a career that put him at risk every day of his life. He was alive, and for that he should've been grateful, not angry and resentful.

"You will follow my directives." Her voice was soft yet threatening. "You need me to feed you and assist you with your personal hygiene." She knew he wouldn't be able to feed himself easily because he was left-handed. "Growl at me one more time and I'll take my time helping you to the bathroom. Lying in one's own waste is not the most pleasant experience."

Jeremy gave Tricia a long, penetrating look. How had she known? He and the three surviving members from a DEA Black Op team of six had hidden out in a swamp in the Peruvian jungle for forty-eight hours before they were rescued. Not only had they lain in their own waste but they'd been bitten repeatedly by insects. His team leader had come down with a fever and died within an hour of being airlifted to safety.

He had no more fight left in him—at least not today. His head felt as if it was exploding. He wanted to tell Tricia that he knew how to use a pair of crutches and hobble, albeit slowly, to the bathroom, but decided not to antagonize her further.

"All right," he said, deciding to concede. "You win, Tricia." And she would remain the winner, but only until his pain eased. "I'll get out of bed." Closing his eyes, he clenched his teeth.

"Are you in pain?"

He squinted. "My head."

"I'll take your vitals, then I'll give you something to take the edge off." Ryan had left a blood pressure kit and a digital thermometer for her use.

Jeremy suffered Tricia's gentle touch and the hauntingly familiar scent of her body as she took his temperature and blood pressure. She gave him a pill and a glass of water, watching closely as he placed it on his tongue. She recorded the readings on a pad and the time she had given him the painkiller.

"Drink all of the water."

He complied, handing her the empty glass. Their gazes met and fused. "Thank you," he mumbled reluctantly.

Her passive expression did not change. "You're welcome."

She was there, and then she was gone, taking her warmth and scent with her. And it had been her smell that, years ago, had drawn Jeremy to Tricia. She always wore perfume when the other girls on the farm smelled of hay and horses.

Sighing heavily, he closed his eyes. His father and brother complained they did not see him enough. And whenever he did return home it was never for more than a few days. There had been a time when Blackstone Farms was his whole world but after joining the DEA, the war on drugs had become his life. He always came back to reconnect with his family, but refused to stay.

He lay in the dimly lit room listening to the sound

of his own heart beating. He hadn't realized he had fallen asleep until he felt the soft touch on his arm and a familiar voice calling his name.

"Wake up, Jeremy. It's time to eat."

Seeing Tricia again, inhaling her familiar feminine scent reminded him of what he'd been denying for nearly half his life. He hadn't returned to Blackstone Farms after graduating from college because of the memories of a young woman to whom he had pledged his future. He had loved her unconditionally while she had deceived him with another man.

Whenever he visited the farm a part of him had hoped to see Tricia, but they never connected—until now. And whenever he asked her grandparents about her, their response was always, "She's doing just fine in the big city."

He shifted on the bed, groaning softly as pain shot through his ankle. Compressing his lips, he managed to somehow find a more comfortable position as Tricia adjusted the bed's tray table.

The moment she uncovered a plate he closed his eyes. "I want some real food."

She placed a cloth napkin over his chest. "This is real food."

He opened his eyes, his expression thunderous. "Broth, applesauce and weak-ass tea!"

She picked up a soup spoon. "You've been on a light diet. It's going to take time before you'll be able to tolerate solids." He clamped his jaw tight once she put the spoon to his mouth. "Open!"

He shook his head, chiding himself for the action. Each time he moved, intense pain tightened like a vise on his head. "No," he hissed between clenched teeth.

Tricia bit down on her lower lip in frustration and stared at the stubborn set of his jaw. Broken, battered and bruised he still had the power to make her heart race. "You're going to have to eat or you'll be too weak to get out of bed."

He glared at her. "Get me some food, Tricia. Now!"

She glared back in what she knew would become a standoff, a battle of wills. "I'm certain I warned you about raising your voice to me. Eat the broth and applesauce and I'll call the dining hall to have them send something else."

"What?"

"You can have either Jell-O or soft scrambled eggs."

"How about steak and eggs?"

"Not yet, hotshot. Once you're up and moving around I'll put in an order for steak and eggs. And if you actually cooperate, then you can have pancakes." Everyone at Blackstone Farms knew how much Jeremy loved the chef's pancakes. He opened his mouth and she fed him the soup.

"Is he giving you a hard time?" asked a familiar voice.

Tricia shifted slightly and stared over her shoulder at Ryan. He had entered the room without making a sound. "No."

Jeremy swallowed the bland liquid. "She's giving me a hard time. This stuff is as bad as castor oil."

Ryan pushed aside the ottoman as he sat on the roomy leather chair. He smiled and attractive lines fanned out around his eyes. He ran his left hand over his cropped hair, and a shaft of light coming through the blinds glinted off the band on his finger. He'd married the resident schoolteacher last summer, and now he and Kelly awaited the birth of their first child together. Ryan had a five-year-old son, Sean, from a prior marriage.

"It can't be that bad, little brother."

Jeremy grimaced. "Worse."

Ryan raised his eyebrows. "You better follow your nurse's orders and get your butt out of that bed as soon as possible."

Jeremy swallowed two more spoonfuls. "Why?"

"Kelly woke up this morning with contractions. They're not that strong, about twenty minutes apart, but there's a good chance she'll have the baby either today or tomorrow, and I know when I bring your niece home you don't want her to see her uncle flat on his back."

Jeremy managed a smile, but it looked more like

a grimace. "I thought Kelly wasn't due until the end of the month." It was now the second week in July.

"She's farther along than was first predicted. Babies are smarter than we are. They know exactly when to make their grand entrance. Don't you agree, Tricia?"

She nodded. The words she wanted to say were locked in her constricted throat. She wanted to tell Ryan that she had given Sheldon Blackstone his first granddaughter. A little girl she'd named Juliet to honor the memory of Jeremy's mother Julia—a little girl who'd been undeniably a Blackstone.

Tricia wanted to run out of the room, leaving the brothers to discuss the upcoming birth of Kelly's daughter. She drew a deep breath, forbidding herself to cry. Not in front of Jeremy.

"Ryan, could you please finish feeding your brother? I'd like to look in on my grandfather for a few minutes." She had to escape before she broke down.

She'd left Gus earlier that morning after Sheldon had come to the bungalow asking her help in caring for Jeremy. The look on the older man's face spoke volumes. It was fear. There was no doubt he was afraid she would become involved with Jeremy again; she wanted to reassure her grandfather that would not happen a second time.

Ryan stood up, exchanging seats with Tricia.

"Take your time with Gus. If I have to leave, then I'll call my father to come and sit."

She took a quick glance at her patient. His chest rose and fell in a measured rhythm. He had fallen asleep. Her gaze softened as she studied his face in repose. Juliet had been a miniature, feminine version of her father.

A shudder shook her as the import of what had become a reality for three short months struck her. She and Jeremy had been parents of a little girl who had righted all of the wrongs—a baby she loved with all of her heart.

Tricia found Gus sitting on the porch, rocking in his favorite chair, eyes closed. She stood on the lower step and stared at her grandfather. Tall and slender, there wasn't an extra ounce of flesh on his spare frame and for the first time she saw him as an old man. He had celebrated his seventy-seventh birthday that spring. She mounted the steps slowly, and he opened his eyes to stare up at her.

"How is he?"

"*He* does have a name, Grandpa."

"Okay. How is Jeremy?"

"He's going to live." Smiling, she pulled over a rattan chair, facing her grandfather.

Gus returned her smile. The gesture took years off his face. "That's good."

"Is it, Grandpa?"

His smile vanished. "I've always liked Jeremy."

"You liked him, but not for me."

"I was trying to protect you, Tricia."

"Protect me from what or whom?" she asked, leaning forward on the cushioned seat.

"I just didn't want you to end up like your mother."

Gus had attempted to protect Tricia, but she did end up like her mother. She'd gotten pregnant and had become a teenage mother. But unlike Patricia, she had not abandoned her baby.

"She could've aborted me, but she didn't."

"I'm thankful she didn't, because who else would I have in my old age."

"You're not old, Grandpa."

Gus sucked his teeth. "I'm old and you know it. And what bothers me is that I've become an old fool. If I hadn't interfered with you and Jeremy, I know the two of you would've married years ago. And there's no doubt I would've had at least two or three great-grandchildren by now."

Tricia stared at the climbing roses on the trellis attached to the side of the house. The roses had been her grandmother's pride and joy. "What's done is done."

Gus stared at his granddaughter's solemn expression. "You still love him, don't you?"

Turning her head, she looked directly at him. "Why would you ask me that?"

"Because I need *you* to tell me the truth, Tricia.

When you called your grandmamma and me to tell us you were marrying that lawyer fellow neither of us could believe it because you never mentioned his name whenever you called us. And when we came up to New York to meet him, the first thing Olga said to me was that you didn't love him. That's why we never told anyone at the farm that you'd married. Olga knew it wasn't going to last. But what hurt most was that a stranger had to tell us that you'd had our great-granddaughter."

"I told you why I did not want to tell you. At that point in my life I wasn't equipped to listen to you preach about how I'd become my mother. What you failed and still fail to see is that I am who I am. I may look like my mother, but that's where the similarity ends. Yes, I had a baby, but I did not desert my daughter.

"Even though I was a full-time student, I got a job, saved my money, passed all my courses and made arrangements for child care before Juliet was born. I managed to hold everything together until the accident. Then, I didn't care whether I lived or died. I'd lost my baby, and then Grandmamma died two years later. I carried a lot of guilt, Grandpa, because I kept telling myself that if I'd come back to the farm when I realized I was pregnant, my baby wouldn't have died."

Leaning back on the rocker, Gus sighed. "But you

didn't come back, because you didn't want to hear me say 'I told you so.'"

"That wasn't the only thing, Grandpa. I wanted to see if I could make it on my own," she half lied. What she had not wanted to do was use her child as a pawn to get Jeremy to come back to her.

Gus shook his head. "Olga, God rest her soul, always told me that I was better with horses than human beings."

Tricia smiled. "That's because horses don't talk back."

"Amen, grandbaby girl." He waved a gnarled hand. "Don't you think it's time you get back to your young man?"

"He's my *patient,* Grandpa, not my young man." She stood up. "Did you eat lunch?" Even though her grandfather had retired at seventy-five he continued to live on the horse farm and rent the bungalow. The cost of meals was included in his monthly rental.

Gus patted his flat belly over a pair of well-washed denim overalls. "I ate a big breakfast."

Leaning over, she kissed his cheek. "Don't forget to eat dinner."

"I won't." He waved his hand again. "Go on!"

Tricia drove the short distance back to Jeremy's house. She was surprised to find Sheldon instead of Ryan sitting in the club chair. He stood up.

"I told Ryan I'd sit with him until you got back."

"I'll take over now."

"Ryan also told me that you haven't eaten, so I'll have your lunch delivered."

"Thank you."

Sheldon walked out, and Tricia sat down on the chair he'd vacated, watching the man she had fallen in love with so many years ago sleep.

Chapter Two

Jeremy woke up, his glazed gaze fixed on the ceiling. "Jump! Jump now, dammit!"

Tricia sat up in a jerky motion like a marionette on a string, her heart pounding wildly in her chest. She shot up from the chair and raced over to the bed. Jeremy's right arm flailed wildly, his elbow striking her shoulder and knocking her backward. Recovering quickly, she lay over his chest, holding his arms at his sides.

"Jeremy, Jeremy," she said, crooning his name over and over. "It's all right. You're safe, darling." The endearment had slipped out unbidden.

He heard the voice, felt the comforting weight of

a soft body and inhaled the familiar feminine fragrance that made him think of other times in his life when two motherless youngsters found comfort in each other's embraces. The frightening images faded as quickly as they had come and Jeremy buried his face in the curly hair grazing his jaw.

"Tricia?"

"Go back to sleep."

"I…I…love…" His words trailed off.

Tricia went completely still. Who was he talking about? Was there a woman who had captured Jeremy's heart the way she'd done? He had come back to Blackstone Farms, but did he have a fiancée somewhere who awaited his return?

Her fingertips massaged his temples in a circular motion. "It's all right, Jeremy. Everything's going to be all right."

"You won't leave me?"

Tricia shook her head before she realized Jeremy couldn't see her. Why did he sound so helpless, vulnerable? "No, Jeremy, I won't leave you."

"Please, get into bed with me."

"I can't."

"Why not? You used to sleep with me."

"That was before and this is now. I'm your nurse and you're my patient."

He gritted his teeth, slowly letting out his breath. He'd gripped her shoulder with his injured fingers. "Please stay with me until I go back to sleep."

Sleeping with a patient was unprofessional and unethical. The difference in having Jeremy Blackstone as a patient was that at one time she *had* slept with him.

Easing out of his embrace, she lowered the railing and lay down on his right side. All the memories of her sharing a bed with him came rushing back as if it were yesterday instead of fourteen years before. She lay motionless as everything about her first lover enveloped her in a longing that she had forgotten.

"Tricia?"

She smiled. Why did he always make her name sound like a caress? "Yes, Jeremy."

"Thank you."

It was the second time he'd thanked her. "You're welcome."

Waiting until she heard the soft snores indicating Jeremy had gone back to sleep, Tricia slipped off the bed. *It's not going to work.* The five words slapped at her. How was she going to share a bedroom, touch her first lover's body and not lose it? She'd had fourteen years to tell herself that she hated Jeremy for deserting her, but just coming face-to-face with him had made a liar of her.

She'd done the very thing her grandfather had warned her against. She had given Jeremy her heart, her innocence and her love, for eternity.

Making her way over to the daybed, she lay down, resting her head on folded arms. Now she knew why

Sheldon wanted a private-duty nurse for Jeremy. They did not want him alone during his flashback episodes. The expression on his face had been one of pure terror, and again she wondered if he had been held prisoner or tortured during his captivity.

The attending doctor at the military hospital had written referrals for Jeremy to see an orthopedist and a psychiatrist, and there was no doubt his body would heal before his mind did.

She remembered what Sheldon had said about Jeremy responding positively to treatment if he was in familiar surroundings. A knowing smile crinkled her eyes. She and Jeremy could not turn back the clock, but she could attempt to recapture some of the magic from their childhood.

Jeremy woke up for the first time, since he'd regained consciousness in the Washington, D.C., hospital, without the blinding pain in his head. He'd lost track of time but knew he was home when he heard the soothing strains of violins playing Mozart's "Serenade in G Major." It had been a long time since he'd heard that selection.

Lifting his head off the pillows cradling his shoulders, he sniffed the air and smiled. He could smell brewing coffee. What he'd liked most about his South American missions had been the coffee. Colombian and Brazilian coffees were some of the best blends in the world. However, he couldn't lie in bed savoring the smell of coffee or listening to music, because he had to use the bathroom. There was one problem: he couldn't get out of the bed without help.

"Hello," he called out.

Seconds later Tricia appeared. She looked different from before. She'd exchanged her blouse and slacks for a sunny-yellow sundress with a squared neckline that skimmed her lush body. Other than her short hair, it had been the changes to her body that had caught his immediate attention. When he'd left Tricia, her body hadn't claimed the womanly curves she now flaunted shamelessly. The pressure in the lower portion of his body increased, and Jeremy knew it had nothing to do with his need to relieve himself.

"Hi."

She flashed a shy smile, her expression reminiscent of one she'd offered him what now seemed so long ago. "Good morning, Jeremy." She looked at her watch. "It's six-twenty."

He scratched his cheek with his right hand at the same time his stomach grumbled. He had been asleep for more than fifteen hours. "I need to use the bathroom."

Nodding, Tricia picked up a pair of crutches. She moved over to the bed, lowered a side rail and handed him the crutches. He took them with his uninjured hand while she gently swung his legs over the side of the mattress.

"Put your left arm around my neck and pull yourself up with your right hand, using the crutches for support."

He completed the task without difficulty, but had to anchor the thumb and forefinger of his left hand over the rubber-covered handgrip. It would be some time before he'd be able to make a fist with that hand.

"Steady, hotshot," Tricia cautioned softly.

Jeremy took several halting steps before he regained his balance. "I've got it."

She looked up at him, her dark gaze fusing with his. "Do you need me to help you?"

His gaze grew wider as he took in everything about her in one sweeping glance. They had lost so much. It had taken them a long time to reunite, but now they were different people. It was as if they'd become polite strangers.

"No, thank you. I believe I have everything under control."

Lowering her gaze, she nodded. "Call me when you're finished." He nodded and hobbled slowly to the bathroom.

Tricia stripped the bed and remade it with clean linens while she waited for Jeremy to call her. She'd gotten up earlier that morning and had taken a tour of his home. It was an exact replica of the one where he'd grown up, except on a smaller scale. The three-bedroom house was constructed with enough room for a family of four to live comfortably without bumping into one another. She'd stood in the middle of the master bedroom suite, wondering if she had come back once her pregnancy was confirmed whether she would have slept beside Jeremy in the king-size wrought-iron bed or sat in the sitting room nursing their daughter.

She'd dismissed those thoughts as soon as they'd entered her head because she could not afford to think of what would've been. And the reality of the present was that she would give Jeremy the next four weeks of her life. No more than that.

The last disc on the CD player ended, filling the space with silence. She glanced at her watch. Jeremy had been in the bathroom for more than a quarter of an hour.

Tricia made her way to the bathroom and knocked on the door. "Jeremy?"

"Come in." His voice was muffled.

She pushed open the door and found him sitting on a stool in front of a generous serpentine-marble washbasin, peering into a marble-rimmed oval mirror anchored to a length of wall mirrors. The mirrors made the space appear twice its size. His jaw was covered with shaving cream as he attempted to shave himself with his right hand. The day before he hadn't wanted to get out of bed, and now he was attempting to groom himself.

Closing the distance between them, she took the razor from his grasp. "Why didn't you call me?"

Jeremy's head came up, and he saw the frown marring Tricia's smooth forehead. "I wanted to see if I could shave myself. I did manage to brush my teeth."

"Brushing your teeth is safer than shaving. What if you'd cut yourself?"

He lifted a thick, curving black eyebrow. "If I cut my throat, then that would let you off the hook."

Her frown deepened. "What are you talking about?"

"I'd bleed to death, then you wouldn't have to take care of me."

Her fingers tightened on the handle of the razor. "Did I say I didn't want to take care of you?"

"I know you don't want to be here with me. You're only doing it because my father asked you."

Tricia crossed her arms under her breasts. "Let's clear the air about something. I'm here because you're my patient, so don't read more into our association than that."

He angled his head, studying her gaze for a hint of guile. "Okay, Tricia, if that's what you want."

"It is," she said quickly.

Shifting, she stood directly in front of him. Cradling his chin in her hand, she lifted his face. Dots of blood showed through the layer of cream. "You've already cut yourself." Turning on the hot water faucet, she rinsed the blade, then began scraping away the wiry black whiskers. His face was leaner, cheekbones more pronounced. He'd lost weight.

Jeremy was hard-pressed not to laugh. Tricia's breasts were level with his gaze. Mesmerized, he watched the gentle swell of dark brown flesh rise and fall above the revealing décolletage.

"Did you bring any uniforms with you?"

Her hand halted under his chin. "No. Why?"

A knowing smile crinkled the network of lines around his eyes—lines that were the result of squinting in the tropical sun. "I'm getting quite an eyeful of certain part of your anatomy with you in that dress."

Her gaze lowered as heat suffused her cheeks. She moved the blade closer to his brown throat. "Don't you know it's risky to mess with a woman who's holding a sharp razor at your throat?"

His eyes darkened until they appeared as black as his pupils. "No more risky than my falling in love with you fourteen years ago."

Her hand trembled slightly. "No, Jeremy," she whispered.

Vertical lines appeared between his eyes. "No! No *what?*"

"Let's not talk about the past."

Reaching up, he wrested the razor from her fingers. "Yes, Tricia, let's talk about it. Let's clear the air so we can move on."

She flinched at the tone of his voice. "I've moved on."

"Well, I haven't."

"Whose problem is that?"

"It's our problem, Tricia." His voice was noticeably softer. "Every time I came back I'd ask your grandfather how you were doing, and he always had a pat answer. 'Tricia's doing well,' or 'she loves living in New York.' You loved New York so well that you moved to Baltimore?"

She nodded. "I moved to Baltimore after my divorce."

He went completely still. Her grandfather never mentioned her marrying. His chest rose and fell as his pulse raced uncontrollably. "You were married?"

"Yes."

Jeremy sucked in a lungful of breath, held it as long as he could before letting it out, feeling himself relaxing, albeit slowly. When he'd least expected it, memories of what they'd shared crept under the barrier he'd erected to keep other women out of his life and his bed. Each nameless face had become Tricia's. Their voices her voice. After a while he gave up altogether and succumbed to prolonged periods of celibacy.

"How long were you married?"

Tricia retrieved the razor and resumed the task of scraping away the coarse black whiskers from his chin and jaw. "Not long." Her voice was as neutral as her touch.

"How long is not long?"

Smoothly they'd slipped back into the comfortable familiarity of confiding in each other, because they'd been friends longer than they'd been lovers.

"It was over before we celebrated our first anniversary."

"What happened?"

"We were not compatible."

"Didn't you know that before you married him?" She nodded. "Why did you marry him, anyway?"

"I was very vulnerable at the time."

"Which meant he took advantage of you."

She shook her head. "No, Jeremy, he did not take advantage of me. I knew what I was doing. It was a period in my life when I did not want to be alone." She put the razor in the basin.

Reaching for a damp towel on the nearby countertop, Jeremy wiped away dots of shaving cream. "Why didn't you come back to live with your grandfather if you didn't want to be alone?"

Tricia took the towel from his loose grip and dabbed at the nicks. "I couldn't come back—at least not to stay."

He curved his right arm around her waist, pulling her closer. For several moments they fed on each other, offering strength and comfort. Resting her chin on the top of his head, Tricia closed her eyes. It was so easy to slip back in time—a time when they could talk about any and everything, a time when they weren't afraid to tell the other their most heart-felt secrets and a time when they were young, fear-less and hopelessly in love with life and each other.

"What about now, Tricia? Are you ready to stay?"

She curbed an urge to kiss his hair as she'd once done. The man embracing her may sound the same, but she knew he was not the same. The short spiky black hair and pierced earlobes belonged to a stranger, someone she recognized but no longer knew.

"No," she said after a pregnant pause.

"Why not?"

"Because I have a life in Baltimore."

He raised his head and his gray gaze searched her face, looking for a remnant of the girl he had grown up with—the one who'd captured his heart with her vulnerability, the one he'd protected from the other children who repeated gossip they'd heard from their parents about her mother.

He flashed a wry smile. "Is there someone wait-ing for you in Baltimore?"

Tricia thought of one of the doctors in the group where she worked. She and Wade had dated casually over the past two months, although he'd expressed a desire for it to become more than casual.

Easing out of his loose embrace, Tricia shook her head. "No," she answered truthfully.

"Then there is a distinct possibility that you could come back to Blackstone Farms to work?"

"And do what?"

"Blackstone Farms Day School will officially operate as a private school this September. Kelly has interviewed and hired teachers for prekindergarten through sixth grade. All of the farm children will attend the school along with additional children from several neighboring farms. I believe there is still an opening for a school nurse."

A lump settled in Tricia's throat, making swallowing difficult. What Jeremy was offering was a perfect solution for her. She could be close to her grandfather and still pursue her career. It had taken Gus more than a decade to apologize in his own way without actually saying he was sorry, but he finally had.

If her grandfather hadn't interfered, she would've married Jeremy and Gus would have had a beautiful great-grandchild to spoil or bounce on his knee. But Tricia was a realist and she knew she could not go back in time to right past wrongs. She'd made a new life for herself and there was no place in her life for Jeremy. She could not trust him not to desert her again.

If she had to take care of her grandfather, once he was no longer able to care for himself, then she would take him to Baltimore with her. The row house she'd purchased in the fashionable suburban community had three bedrooms—more than enough room for her and Gus.

"I'm certain becoming a school nurse would be a new and wonderful experience for me, but I like where I live and I love what I do."

Angling his head again, Jeremy stared up at her through half-closed eyes. She liked where she lived and loved her career, while he felt as if he were swimming through a haze of doubt and uncertainty. His injuries and the possibility that he might never be medically cleared to participate in future undercover missions made Jeremy consider his future.

He had wasted too many years running away when he should've stayed and confronted Tricia about Russell Smith. He'd realized that the afternoon he lay in bed in a Richmond hotel, staring at the clock, aware that she was on a jet flying to New York.

He had come back over the years to see his father, brother, nephew and sister-in-law, but he also had come back to see Tricia—to ask her why.

"Are you ready for your shower?"

Tricia's soft voice broke into his thoughts. "I will be, after you answer one question for me."

"What's that?"

"Why did you ever sleep with Russell Smith?"

Chapter Three

Tricia blinked once, as if coming out of a trance, not certain whether she had heard Jeremy correctly. Had he asked her if she had slept with Russell Smith? It had been years since she had given the man a passing thought, and that was to tell her grandfather she did not want Russell's graduation gift. She'd told Gus to return it sight unseen.

"Do you actually expect me to answer that?" she retorted with cold sarcasm.

Jeremy nodded. "I'd like you to."

She stared wordlessly at him for several seconds. "This is not about what you'd like, Jeremy." Tricia was surprised her voice was so calm when her heart was pounding an erratic rhythm. "If you'd asked me that question fourteen years ago I would've given you an answer. But there has been too much time between us. I've changed, while it's apparent you haven't. I'm your nurse, not your girlfriend. As long as you remember that, we will get along famously."

Jeremy's luminous eyes widened as he glared at her. "You weren't my girlfriend, Tricia. You were my fiancée. I'd offered to give you a ring, but it was you who wanted to wait until after we'd graduated from college. If you had been wearing my ring, then that would've kept the other boys from following you around."

"The only one who followed me was you, Jeremy. And it wasn't until I stood still long enough that you caught me."

His black lashes concealed his gaze from hers as he stared at the thick plaster cast protecting his shattered ankle. "Did you regret it?"

"No." His head came up and she met his direct stare. "I didn't regret it, because at that time I was ready to give up my virginity. And, why not to the boss's son?"

If Tricia had sought to wound Jeremy as much as he had her, then she knew she succeeded when she saw his expression. His black eyebrows were drawn together in an agonized expression.

Jeremy swallowed back curses—raw, ugly,

violent, crude ones he hadn't spewed in years—
curses that used to bring tears to his mother's eyes
and a threat to wash his mouth out with soap. He had
continued to swear until her threats became a reality.
Despite detesting the taste of lye soap he had still
cursed, but tried never to do it in her presence.

Tricia did not have to tell him if she'd slept with
Russell, because her response validated Russell's
claim: *She doesn't mind sharing her goodies with the
hired help as long as she can hold on to the boss's
son.*

He wasn't angry with Tricia but himself, because
he had opened a wound he had permitted to heal, a
wound with a noticeable scar. Now he was bleeding
again. No, he told himself. What he'd had with Tricia
was over, never to be resurrected.

With his jaw clenched, he captured and held Tricia's dark, slanting eyes. "You're right about our roles
as nurse and patient. I'll make certain never to forget
that as long as you're here. Now, if you don't mind
I'm ready to take my shower."

The short, curling hair on the nape of Tricia's neck
stood up. It wasn't what Jeremy had said but how he'd
said it that held a silken thread of warning.

Nodding, she relieved him of the T-shirt. Her
mouth went dry as she stared at a broad chest covered with thick black hair. Jeremy's upper body was
magnificent: defined pectorals, massive biceps and

flat abs. Despite his broken ankle, he was in peak condition.

She kept her expression and touch neutral as she relieved him of his shorts, underwear and covered his left leg and foot with the plastic cast sheath, tightening the Velcro band around his thigh. Jeremy hobbled on crutches to the circular shower and sat down on a stool under a ten-inch showerhead that was centrally positioned overhead. She handed him a plastic bottle filled with liquid soap, a cloth, and removed an auxiliary hand shower from the wall.

She picked up the crutches. "Do you want me to turn on the water?" The faucets were within arm's reach.

Jeremy shook his head. "No, thank you. I'll manage."

Tricia met his impassive gaze. "Call me when you're finished." Not waiting for his reply, she walked out of the bathroom.

She stood next to the hospital bed and sucked in a lungful of air. It had taken every ounce of her willpower not to glance below his waist. She had concentrated on the bruises dotting his body instead.

She had told herself that she was a nurse and as one she had seen countless nude men in various stages of arousal during her nursing school training. Some thought they could shock her whenever they summoned her to their beds to look at what they'd considered their masculine prowess, but what they did not know was that none of them would ever affect her the way her first lover had done. It wasn't until after she'd married Dwight that she realized she was a one-man woman. That man was Jeremiah Baruch Blackstone. And she had not wanted to look at her first lover to see whether he still turned her on, because she knew she wasn't as immune to him as she wanted to be.

And if the truth be told, she still wanted him in her bed. She had never stopped wanting him in her bed.

As directed, Jeremy called out to Tricia that he had finished his shower. She reentered the bathroom, and the lingering steam settled around her, dampening her face and hair. His stare was fixed on her grim expression as she dried his wet body with a thirsty terry cloth towel. She removed the plastic covering from his leg, checking for moisture seepage. Twenty minutes later he sat at a table on the porch, wearing a T-shirt and shorts, his left foot propped up on a low stool.

He watched Tricia like a hawk as she set a table with china and silver. She had only put out one serving. "Aren't you going to eat?"

Her head came up. "I'll eat later."

"I'd like you to eat *now*."

Tricia held his gaze. "If you want me to eat with you, why not ask me to…politely."

A slight smile tugged at the corners of his mouth. "I want you to take *all* of your meals with me."

Tricia had forgotten that Jeremy never ate alone after his mother's untimely death. Even though the farm had a resident chef, Julia Blackstone had always cooked dinner. That had been her time to bond with her husband and sons.

She nodded. "I'll get another place setting."

He sat motionless, staring out at the lushness of the property surrounding his house. Massive oak trees with sweeping branches provided a canopy of shade for the manicured lawn that resembled an undulating green carpet.

A knowing smile softened his mouth and crinkled the skin around his eyes. Blackstone Farms was beautiful, almost as beautiful as the primordial jungles of South America.

He closed his eyes and thought about the men on his team, men who had lived together for so long they knew the others' thoughts, men who, over the course of several years, had become as close as brothers. The six of them had trained together in Quantico, Virginia, honing their physical and mental skills. He'd become an expert in firearms, fitness and defensive tactics, as well as defensive driving training. His olive coloring and fluency in Spanish and additional intelligence training courses made him a natural candidate for undercover missions in Latin America.

He opened his eyes, reached up with his uninjured hand and ran his fingers through his short damp hair. He had been debriefed by his superiors and informed that the probability of his returning to undercover work was questionable. The orthopedist's prognosis stated that although he would walk again without too much difficulty, the damage to his ankle would never withstand the rigors of duty in the field.

All thoughts of his future with the Drug Enforcement Administration vanished as Tricia reappeared.

"I called the dining hall and put in a request for grits and eggs."

Jeremy's smile was dazzling. "What about bacon or sausage?"

A flash of humor crossed her face. "You really must be feeling good because there's nothing wrong with your appetite."

"I'd have to be dead not to eat."

She went completely still, her gaze fusing with his. "Please, Jeremy. Don't talk about dying." She didn't think she would ever forget the image of the tiny white coffin with their child being lowered into a grave.

He sobered quickly. "I'm sorry." He didn't know why he'd mentioned the word. He reflected again on the three members of his team who would never see their loved ones again. The jungle had claimed all of them.

The telephone rang, interrupting both their gloomy musings. Tricia straightened. "I'll answer it." Turning, she went back into the house and picked up the receiver to the phone on a side table in the entryway.

"Hello."

"Good morning, Tricia."

She recognized the distinctive drawling voice. "Good morning, Sheldon."

"How's Jeremy today?"

"He's sitting on the porch. I'm waiting for breakfast to be delivered."

"Good. I'm glad he's out of bed. Let him know that Ryan just called with the news that Kelly had a little girl. Mother and baby are doing well."

She bit down on her lower lip, remembering her own joy the instant she saw her daughter for the first time. "Congratulations, Sheldon."

"Thank you. Please let Jeremy know that Sean and I will be over later this morning."

"Okay." She hung up the phone, waiting until she was in control of her emotions, then returned to the porch.

One of the young men who worked in the dining hall had arrived and emptied a large wicker basket filled with serving dishes, a carafe of coffee and a pitcher of chilled orange juice onto the cloth-covered table on the porch.

"Thank you, Bobby," Tricia said, her soft voice breaking the silence.

Robert Thomas smiled at Tricia, blushing to the roots of his flaming red hair. "You're welcome, Miss Tricia. I'll pick up the dishes when I come back with lunch."

Jeremy noticed the direction of the adolescent's gaze. It was fixed on Tricia's neckline. He'd told her about that doggone dress. Every time she inhaled or bent over the sight of her breasts made the flesh between his legs stir.

"Are you finished, Bobby?" His voice snapped like the crack of a whip.

His head swiveling like Linda Blair's in *The Exorcist,* Bobby stared at Jeremy. "Yes, sir."

"If that's the case, then beat it!"

Tricia opened her mouth to censure Jeremy for his rudeness, but the retort died on her tongue as she reminded herself that Jeremy was an owner of Blackstone Farms and Bobby an employee. She did not want to undermine Jeremy's authority in front of his workers.

Bobby managed to look embarrassed. "Yes, sir, Mr. Blackstone." Picking up the wicker basket, he made his way off the porch and raced to the SUV he had parked in the driveway.

Pulling out a chair, Tricia sat across the table from Jeremy. She uncovered a serving dish with fluffy scrambled eggs, another with steaming creamy grits and a third with a rash of bacon, spicy beef sausage links and strips of baked ham. She reached for his plate, filled it with grits and eggs and placed it in front of him.

"I didn't know bullying was a requisite for becoming a special agent with the DEA."

Jeremy's grip on his fork tightened. "What are you talking about?"

A slight frown marred her smooth forehead. "You didn't have to talk to Bobby like that." Bobby had been a toddler when she left the farm to attend college.

"It was either send him on his way or have him salivating over your cleavage."

Tricia placed a hand over her chest. "Do you have a problem with my dress?"

"It's not the dress, but what's in your dress." He lifted his eyebrows. "Or should I say what is spilling out of your dress."

She lowered her hand, deciding to ignore his ribald comment and served herself. "That was your father on the phone," she said, smoothly changing the topic. "Kelly had a girl, and both mother and baby are doing well."

Jeremy clenched his right fist. "Boo-yaw!"

Tricia felt his enthusiasm. "Congratulations, Uncle Jeremy."

He stared at her, his eyes brimming with tenderness. "Thank you, Tricia."

Her lower lip trembled as her mind fluttered in anxiety. She dropped her gaze and concentrated on the food on her plate, hoping to bring her fragile emotions under control because she had involuntarily reacted to Jeremy's gentle look.

She had told herself it wasn't going to work, and now she was certain. All Jeremy had to do was look at her with a gentle yearning and she was lost—lost in her own yearning that pulled her in and refused to let her go.

There was a time when he had become her knight in shining armor, protecting her from the taunts of the other farm children. He had taught her how to love herself and in turn she had fallen in love with him.

Tricia watched Jeremy as he attempted to feed himself. His right hand trembled noticeably and a muscle in his jaw twitched. She put down her fork. "Would you like something to take the edge off?"

Jeremy's head came up slowly. The blinding headache had returned. "I don't know."

"What don't you know?"

"I'm losing track of time. Whenever I wake up I don't know what day it is or whether it's day or night."

"Time should be the least of your concerns, Jeremy. You're not going anywhere for a while." She touched the corners of her mouth with a cloth napkin. "As soon as you're finished eating, I'll bring you your medication."

He nodded, then chided himself for the action. Each time he moved his head it felt as if it was going to explode.

Tricia aided Jeremy as he made his way over to a chintz-covered chaise at the opposite end of the porch. He lay motionless as she raised his injured foot to a pillow. She took his vitals and gave him the pill. Sitting on a matching rocker, she waited until his lids closed and his chest rose and fell in an even rhythm, indicating he had fallen asleep.

She sat, studying his face in repose, noting the lean jaw, aquiline nose and firm chin—features their daughter had inherited. Juliet had been a feminine version of her father with the exception of her mouth. Her mouth had been Tricia's.

She pushed off the rocker and began clearing the table. She washed the dishes, then carefully dried the china and silver and put them away. She returned to the porch, book in hand and sat down on the rocker.

The sound of an approaching vehicle shattered the stillness of the morning. Glancing up, she saw Sheldon's pickup truck maneuvering into the driveway. Tricia was on her feet, watching as Sheldon helped his grandson out of the truck. Sean Blackstone raced up the steps of the porch, his dark-gray eyes sparkling with excitement.

"I have a sister, Miss Tricia!" His high-pitched voice startled several birds perched on the branches of a nearby oak tree. They fluttered and chattered noisily before settling back under the cool canopy of leaves.

She stared down at the young boy, smiling. There was no doubt that he was Ryan's son. Tricia ruffled his black curly hair. "Congratulations on becoming a big brother."

"Daddy said I can't see my baby sister until she comes home with Mommy." Sean's gaze shifted, resting on his uncle on the chaise. "What happened to Uncle Jeremy, Miss Tricia? Why is his leg wrapped up like that?"

Tricia stared at Sheldon who now stood on the porch. It was obvious Sean hadn't been told about his uncle's injuries.

Resting a large hand on his grandson's shoulder, Sheldon let out his breath in an audible sigh. "Your uncle Jeremy had an accident. He fell and hurt his leg."

Sean's head came up and he stared at Sheldon. "Like a horse?"

Sheldon nodded. "Yes, like a horse."

"Grandpa, did he hurt his face when he fell down?"

"Yes, Sean. He also hurt his face when he fell," Sheldon said in a quiet voice. "Why don't you go for a walk with Miss Tricia while I sit with Uncle Jeremy?"

Tricia reached for Sean's hand. "Come with me. I'm going to see my grandfather." She knew Sheldon wanted to be alone with Jeremy, even though he was sedated.

"Take my truck, Tricia," Sheldon called out as he sat on the rocker she had just vacated. Everyone who lived or worked at the horse farm always left the keys in the ignition of their vehicles.

Tricia helped Sean into the pickup and belted him in before she sat behind the wheel and started the engine. It had been a while since she had driven a standard vehicle. She, like most of the children living at Blackstone Farms, had learned to drive a tractor as soon as their legs were long enough to reach the pedals.

She arrived at Gus's house and found his pickup missing. Turning to Sean, she smiled at him. "How would you like to help me cut some flowers to make a bouquet for your mother and little sister to welcome them home?"

Sean flashed a wide grin. "Yes, Miss Tricia."

Fifty minutes later Tricia drove back to Jeremy's house with a basket filled with pink and white roses, a vase and spools of pink ribbon in varying shades. Her grandmother had taught her the intricacies of floral arranging. Tricia had also changed out of her dress and into a pair of black capris and a white camp shirt.

She stared at Jeremy. He was still asleep. "How was he?" she asked Sheldon in a quiet voice.

Sheldon cupped her elbow arm and led her away from where Sean sat next to his uncle. "He was talking in his sleep, Tricia."

Her heart stopped, then started up again. "What did he say?"

A knowing gaze pinned her to the spot. "He kept mumbling, 'I'm sorry, Tricia.'" A frown creased Sheldon's forehead. "What happened between you and my son?"

"I don't know what you're talking about."

Sheldon decided to be candid. "Were you the reason he joined the Marines instead of coming home?"

She met his accusing gaze without flinching. "I

don't know why Jeremy joined the Marines. But, if you want answers as to what went on between me and Jeremy, then you're going to have to ask him."

Sheldon released Tricia's arm. He had many unanswered questions about Jeremy and Tricia's past relationship and he was determined to get some answers. He'd lost his son once, but he had no intention of losing him again.

He inclined his head. "Thank you again for taking care of Jeremy. We'll talk about you and Jeremy later."

She nodded, and, turning on his heel, Sheldon went to Sean and took his hand. Together they walked back to the truck.

Tricia stood watching uneasily until the departing vehicle disappeared from view.

Chapter Four

Tricia moved closer to Jeremy and held his uninjured hand as he sat on an examining table, while the nurse cut through the plaster cast on his ankle. The whirring sound of the drill set her teeth on edge. The plaster cast would be replaced with one made of fiberglass, but only after the removal of the surgical staples and an X-ray.

She noted the tense set of his jaw. "Are you all right?" she whispered close to his ear.

He turned his head, met her gaze and nodded. Their mouths were mere inches apart. His breath swept over her cheek. "Thank you for being here." Leaning forward, he brushed his mouth over hers with the softness of a breeze. There was no intimacy in the kiss, but that did not stop Tricia from reacting to the slight pressure. Unable to move, she felt her pulse race uncontrollably.

She wanted to tell Jeremy that she did not want to be here—with him—because with each sunrise it was becoming increasingly more difficult to sleep under his roof, to wake up and see him and not be affected by the sensual memories of what had been between them.

Jeremy stared at the rapidly beating pulse in Tricia's throat. He had only touched his lips to hers, when he'd wanted to do so much more. He wanted to ravish her mouth. He felt like a starving man craving food or a man dying of thirst needing water. He wanted to kiss her so badly.

He and Tricia could not go backward, yet despite her duplicity and infidelity he still wanted her. It no longer mattered that she had married or slept with other men. In spite of the anguish tormenting him for fourteen years he still wanted her in his bed.

He drew in a sharp breath with the removal of the first staple. A second one followed, then a third. He lost count of the biting sensation after fifteen. Closing his eyes, he rested his head against her shoulder. When the last staple was removed, he was helped into a wheelchair and pushed into another room where a technician X-rayed his hand and foot.

* * *

Tricia opened the passenger-side door, holding Jeremy's crutches. Moving slowly, he swung his legs around until his feet touched the macadam. She handed him the crutches and he pulled himself into a standing position.

It took him five minutes to make his way from the car to his bed, every step torture. He sat down heavily on the side of the bed and fell back on the mattress.

Tricia stood over him, hands on her hips. "I'm going to give you a pill."

Jeremy rested an arm over his forehead. "No, Tricia. I don't want it."

Reaching out, she placed her hand alongside his cheek. "Yes, Jeremy."

He caught her hand and kissed the palm. "Just let me rest for a little while."

"Are you sure?"

He smiled, the expression resembling a grimace. "Yes."

She eased her hand from his loose grip, removed his running shoe and the shapeless boot with Velcro fasteners from his injured foot, then raised his legs to the bed.

"I'll be nearby if you need me."

"Thank you, Tricia." He gave her a wry smile. "I seem to be thanking you a lot lately."

Tricia resisted the urge to kiss him, because at

that moment he appeared boyish and carefree. The way she had remembered him. "Hush, now, and try to get some sleep."

Grinning, he saluted her. "Aye, aye, ma'am."

She sat on the club chair, slipped out of her sandals, rested her bare feet on the ottoman and closed her eyes. She was exhausted. Jeremy rarely slept throughout the night and whenever he moaned or cried out in his sleep she left her bed to check on him. She always held him until he settled back to sleep, listening in shock as he mumbled about the horrors he had experienced during his ill-fated mission. These were the times when she felt like a voyeur. Willing her mind blank, she felt her chest rise and fall in an even rhythm, and she fell asleep.

Noise startled her, and she was jolted awake. Tricia sat up and stared at Jeremy. He was talking in his sleep again. She pushed up off the chair and sat on the side of the mattress.

"It's all right, Jeremy," she crooned softly.

"Forgive me, Tricia."

She leaned over him. "It's all right, darling. I forgive you."

"I…I did not want to…to leave…you," he mumbled, still not opening his eyes.

Getting into the bed with him, Tricia rested an arm over his chest, blinking back tears. "I love you," she whispered in his ear. Rising on an elbow, she kissed him.

Without warning Jeremy's eyes opened and he stared at her as if he had never seen her before. Tricia's heart beat a double-time rhythm. Had he heard her?

She met his questioning gaze. "You were talking in your sleep again."

"What did I say?"

She decided to tell him the truth. "You asked me to forgive you."

He closed his eyes, long black lashes resting on his high cheekbones. "For what?"

She hesitated and he opened his eyes. "For leaving me."

Jeremy's gaze fused with her dark-brown eyes. "I should've never left you, Tricia, but I took the coward's way out and ran, after Russell told me about the two of you."

She gasped, her mind reeling in confusion. Was that why he'd asked her if she had slept with Russell? Her breath burned in her throat as she swallowed the hateful words poised to explode from her mouth. They had wasted too many years, and she had lost a child because she'd refused to come back to the farm because of a spiteful man's lies.

"I don't care what Russell told you, but I never slept with him."

Jeremy's raven eyebrows lifted as he pushed up on an elbow. "He lied?"

"Of course he lied," she spat out. "Why didn't you ask *me,* Jeremy?"

A muscle quivered at his jaw. If he ever ran into Russell again he would make him sorry he ever drew breath. The SOB had lied to him about sleeping with Tricia.

"Why didn't you ask me?" she asked again.

Jeremy shook his head. He did not have an answer. "I don't know. And don't think I haven't asked myself the same question over and over every time I came back here."

A look of distress crossed her face. "What hurts most is that you did not trust me. How could you profess to love me when you didn't trust me to be faithful to you?"

He frowned. "Loving you had nothing to do with not trusting you."

Tricia sat up. "Love *is* trust. You cannot have one without the other."

There was a prolonged silence before Jeremy said, "Do you still love me, Tricia?"

She felt as if all of her emotions were under attack and wanted to lie. But only minutes before she had openly confessed to loving him.

He had been her first lover, the man who unknowingly had made her a mother. She shook her head. "No," she said softly, "not the way I used to love you."

"Do you hate me?"

Smiling, Tricia shook her head again. "No, Jeremy, I don't hate you."

Sitting up, Jeremy shifted to his right side and kissed her. He inhaled the very essence of Tricia: her smell, the velvet softness of her mouth, the press of her breasts against his arm. He took his time kissing her mouth, eyes and face. She trembled when his lips brushed the curve of her eyebrows.

Tricia opened her mouth to his probing tongue, swallowing his breath. What had begun as a soft, tender joining flowed into a dreamy intimacy she had forgotten existed.

Jeremy eased back, staring at her. "Do you know how long I've waited to kiss your mouth, eyes?"

Her gaze widened. "No." The single word was whispered.

"Forever," he whispered back, then took possession of her mouth again.

She emitted a soft moan. "We shouldn't be doing this."

"Why not?"

"Because I'm your nurse."

"That excuse is starting to sound lame," he crooned, gently biting her earlobe.

Tricia fortified herself against his sensual assault and placed a hand in the middle of his chest. "We can't go back to who we were. Too much time has passed and we're not the same people. I've changed and you've changed."

Reaching out, he pulled her effortlessly to sit on his lap, her back pressed to his chest. Her legs were cradled between his outstretched ones. "I don't want to go back, Tricia," he whispered in her ear. "Why can't we move forward?" He tightened his hold under her breasts.

A wave of desire flooded Tricia's body and she melted against the hardness of his chest. "That's not possible."

"Why not?"

"We don't have the time. I'm only going to be here for another three weeks."

Jeremy stared at the back of her head. He kissed her nape. "Three weeks is more than enough time." What he did not tell Tricia was that each hour, minute and second was precious, because he remembered counting down the seconds, minutes and hours while he and the others on his team lay waiting for death.

He wanted Tricia without a commitment or declaration of love. He wasn't ready to risk losing his heart to her again. "I've never asked anything from you, sweetheart," he continued, unaware that the endearment had slipped out, "not your love or your body. Those you gave willingly. What I am asking for is the next three weeks of your life."

Tricia was certain Jeremy could feel the flutters in her chest. "What happens after that?"

"Whatever it is you want to happen."

Shifting on his thighs, she turned in his loose

embrace. His gaze was steady. "I'm leaving as planned on August fifteenth, so whatever we will share up to that time will become a part of our past."

Jeremy lifted his eyebrows. "Okay," he agreed. "When it comes time for you to leave I promise not to put any pressure on you to force you to stay."

Lowering her gaze, she smiled. "Thank you."

He angled his head and kissed her again. "Will you go out with me tonight?"

She gave him a sassy smile. "Are you asking me on a date?"

Pressing his forehead to hers, Jeremy flashed his brilliant white-toothed smile. "As a matter of fact, I am."

"Where do you want to go?"

"Out to dinner, then we'll take in a movie."

Tricia chuckled. "I believe we should begin with dinner. Sitting in a movie theater with your leg in a cast is a stretch."

Jeremy kissed the end of her nose. "I wasn't talking about a movie theater. We can eat out, then come back here and watch a movie."

He had used the home theater in the family room exactly twice since he'd purchased it two years before. A collection of DVDs stacked on several shelves were still in their original cellophane packaging. Whenever he came home on leave, he stayed in his house because he had come to value his privacy. But it had never felt like home…until now.

Curving her arms around his neck, Tricia rested her head on his shoulder. "You've got yourself a date. I'll call the dining hall and cancel dinner," she said, and rose to leave.

"And where do you think you're going?" he asked.

"I'm going over to my grandfather's to find something to wear."

Jeremy chuckled, the sound coming from deep within his chest. "I hope you're not going to wear that yellow dress."

Tricia gave him a long, penetrating stare. "What's with you and that dress?"

A sensual flame fired his eyes like flints of steel. "Nothing."

"If that's the case, then I'll wear it tonight."

His expression changed, becoming tight, strained. "Please don't, Tricia." He held up his left hand. "I still can't quite make a fist, so I won't be able to punch out some guy for leering at your breasts."

She sucked her teeth. "I thought you gave up brawling a long time ago."

"I did. Remember, the only times I got into fights were because of you."

Tricia ran a finger down the length of his nose seconds before she pressed her mouth to his. "I never wanted you to fight for me."

"Someone had to protect you."

"And you did, Jeremy." She'd lost count of the number of black eyes and bloody noses he had inflicted on a few of the farm kids. "I wrote in my diary that you were my knight in shining armor. I used to refer to you as Sir Blackstone, the Black Knight."

He nuzzled her neck. "Do you need my protection now?"

"No," she said in a quiet voice. "I've learned to protect myself." She slipped off the bed and put on her shoes. "Please stay in bed until I get back."

Jeremy's expression was one of faint amusement. He wanted to tell Tricia that he was quite capable of getting in and out of bed without her assistance as long as the crutches were within reach. Already he could groom and dress himself, navigate the stairs and feed himself. He still couldn't drive or walk distances, but, that would come in time.

He winked at her, then rested his head on the pillows and waited for her return.

When Tricia arrived at her grandfather's house, his truck wasn't in its usual parking space, which meant he was probably having dinner in the dining hall. The temporary solitude gave Tricia a chance to think about her relationship with her grandfather.

She usually visited with him every morning after Sheldon came to see Jeremy. She'd sit with Gus on the porch in easy silence. In the past, their relationship had been anything but easy. In fact, Gus still did not approve of her involvement with the owner's son. She wanted to tell Gus there was no need to torment himself about her and Jeremy because in three weeks she would leave Blackstone Farms, her ex-lover and return to her orderly life in Baltimore. However, this time when she left Virginia it would be without the tortured questions and memories.

She went into her bedroom and selected a black linen dress. Black lacy underwear and strappy black sling-back sandals completed her outfit. She showered, dressed, applied a light coat of makeup and set out for Jeremy's house. He was sitting on the porch waiting for her.

Her gaze raced over his off-white linen suit, matching shirt and tie. He wore the shapeless boot with Velcro fasteners and a black loafer. Walking slowly up the porch stairs, her gaze widened in appreciation. The light color of the suit was the perfect foil for his deeply tanned olive coloring.

Reaching for the crutches, Jeremy pulled himself up. "I thought I'd save some time and change before you got back."

She stared at his clean-shaven jaw. "I told you to wait for me."

Jeremy rested the crutches under his armpits. "I wasn't alone. Ryan came over with the baby. He left just before you drove up." A wide grin crinkled the skin around his luminous eyes. "Even though Vivienne is only a few days old, she's a beauty. She looks just like Kelly. To say that Ryan is a proud papa is putting it mildly," he said. "I don't remember Ryan being this excited when Sean was born."

Tricia returned his smile. "That's because this time he can really appreciate what it means to be a father."

"I guess you're right." He angled his head and looked her up and down, his gaze lingering on her long legs in the three-inch heels. "By the way, you look stunning."

She could not stop the heat from stealing into her cheeks. "Thank you."

Jeremy took a step. "Are you ready?"

Tricia nodded. "Yes."

She was ready, ready for Jeremy and the next three weeks.

Chapter Five

Tricia turned the key in the ignition, adjusted the air-conditioning, backed out of the driveway and drove along the main road that led away from Blackstone Farms.

She gave Jeremy a sidelong glance. "Where are we going?"

"Take 64 to 81, then I'll tell you where to turn off."

"How far is it from here?"

"About thirty clicks."

She smiled. How could she have forgotten that Jeremy had been a Marine and was now a special agent with the DEA? The military jargon had just slipped out.

Nodding, she concentrated on driving instead of on the man sitting next to her. She had agreed to become involved with him again, but refused to think of the depth of their involvement. She doubted whether they would make love, because of his injury, but having an emotional relationship rather than a physical one was not an option either. If they became emotionally involved it would make their eventual separation that much harder…at least for her. Besides, it had been more than ten years since she had slept with a man.

Tricia increased her speed, passing the Blackstone property marker and headed for the interstate. Security devices and closed-circuit cameras mounted on poles and fences surrounding the horse farm monitored everyone entering or leaving the ten-thousand-acre compound.

Her narrowed gaze lingered on the dark clouds in the distance. "It looks like rain."

Jeremy studied the gunmetal-gray sky. A heat wave had held the Shenandoah Valley and the surrounding environs in a brutal grip for a month. Sheldon had ordered the trainers to limit most outdoor activities for the horses until the ninety-plus degrees and oppressive humidity eased, while in-ground sprinklers worked around the clock to keep the grazing pastures verdant.

"We need more than a passing thunderstorm," he stated matter-of-factly. As soon as the words were out of his mouth a roll of thunder shook the earth, followed by a flash of lightning that came dangerously close to the ground.

Tricia's jaw tightened as she stared straight ahead. The daytime running lights on her car shimmered eerily in the encroaching darkness. It was only minutes after seven.

"Pull off at the next exit," Jeremy ordered in a strained voice.

"Why?"

"Because I don't want you to drive."

She frowned. "But, you can't drive."

"I know I can't drive," he snapped angrily. "I'm not going to let you drive along a mountain road during a thunderstorm." Having grown up in the western part of the state, both Tricia and Jeremy knew of the number of accidents and fatalities that resulted from landslides and falling rocks during violent storms each year.

"Where do you want me to go?"

"I don't know. There's bound to be a motel close by."

Tricia left the interstate and drove along a county road. There came another roll of thunder, followed by lightning, then rain. Fat drops spattered the windshield.

Jeremy was hard-pressed not to tell Tricia to pull

over on the shoulder and switch seats with him. Her car was an automatic and he didn't need his left foot to drive.

"Over there," he said, pointing to his right. A sign advertising a bed-and-breakfast appeared out of nowhere. The outline of a large white Victorian structure came into the sweep of the headlights.

Decelerating, Tricia maneuvered along a path leading to the Lind Rose bed-and-breakfast, parking under a porte cochere behind several SUVs. She cut off the engine, stepped out into the oppressive humidity and came around to assist Jeremy.

A side door to the three-story house opened and a tiny woman with short snow-white hair emerged. "Oh, you poor dears. Please come in out of the rain." The shadowy figure of a tall man joined her.

Tricia lagged behind Jeremy as he made his way toward the couple. He had left his jacket in the car, and despite the air-conditioning his shirt was pasted to his back. She felt her mouth go dry as she studied his broad shoulders under the finely woven shirt, the slimness of his waist and hips and long legs. His beautifully proportioned body equaled his classically handsome features.

"Welcome to the Lind Rose," a deep voice rumbled in the darkness. "I'm Lindbergh and this is my wife, Rose. We just heard on the scanner that the storm is a bad one. Hear tell a bridge near Craigsville was washed out, and the state police just shut down a portion of the interstate outside of Staunton."

Jeremy smiled at the tall gaunt man with a head of shocking white hair as he neared him. "I'm glad we stopped because we were planning to go through Craigsville."

"You're in luck tonight," Rose said, gesturing toward Jeremy's leg with the unattractive boot. "We happen to have a room on the first floor. Most folks who come here want to stay on the second or third floor because they want to sit out on the veranda and look at the mountains."

Jeremy nodded. "My wife and I need a room, and if it's not too late we'd also like to have dinner." The request had come out as if Jeremy had said it many times before.

Tricia stared at the smooth, taut, olive skin over the elegant ridge of his high cheekbones, her breath catching in her chest. He had referred to her as his wife.

Rose smiled. "Would you like to eat in the dining room or in your room?"

"The dining room."

"In our room." Tricia and Jeremy had spoken in unison as the older couple exchanged a knowing glance.

"Sweetheart, if it's all right with you I'd like to get off my feet," Jeremy said in a quiet tone.

Tricia wanted to glare and bare her teeth at him,

but smiled sweetly instead. "Of course, *darling.* We'll dine in the room."

Reaching into his pocket, Jeremy withdrew a small leather case and extended it to Tricia. "Please take one of the cards." She reached for an American Express card and handed it to Rose. "We're also going to need some toiletries."

Rose gave the credit card to her husband. "All of the rooms come with baskets of complimentary grooming samples. You'll also find bathrobes and slippers. We ask that you leave them, but if you want them as souvenirs just let us know and we'll add the cost to your bill. Come with me and I'll show you your room."

Lindbergh stared at the name on the credit card before peering closely at Jeremy. "Are you one of those Blackstones from the horse farm?"

Jeremy's expression was impassive. "Yes."

Lindbergh reached for Jeremy's right hand and pumped it. "My pleasure, Mr. Blackstone." He nodded at Tricia. "Mrs. Blackstone."

"Let go of the man's hand, Lind," Rose admonished softly. "Don't you see he's hurting?"

Tricia moved closer to Jeremy and studied his face. Moisture dotted his forehead and his mouth was drawn into a tight line. There was no doubt he was uncomfortable.

He was in pain and his medication was back at

the farm. She touched his shoulder. "Let's go to the room," she said softly.

Tricia and Jeremy followed Rose down a carpeted hallway to a room at the opposite end of the hall. Rose opened the door and flipped a wall switch. Table lamps filled the space with a warm, soft golden glow, highlighting an exquisite queen-size sleigh bed with a lace and organza coverlet and pillows. A table, doubling as a desk, held a vase of fresh white roses and a supply of candles next to a quartet of hurricane lanterns. The room also had a sitting area with a round table and two chairs, and an adjoining bathroom. Bundles of dried herbs lay on the grate in a stone fireplace instead of the usual logs.

Tricia smiled. "It's beautiful."

Rose beamed. "I'm glad you like it." She walked over to the table in the sitting area, picked up a small leather-bound binder and handed it to Tricia. "I'm certain we'll have most of what you'll need to make your stay comfortable. We also offer laundry service. If you want something washed, just put them in the bags you'll find on a shelf in the closet and hang it outside your door tonight. You'll also find today's menu in the binder. If there's anything you need other than what is listed, please let me or Lind know."

Walking slowly over to an overstuffed armchair, Jeremy sat down heavily. His ankle was throbbing. The orthopedist had warned him that atmospheric changes would affect the metal in his foot. He closed his eyes, praying the pain would go away.

Tricia placed her purse on a table near the bed and opened the binder. The entrées included roast chicken, filet mignon and broiled trout. The bed-and-breakfast also offered a variety of dishes for vegetarians and those on restricted diets.

"What do you want to eat?" she asked Jeremy.

He waved a hand, not opening his eyes. "Please order for me."

She spoke quietly with Rose, ordering the chicken and fish entrées with steamed vegetables. Once Rose left to put in their order, she went over to Jeremy.

"Would you like to eat in bed?"

He opened his eyes and his head came up slowly. A slight smile played at the corners of his mouth. Had Tricia realized what she'd asked? Her naive question elicited erotic musings that made him temporarily forget about his pain. Yes, he wanted to eat in bed, taste every inch of her smooth fragrant skin from her face to her toes.

The notion of making love to her elicited a longing and a desire he had long thought dead. Whenever he made love to other women it was only for sexual release. But it had never been that way with Tricia. He hadn't consciously planned to seduce her, to get her into his bed, but the fact that they would share the same bed was now beyond her control, their control.

"Yes." The single word came out like a silken growl. His steady gaze met and fused with hers.

A minute passed before Tricia dropped her gaze. Turning on her heel, she went over to the bed, shifted the pillows and shams and turned back the coverlet. She went completely still when she registered the heat from Jeremy's body seeping into hers as he closed the distance between them. She shivered as his moist breath swept over the nape of her neck. She hadn't heard him get up.

"Help me into bed, sweetheart."

She took his crutches, propping them in a corner as he sat down heavily on the mattress. Bending over, she removed his shoe. Her motions were measured, precise as she placed an arm under the back of his knees and lifted his legs onto the bed.

"Are you in pain?" she asked after he'd slumped back to the pillows.

"It's bearable."

"That's not what I asked."

He glared at her. "I said it's bearable."

She did not believe him, but decided not to press the issue. Reaching for the telephone on the nightstand, she dialed the number for room service. She would order something that would not only dull his pain but also his senses temporarily.

"This is Mrs. Blackstone. I'd like to order a bottle of Chardonnay." She ignored Jeremy's questioning look. "Yes. Thank you."

"When did you start drinking?" he asked after she ended the call.

At fifteen they'd taken two bottles of wine from the dining hall's wine cellar and finished one in less than an hour. Jeremy had been slightly tipsy while Tricia spent half the night in the bathroom, retching violently. Once she recovered she swore she would never drink again.

"I sometimes have a glass or two for special occasions."

He lifted an eyebrow. "Is this a special occasion?"

A smile softened her mouth. "I'd say it is."

His smile matched hers. "What are we celebrating?"

"A truce, Jeremy."

His smile faded. "I'd like to think of it as a reconciliation, *Mrs. Blackstone*."

"Don't get carried away with yourself. I couldn't tell them I'm Miss Parker after you introduced me as your wife."

A muscle quivered at his jaw. "But you *could've* been Mrs. Blackstone."

She stared back at him for a long moment. "I could have been, but you chose to believe a lie."

Jeremy's eyes darkened with pain. Tricia did not know how many times he had punished himself for his cowardly actions. He'd run instead of staying to confront her. Even if she had lied about sleeping with Russell Smith, it still would have been better than not knowing.

"How long will I have to pay penance for deserting you, Tricia?"

"Fourteen years, Jeremy," she spat out angrily. "I loved you even when I became another man's wife. Every time he touched me I cursed you, because it was you I wanted to make love to, not Dwight. There were nights when I feigned sleep so I wouldn't have to make love with him. I punished Dwight when he didn't deserve to be punished." Her eyes glistened with unshed tears. "He was kind, patient but after a while even he couldn't put up with a cold and unresponsive wife."

Jeremy felt Tricia's pain as surely as if it was his own. He had hurt her—deeply. "I'm sorry. I know it sounds trite, but there's nothing else I can say. I'm sorry and I don't want you to leave the farm."

Straightening her spine, she stared down her nose at him. "What I promised to give you is three weeks. Please don't ask for more."

A sixth sense told him that something traumatic had happened to her during their separation. Something he knew he had to uncover before she left Blackstone Farms again.

He waited until Tricia walked into the bathroom, closing the door behind her, and leaned over to pick up the telephone receiver. He punched in several numbers. His call was answered after the third ring.

"Hey, Pop."

"Where the hell are you and Tricia?"

Jeremy ignored his father's sharp tone. "We're holed up at a bed-and-breakfast outside of Craigsville."

A heavy sigh came through the wire. "Dammit, Jeremy, you're going to put me in an early grave. Have you forgotten that everyone checks in during bad weather?"

Jeremy was aware of the mandated farm telephone chain that every resident check in with one another during violent weather.

"Half the county is blacked out because of downed power lines," Sheldon continued. "Poor Gus nearly passed out when I told him that I hadn't heard from you or Tricia."

"Tell Gus Tricia is safe. We plan to spend the night here."

There was a noticeable pause before Sheldon asked, "Is there something going on between you and Gus's granddaughter?"

Jeremy hesitated, then said, "Yes, Pop. There's something going on between Tricia and me, but it's something we have to work out by ourselves."

"I asked Tricia if she was the reason you joined the Marine Corps instead of coming back to the farm and she said I had to ask you."

"Since you've asked, I'll give you an answer. I

ran away instead of confronting her about something someone told me."

"Are you still running, son?"

Jeremy smiled. "No, Pop."

"Does this mean I can retire?"

"No. You're too young to retire."

"I'm tired, Jeremy. Thirty years in this business is enough. Now all I want to do is fish and spoil my grandchildren."

Jeremy closed his eyes and took a deep breath. "Can we talk about this another time?"

There was silence before Sheldon said, "Sure."

"Good night, Pop." He hung up the phone at the same time Tricia walked out of the bathroom.

"Who were you talking to?"

"My father. I called to let him know we're safe. He'll let your grandfather know that we're together."

Tricia nodded. It was one thing to sleep under Jeremy's roof and another to sleep with him—in the same bed—at a bed-and-breakfast. She did not have to be a clairvoyant to know Gus Parker's thoughts once Sheldon told him she and Jeremy were spending the night together away from the farm. Her grandfather had warned her repeatedly not to become involved with Jeremy...and she knew instinctively his warning had something to do with her mother.

Every time she'd asked her grandparents about her father they went mute. Had Patricia Parker become involved with someone who had been a boss's son?

Reuniting with Jeremy had changed her because she now had answers to her past—all but the identity of her father. As soon as she returned to Blackstone Farms she intended to confront her grandfather about her mother *and* her father.

Tricia sat down on a chair beside the bed and stared at Jeremy. He lay, his head and shoulders cradled on a mound of pillows, staring up at the ceiling. A comfortable silence filled the space as the sound of rain lashed at the windows. She moved off the chair when a knock on the door signaled the arrival of their dinner.

Chapter Six

Tricia turned off the lamp and slipped under the cool crisp sheet. The heat from Jeremy's nude body was overwhelming as he shifted on his side and rested an arm over her bare hip.

He nuzzled her ear. "How are you feeling?"

She smiled in the darkness. She could not remember the last time she'd felt so relaxed. "Wonderful. Why?"

Jeremy chuckled. "I don't want to take advantage of you if you're under the influence." He had drunk three glasses of wine to her two.

Turning to face him, Tricia looped an arm over his shoulder. "You're in no condition to talk trash, hotshot. Especially not with a busted ankle."

"My busted ankle has nothing to do with my ability to make love to you," he countered softly.

She snuggled against his chest. "Go to sleep, Jeremy."

"I don't think so."

Tricia went completely still. "You're kidding, aren't you?"

"No," he whispered against her moist parted lips. "I want you."

Pulling out of his embrace, she sat up and turned on the lamp on her side of the bed. Her heart fluttered wildly in her chest when she saw the direction of Jeremy's gaze. He was staring at her breasts, and she resisted the urge to pull the sheet up to her neck.

"I'm not going to lie and say I don't want you," she whispered. "But…" Her words trailed off.

He pushed up on an elbow. "But what, Tricia?"

She bit her lower lip. "Making love will complicate things."

"What things?"

"My having to leave you."

Jeremy held her gaze. "Didn't I tell you that I wouldn't try to pressure you to stay?"

When it comes time for you to leave I will not put any pressure on you to force you to stay. His declaration had stayed with Tricia, she wanted to believe him.

"You promise?" Her voice was soft, childlike.

"Have I ever lied to you, Tricia?"

A smile trembled over her lips. "No, Jeremy. You've never lied to me." Leaning forward, she kissed him, her lips caressing his. "No," she whispered over and over as she kissed his chin, jaw and forehead. Moving over him, she lay between his legs and kissed every inch of his face before her tongue mapped a path down his chest to his flat belly.

Jeremy felt a swath of heat race down his body. It settled in his groin, and his sex hardened quickly. He had waited years, more than a decade to experience the unrestrained, uncontrollable desire Tricia wrung from him. While he lay hidden in a swamp in a South American jungle he'd thought of her and the times they'd made love. He had forced himself to remember all of the good times in his life while he awaited death either from venomous insects, reptiles or the men searching for the team of DEA agents who'd inadvertently stumbled upon their cocaine factory.

He closed his eyes, curled his fingers into a fist and reveled in the sensual waves rippling up and down his body, letting his senses take over. He heard the rain slashing at the windows, felt the sweep of Tricia's breasts as she slid down his body and inhaled the fragrance of her perfume mingling with the rising scent of her desire. He did not know how, but he'd always been able to detect desire rising from the pores of her velvety skin.

Tricia had confessed to wanting him, even though she'd married another man, and it had been the same for him. Every woman he'd ever known had become Tricia Parker.

Unclenching his hands, he reached down and pulled her up before he climaxed. What he wanted— more than anything—was to explode inside her hot fragrant body.

Tricia tried freeing herself from Jeremy's grip, but she was no match for his superior strength as she lay over his chest. The soft light from the lamp spilled over his features. His eyes were dark and unfathomable.

"Sit on me," he ordered quietly.

She shook her head. "No, Jeremy. I don't want to hurt you."

He covered a breast with his hand, measuring the shape and weight of the full, ripe globe. His thumb made sweeping motions over the nipple. It hardened quickly.

"Another part of my body is hurting right now, and it's definitely not my foot."

Tricia knew if she permitted Jeremy to penetrate her without using protection, then there was the possibility of her becoming pregnant. She could not forget how easily she had conceived a child with him fourteen years before.

She shook her head again. "Not without protection, Jeremy."

His mouth twitched in amusement. "There are condoms in the bathroom."

Her jaw dropped. "You brought condoms with you?"

Jeremy was amused by her reaction. "No. There are a few in my grooming basket. Either you get them or hand me the crutches and I'll get them."

Tricia leaned closer and pressed her breasts to his chest. The strong, steady pumping of his heart echoed hers. "Let me make love to you without you penetrating me," she whispered close to his ear.

He smiled. "The next time you can make love to me. Tonight we'll make love to each other. I want to be inside you."

Tricia wanted Jeremy inside her, so deep he touched her womb, deep enough to make her sob in ecstasy as he'd done when she was a girl. She wanted him so deep inside her that they'd cease to exist as separate entities. But as much as she wanted Jeremy, Tricia feared becoming pregnant again.

"Please don't make me beg, sweetheart," Jeremy whispered.

He was asking what she'd wanted for years, what she wanted each time she'd permitted her ex-husband to make love to her. She'd spent years since she'd left the farm fantasizing about sleeping with Jeremy, and now that she was given a second chance she found herself balking.

She'd had and lost their baby. In that instant, Tricia vowed that if she were to become pregnant again, this time she would tell Jeremy. She kissed him deeply, her tongue meeting and curling around his in a sensual dance of desire.

"Don't go away. I'll be right back."

Jeremy's gaze followed her as she slipped off the bed and made her way to the bathroom. She had gained weight in all the right places. Her body was full and voluptuous. It reminded him of lush, sweet overripe fruit. Tricia's footfalls were silent as she returned to the bed. Extending her hand, she dropped a small square packet onto his chest.

Smiling, Jeremy picked it up and tore open the foil covering and took out the latex sheath. "Can you please put it on?" He held it up with his injured left hand.

Tricia rested her hands on her hips, her eyes narrowing. "You're really pushing it, aren't you?"

He lifted a raven eyebrow. "It's your call, Tricia. It wouldn't bother me if you rode bareback."

She shook her head. "No, Jeremy. I can't afford to get pregnant."

Jeremy sobered and pushed himself into a sitting position. "You know I always wanted you to be the mother of our children."

What Tricia wanted to tell him was that she'd had his child—a daughter who'd looked so much like him. Taking the condom, she slipped it on. She had barely completed the task when she found her face pressed to Jeremy's hard shoulder, his hand cupping the back of her head.

She felt like crying as she wound her arms around his neck. Easing back, she kissed him tentatively, inhaling his breath and masculine scent. He'd just echoed what lay in her heart.

"Don't talk, Jeremy. Just love me," she whispered, repeating the entreaty she'd uttered the last time they'd made love.

Jeremy's hands moved up and down her back, his fingertips trailing over her skin until she shuddered and moaned softly. He loathed the temporary disability that would not let him move and become an active participant; he wanted to use every inch of the large bed, trail his tongue along the length of Tricia's spine and he wanted to bury his face between her scented thighs and sample her feminine nectar. But more than anything he wanted to sheath his flesh inside her, feel her moist heat, the orgasmic convulsions that never failed to bring him to a free fall that would make him forget everything except Tricia.

Tricia took her time reacquainting herself with her ex-lover's body. She kissed his ear before tracing its shape with her tongue. She placed light kisses over the curve of his arching eyebrows, pressed her lips to the pulse in his throat, ran the tip of her tongue around the circle of his nipples until he moaned deep in his chest.

What had begun as slow, seductive foreplay

turned into a sensual dance of desire. She lost track of time and place as her blood raced through her veins. As Jeremy became more aroused she felt herself losing control. Shifting, she fitted her hips over his.

A slight gasp escaped Tricia as Jeremy raised his hips off the mattress and he stared at the shocked expression on her face. She was as tight as she had been as a virgin, and he wondered how long it had been since she'd slept with a man.

He cradled her bottom. "Do it slow. That's it," he urged as she lowered herself, inch by inch over his aroused flesh. It was his turn to gasp as her tight, hot walls closed around him. They moaned in unison once he was buried inside her.

Bracing her hands on his shoulders, Tricia stared at Jeremy staring up at her. She moved slowly at first, then quickened her motions when he cupped her breasts, squeezing them gently. There had been a time when Jeremy's hands could easily cover her breasts, but that time had passed. Pregnancy and breast-feeding had sensitized her nipples and increased her bust size from a 34B to a 38D.

Hypnotized by his touch, she trembled under his fingertips and closed her eyes as her body vibrated with a fire that threatened to ignite her into a million pieces where she would never be whole again.

Jeremy let go of Tricia's breasts and curved his arms around her waist until she lay flush on him.

Her soft moans of pleasure against his ear became his undoing. He arched his hips, meeting her as she rose and fell over his rigid flesh, the flames of passion burning hot—hotter than it had ever been for them.

This truce, their reconciliation had become a raw act of possession as he sought to leave his brand not only on her body but also in her heart. Silently, wordlessly he implored her to stay.

He closed his eyes, gritting his teeth as Tricia's flesh convulsed around him, she moaning softly as liquid heat flowed from her. Seconds later he abandoned himself to the rush of pleasure that left him weak and light-headed.

Jeremy emitted a low, guttural moan as Tricia's still-pulsing flesh milked the remnants of his release. He tightened the hold on her waist, not wanting to move or let her go.

He felt like a hypocrite. He'd sworn an oath to bring to justice those who sold drugs. Meanwhile, he had become addicted not to illegal substances but to a woman. Tricia had become his drug of choice.

"Jeremy?"

Her husky voice broke into his musing. "Yes, baby?"

"Did I hurt you?"

Turning his head, he dropped a kiss on her damp curly hair. "No, darling. Did I hurt you?"

"No." Tricia had told him no even though she

knew she would probably experience some discomfort in a few hours. Muscles she hadn't used in years were certain to be tender.

He kissed her forehead. "How long has it been?"

She knew he wanted to know how long it had been since she'd shared her body with another man. She waited a full minute, then said, "Ten years."

Staring up at the ceiling, he cursed mutely, cursed the time they'd been apart and cursed his own pigheadedness.

The rain stopped an hour before dawn, and it was late morning when Tricia finally maneuvered into the driveway leading to Jeremy's house. The storm had downed tree limbs and scattered debris for miles. She came to a complete stop as a tall figure rose from a chair on the porch. Sheldon had been waiting for them.

She glanced at Jeremy's stoic expression. "I'm going over to see my grandfather and get a change of clothes." Not waiting for a reply, she got out, retrieved the crutches resting behind the rear seats and handed them to Jeremy, who anchored them against his ribs.

Lowering his head, he brushed a kiss over her mouth. "I'll see you later." He stood motionless, watching as she got back into the car and drove away, then turned and stared up at his father. Sheldon leaned against a porch column, arms crossed over his chest.

"What's up, Pop?"

Sheldon's expression was a mask of stone. "Nothing."

Jeremy slowly made his way up the porch steps and sat down on the chaise. "I told you last night Tricia and I were okay."

Pushing off the column, Sheldon pulled over a rocker to face his son. He sat down and clasped his large hands together. "I wanted to see for myself that you were all right."

"You used to say that when I was fifteen. Have you forgotten how old I am?"

Sheldon's expression was one of pained tolerance. "I know how old you are, Jeremy," he snapped.

"What's this all about, Pop?"

"It's about me being a father, Jeremy." He frowned, his steely eyes shooting off angry sparks. "It's about me worrying about my son, and if I live to be ninety and you're seventy I still have the right to worry. It comes with the territory. But that's something you wouldn't understand because of your selfishness. You left here at eighteen, and over the past fourteen years you've become a drifter. You're here for a day or two, then you're gone.

"Half the time I don't know where you are or whether you're dead or alive. Every night I say a prayer of thanksgiving because someone from the

Justice Department did not show up with an announcement that my son died in the line of duty."

A shadow of annoyance tightened Jeremy's features. "If you're trying to make me feel guilty about my career choice, then forget it."

"It's not about guilt, Jeremy. It's about being responsible. I've worked my ass off for the past thirty years to make this horse farm a success, because I wanted to give you and Ryan things I didn't have. I'm retiring next year whether you stay on or not. And if Ryan isn't able to hold everything together, then I'm going to sell the farm."

Jeremy stared at Sheldon, complete surprise on his face. "You can't sell it."

Sheldon angled his head and lifted his eyebrows. "You think not?"

"But you promised my mother on her deathbed that you'd never sell the farm." It was with Julia's inheritance and her urging that prompted Sheldon to purchase his first Thoroughbred.

"Your mother's gone and I'm here," Sheldon countered as he rose to his feet.

Shock quickly turned to fury as Jeremy glared at his father's retreating back. He resented Sheldon's attempt to pressure him to give up his law enforcement career with the DEA.

He sat on the chaise recalling his passionate encounter with Tricia, temporarily forgetting Sheldon's threat to sell Blackstone Farms.

Three weeks.

The two words nagged at Jeremy because, after re-capturing the passion that had eluded him for years, he had to ask himself if he was prepared to lose Tricia a second time.

Chapter Seven

Tricia walked into Gus's house with a determined stride. It had been years since she'd asked her grandfather about her parents, and his answer had always been "Let sleeping dogs lie."

Well, she was ready to wake up the dogs and didn't care whether they barked, snarled or bit. She was thirty-two years old—old enough to accept the truth no matter how shocking or painful.

"Grandpa," she called out as she walked through the living room. Bright sunlight coming through the windows revealed a light layer of dust on the coffee table. She made a mental note to come by later to dust and vacuum. It had been her grandmother who had kept the house immaculate.

Gus wasn't there even though his truck was parked in its usual spot. Shrugging a shoulder, Tricia showered and dressed. Jeremy was scheduled to see a psychiatrist later in the afternoon. She lingered long enough to tape a note on the refrigerator for Gus to call her at Jeremy's house. They had to arrange a time to sit down and *talk*.

Tricia sat in the doctor's waiting room, flipping through magazines as she waited for Jeremy. She glanced surreptitiously over the magazine at a woman who had tried unsuccessfully to calm her young son. He talked incessantly while fidgeting. The boy ignored his mother, sliding off his chair and onto the floor. His motions mimicked making a snow angel. There was no doubt the child was there to be evaluated for ADHD: attention deficit hyperactivity disorder. She smiled at the boy as he got up and approached her. His dark eyes gleamed and he returned Tricia's smile.

She was surprised when he sat down next to her, and she surmised he was either four or five. Reaching for one of the books stacked on a nearby table, he handed it to her.

"Read," he ordered in a manner that said he was used to being obeyed.

The book was Dr. Seuss's *Green Eggs and Ham*.

She opened to the first page and began reading. The little boy sat quietly, listening to her soft voice as she read the entire book. She closed it, glanced up and saw Jeremy leaning on his crutches. He stared at her with a strange expression on his face.

Handing the book back to the child, she smiled. "I have to go now."

The boy pointed at Jeremy. "Is he your father?"

Tricia laughed. Jeremy certainly did not look old enough to be her father. "No, he isn't."

"What is he?"

She took a quick glance at Jeremy, who'd raised his eyebrows in a questioning gesture. "He's my—"

"I'm her boyfriend," Jeremy said. Taking in her annoyed expression, he smiled for the first time since he'd entered the medical building. Tricia seemed so at ease with the child. There was no doubt she was a wonderful pediatric nurse and probably would have been an excellent pediatrician.

His smile faded. His session with the psychiatrist had not gone well. The doctor had asked him questions he could not and did not want to answer. Jeremy was certain that a copy of the doctor's evaluation of his condition would be faxed to Special Operations in Washington, D.C., and placed in his personnel file.

Tricia stood up and walked over to him. "Are you ready?"

He did not move. "Am I, Tricia?" he asked softly.

"Are you what?"

"Your boyfriend?"

"Definitely not. You're my patient," she answered.

Jeremy stiffened as if Tricia had struck him, and a shadow of annoyance crossed his face seconds before he walked to the door. He paused as she held the door open for him, then he made his way down a ramp to where she had parked her car.

Waiting until she was seated behind the wheel, he turned and glared at her. "What am I to you, Tricia?"

Taken aback by the question, she stared at him with wide eyes. "Let it go, Jeremy."

"I don't want to let it go," he countered, his voice rising slightly.

"If you're looking to argue with me, then you're out of luck today."

Jeremy refused to relent. He had to know where he stood with her. "I don't intend to argue, Tricia. Just answer the question."

There was one thing she knew and remembered about Jeremy and that was his stubborn streak. Once he believed in something, no one could get him to change his mind. He'd believed Russell Smith's lie about them sleeping together and in the end it had cost them a future together.

"You're someone I grew up with and slept with, someone to whom I gave my heart and innocence, someone I fell in love with, someone who did not trust me enough to believe I'd be faithful. And I am someone who on August fifteenth will get into my car and drive back to Baltimore and the life I've made for myself." She took a deep breath. "Does that answer your question, Jeremy?"

A lethal calmness shimmered in the dark-gray eyes that held her gaze. "Yes, Tricia, it does."

The ride back to the farm was accomplished in complete silence. Tricia hadn't turned on the radio and with each passing mile the silence swelled until it was deafening.

She didn't know what Jeremy wanted from her. He'd asked her to forgive him, and she had. They'd reconciled, made love and chances were they would continue to sleep together up until the time her vacation ended. Jeremy said he wouldn't pressure her to stay, but he also hadn't offered her anything that would give her a reason to stay.

She drove through the electronic gate and maneuvered onto the road where several Thoroughbreds grazed behind a fence. Slowing, she came to a complete stop. Her gaze was glued to a small figure sitting astride a magnificent black horse racing around the winding, muddy track. Three men stood outside the fence screaming at the top of their lungs, while a fourth sat on the top rail, holding a stopwatch. Tricia's breath caught in her throat.

"Oh—" Jeremy swallowed an expletive as he watched jockey and horse become one as they appeared to fly over the track. His heart was pounding in his chest by the time horse and rider crossed the finish line. A loud roar rent the air. The jockey jumped off and pumped a gloved fist in the air.

Tricia stared numbly as the jockey took off his headgear and a tumble of dark hair floated around his shoulders. It wasn't until he turned that she realized he was a she.

She turned and stared at Jeremy, the pulse in her throat fluttering wildly. This is what she'd missed about Blackstone Farms: the excitement of prerace activity.

"Who is she?"

"Her name is Cheryl Carney, also known as Blackstone Farms's secret weapon. She's Kevin Manning's niece. Pop claims she's a horse whisperer and that she and Shah Jahan can communicate telepathically." Kevin Manning had taken over as head trainer after Russell Smith's father moved his family to the West Coast.

"Has Jahan raced competitively yet?" Tricia asked when she recalled the celebration following the ebony colt's birth.

"Not yet. Pop wants to wait until he's two. He's still too skittish to compete because whenever he's on the track with another horse he has to wear blinkers."

"There's no doubt he's destined for greatness."

Jeremy nodded. "Ryan predicts that if he stays

healthy, then he'll become the farm's first potential Triple Crown winner."

Tricia raised her eyebrows. "He's that good?"

"With Cheryl riding him there's no doubt he'll become a winner." You and I were that good, he added silently.

Tricia shifted into gear and drove past the stables. She never realized how much she missed the horse farm until she returned. The smell of horseflesh, hay and fields of heather and lavender growing in the undeveloped north end of the property were like an aphrodisiac. She visited on average twice a year: summer and winter. This was the first time she had decided to spend an entire month.

She drove past the schoolhouse made up of four connecting buildings. She thought about Jeremy's offer to become a school nurse and quickly dismissed it. It wasn't that being a school nurse would be unrewarding. It was just that she enjoyed working with the four pediatricians who had set up one of the largest practices in downtown Baltimore.

"Do you miss the farm, Tricia?"

Jeremy had read her mind. "Yes, I do," she answered truthfully.

"What do you miss most?"

She gave him a quick glance. "The people. They're like my extended family. I may have been an only child, but I fought and argued with the other kids as if we were brothers and sisters."

Jeremy nodded, smiling. He had become known as the Blackstone brawler. At that time it was not in his psychological makeup to walk away from a fight, and the number of encounters escalated after his mother's death. He'd been filled with rage because Julia had chosen to hide her illness from everyone until it was too late for her to seek medical treatment.

Resting his left arm over the back of Tricia's seat, his fingers feathered through the soft curls on the nape of her neck.

"Could you please drop me off at Ryan's?"

She made a right turn and less than a minute later she maneuvered into the driveway to Ryan and Kelly's home. Tricia parked, got out of the car and handed Jeremy his crutches.

"Aren't you coming in?" he asked as she turned to get back into the vehicle.

She shook her head. "No."

Jeremy studied her thoughtfully. "Don't you want to see the baby?"

Tricia forced a smile she did not feel. "I'll see her another time." Interacting with newborns was something she did often, but it would be different with Vivienne. She was a Blackstone, Sheldon's granddaughter, just like Juliet, and the image of Juliet's tiny lifeless body was still imprinted on her mind. Even after so many years, that image was still painful for Tricia to bear.

She wondered if she would be able to cradle Vivienne and successfully hold back tears and not relive the joy of becoming a mother and the pain of burying a part of herself. And she knew the answer before she had formed the question—no, not yet.

"I have to talk to my grandfather about something." Tricia glanced at her watch. "I'll come back at six to pick you up for dinner."

"Where would you like to eat tonight?"

"The dining hall," she said quickly.

Jeremy's dark eyebrows slanted in a frown. He did not want to eat at the farm. He wanted a repeat of what he and Tricia had had the night before.

"We can eat at the dining hall tomorrow night." There was a thread of hardness in his statement.

"You asked me where I wanted to eat and I said the dining hall," Tricia retorted.

He refused to relent. "Perhaps I should've said that we *are* eating out tonight."

Tricia reacted quickly to the challenge in his voice. "Perhaps not, Jeremy." She gave him a hostile glare. "Let me remind you that I don't work for *you*. Your father asked me to help you. He asked, not demanded, Jeremy. If you want me to do something, then I suggest you ask politely."

Not giving him the opportunity for a comeback, Tricia got into the car and drove away. She glanced into the rearview mirror and found him leaning on his crutches. His image stayed with her even after she'd walked into Gus's house and found him sitting in his favorite chair, dozing.

Why didn't I wait until he got into the house? What if he had fallen trying to make it up the porch steps?

Concern for Jeremy continued to haunt her until she shook Gus gently to wake him. Gus's eyes opened and he seemed surprised to see her.

"Grandpa, you shouldn't sleep sitting up. It's not good for your circulation."

Gus affected a slow smile. "Don't worry yourself about me, baby girl. Since I stopped salting my food, my ankles don't swell up like they used to."

Tricia held out a hand. "Come sit with me on the love seat. I want to talk to you about something."

"I saw your note."

"Did you call me?"

Shaking his head slowly, Gus said, "No, because I know what it is you want to talk about."

"I need answers."

"Let it go, Tricia."

"I can't, Grandpa. I'm not a little girl. I'm a grown woman. I have a right to know something about my mother and my father."

Gus closed his eyes. "Let sleeping dogs lie, Tricia."

"I can't and I won't!"

He opened his eyes and stared up at her, and it was

then Tricia realized she had yelled at her grandfather. A strange expression crossed his face seconds before he placed a gnarled hand over his chest and slumped forward, his chin resting on his chest.

Tricia was galvanized into action. She caught Gus's wrist, measuring his pulse. It was slow, weak.

Somehow she managed to get him off the chair and onto the floor and began cardiopulmonary resuscitation. Each time she compressed his chest, she prayed, Please don't let him die.

Ryan opened the door for Jeremy. His expression registered shock seeing his brother standing on his porch—alone. "How did you get here?"

"Tricia drove me."

Peering around Jeremy's shoulder, Ryan asked, "Where is she?"

"She went to see her grandfather. Are you going to let me in, or are you going to wait for me to fall?"

Ryan, deciding to ignore Jeremy's acerbic tone, took a step backward and opened the door wider. "Please enter, sir prince."

Jeremy rolled his eyes at his older brother and made his way slowly into the living room. He sat down on a deep club chair, placed his crutches on the floor and raised his left leg onto a footstool.

Ryan sat in a facing armchair and ran a hand over his close-cropped hair. "If you've come to see Kelly and the baby, you're out of luck because they're napping. However, if you've come to bitch and moan, then I'm all ears."

Jeremy frowned. "Who's bitching and moaning?"

"Pop."

"What's up with him?"

Ryan hesitated, then said, "You are."

Jeremy groaned softly. "What now?"

"He's going to sell the farm."

"Sell or he's threatening to sell?"

Ryan's expression was a mask of stone. "Sell, Jeremy!"

"Pop is being manipulative."

"Wrong. Pop is being Pop. I told you last year that he's tired."

Jeremy frowned in cold fury. "I know what brought on his tirade." He revealed to Ryan what he and Sheldon had talked about after he and Tricia returned from spending the night at the bed-and-breakfast."

A slow smile formed on Ryan's lips. "You and Tricia Parker?"

Jeremy smiled in spite of himself and nodded. "Yeah."

"Damn, brother, you sure had me fooled. I thought you and Tricia were just good friends."

"We started out as friends, but the year we turned eighteen something happened."

"Was that little something called love?"

Before Jeremy could answer Ryan's query, the

telephone rang. Reaching for the phone on a nearby table, Ryan spoke softly into the mouthpiece. His expression changed as he stood up. "Stay with him, Tricia. I'll be right there as soon as I call the hospital. No, don't try to move him." He depressed a button, then two others. The speed dial connected him to the local hospital.

Jeremy reached down for his crutches and was on his feet the moment he heard his brother mention "possible heart attack," and Augustus Parker's name.

"I'm coming with you," he said.

"Try to keep up," Ryan said over his shoulder as he raced out of the house.

Chapter Eight

"Stop beating up on yourself," Jeremy whispered to Tricia for what seemed like the hundredth time since Gus Parker was wheeled into the emergency room.

She closed her eyes and rested her head on his shoulder. "I should never have argued with him."

Jeremy tightened his grip around her waist as they sat together on a love seat in a waiting area. "You snapped at me earlier about ordering you about, and now I'm going to do exactly that. I want you to stop blaming yourself for Gus's heart attack. If it hadn't happened now, there's nothing to say it wouldn't have happened after your return to Baltimore. Gus seeing your face once he comes out of surgery is certain to lift his spirits."

Tricia nodded. She opened her eyes to find Sheldon sitting several feet away staring at her and Jeremy. Ryan had driven Gus to the hospital and stayed to confer with the cardiologist who was scheduled to perform open-heart surgery. Ryan then called Sheldon and informed him of Gus's condition. Sheldon had driven from the farm to the hospital in record time.

Pushing off his chair, Sheldon stood up. "I'm going to get some coffee. Would either of you like some?"

Jeremy straightened and removed his arm from Tricia's waist. "How do you want yours?"

Tricia seldom drank coffee, but this was one time when she needed a jolt from the caffeine. "Black."

"Make that two blacks, Pop."

Waiting until Sheldon walked away, Jeremy leaned closer to Tricia, held her hand and pressed a kiss to her cheek. "He's going to be all right." Gus had been in surgery for more than two hours.

Turning her head, she smiled at him. "I want to thank you for being here for me."

"There's…"

The cardiologist walked into the waiting room preempting whatever it was Jeremy planned to say. Tricia stood up on trembling legs as Jeremy came to his feet.

She bit down on her lower lip, gathering courage. "How is my grandfather?"

He offered her a comforting smile. "He has been stabilized and is in the intensive care unit."

"When can I see him?"

"Not until tomorrow."

A flicker of apprehension coursed through Tricia. "What aren't you telling me, Dr. Lawrence?"

"It's apparent your grandfather suffered a mild heart attack in the past which weakened the heart wall. He's going to have to take it easy so the muscles can heal."

"My grandfather never had a heart attack," she argued softly.

"Perhaps he'd experienced chest pains in the past but ignored them. But I can assure you that there is evidence of some heart damage."

"How long will Mr. Parker have to remain in the hospital?" Jeremy asked as he moved closer to Tricia's side.

"At least a week," Dr. Lawrence replied, "followed by a minimum of six weeks of limited activity. After he's reevaluated, then he will have to undergo physical therapy that will help him regain some endurance." He stared at Tricia. "Is there someone at home who can take care of him?"

"I'll take care of him," she said, not hesitating. Her grandfather's heart attack meant she would not return to Baltimore as planned. "I'm going to need medical documentation to take Family Leave."

"You can pick up a form at the business office in the morning." The cardiologist patted her shoulder. "Go home and get some rest. We'll make certain your grandfather receives the best medical care available today."

She managed a weak smile. "Thank you, Dr. Lawrence." He nodded, turned and walked away.

"Gus can move into my house," Jeremy said close to her ear. "I already have the hospital bed and a wheelchair."

Tricia gave him a startled look. "Where will you sleep?"

"I can sleep on the daybed while you can use an upstairs bedroom. I'll make certain someone will keep Gus's place clean and aired out until he's able to live alone."

She was puzzled by Jeremy's offer to open his house for her grandfather's convalescence. "Why are you doing this, Jeremy? You and my grandfather have never been fond of each other."

"How Gus and I feel about each other is irrelevant, because he is still a member of the farm's extended family. Just like you are," he added in a soft tone. "And you know we always look out for one another."

Tricia nodded. "You're right." She managed a weak smile. "Thank you."

His gaze widened. "There's no need to thank me. I would do the same for anyone at Blackstone Farms."

Tricia did not know why, but at that moment she did not want Jeremy to offer his home to Gus just because the elderly man had been a long-time employee of Blackstone Farms. She wanted it to be because he still felt something for her beyond their sleeping together.

She had promised to give him the next three weeks when in reality she wanted it to be the rest of her life. The harder she had tried to ignore the truth the more it nagged at her, for it had taken only one night of passionate lovemaking to conclude that she still loved Jeremy and would love him for the rest of her life.

Sheldon walked into the waiting room as silently as a large cat. He stopped, watching the interaction between his son and Tricia. Clearing his throat, he moved closer as Tricia and Jeremy sprang apart. "If there's anything you need me to do for you and Gus, just ask, Tricia."

Tricia smiled at Sheldon. "Thank you, but Jeremy has offered to let Grandpa stay in his house until he's able to live alone again."

Sheldon lifted an eyebrow, stared at his son and wondered if Jeremy and Tricia had made other plans that perhaps he should know about. Maybe, just maybe, he would be given the opportunity to retire, gain another daughter-in-law and, if he was lucky, another grandchild.

His gaze shifted to Tricia. "Never forget that you're family, Tricia. Everyone connected to the farm is family." He lifted the cardboard container cradling three foam cups. "Let's go somewhere and get some coffee that doesn't come out of a vending machine looking like mud."

Turning, Sheldon led the way out of the hospital, Tricia and Jeremy following.

"Why don't we finish this some other time?"

Sheldon's voice broke into Jeremy's thoughts, his sharp tone filled with annoyance. "No, Pop," he countered. "Let's get it over with now. My recommendation is that you sign for a short-term, high-interest loan to ease your cash flow. Once you sell the mares you can pay it off interest free."

Sheldon nodded. "In other words I would use or borrow the bank's money at no cost to me."

"Exactly," Jeremy concurred, smiling. "Borrow a little extra because you may see some stock you hadn't planned on buying."

"Now you sound like Ryan."

"I'm not into horses like you and Ryan, but I do know horse farms need an infusion of new bloodlines every three to five years. And what Blackstone Farms needs is a three-year-old who will be eligible for next year's Kentucky Derby."

Nodding in agreement, Sheldon closed the ledger, pushed it aside and watched his son massage his forehead with his fingertips. "Do you still have headaches?"

Jeremy lowered his hand. "They come and go."

"Do you want me to go back to your place for your medication?"

"No. I've stopped taking it."

"Why?"

"Because I don't like not being in control of what I do or say."

Sheldon gave him a long, penetrating look. "You can tell me it's none of my business but—"

"But you're going to say it anyway," Jeremy countered, smiling.

A rare smile deepened the lines around Sheldon's eyes. "Yes, I am going to say it anyway." He sobered quickly. "What's going on between you and Tricia?"

Jeremy did not move, not even his eyes. "There's nothing going on?" Nothing except that they were lovers once again.

"Do you love her?"

"I'll guess I've always loved her."

"Have you told her how you feel?"

"No."

"Why not?"

Jeremy shrugged a shoulder as he continued to massage his forehead. "We've been apart for too long. I've changed and she's changed. If we had reconnected ten years ago or even last year, then I believe things would be different."

"Why would you say that?" Sheldon asked.

"Look at me, Pop. Whenever I have the flash-backs, I feel as if I'm losing my mind. Tricia remembers me whole and sane, not crippled and crazy."

Sheldon leaned forward. "You're not a cripple."

"Get real, Pop. The doctor says I'm healing nicely, but he knows and I know that I'm through with undercover assignments."

"I'm going to be honest when I say I'm not sorry about that."

"That's because you never supported my career choice."

"You belong here, Jeremy. You should've come back after you graduated from college."

"I couldn't come back."

"Why not?"

Sheldon sat silently as Jeremy repeated what Russell Smith and Gus Parker told him that fateful night fourteen years before. "I've spent years beating myself up for breaking up with Tricia. I wanted to hate her, but every time I came back to the farm I prayed she'd be here."

"Has she forgiven you?"

A smile inched its way through the uncertain expression on Jeremy's lean face. "As much as she can, given the circumstances. Before Gus's heart attack she said she'd give me three weeks."

"Is that what she said?"

Jeremy nodded. "Loud and clear."

Sheldon ran a hand over his face. "Damn. She's as stubborn as Gus," he drawled. He angled his head. "I stopped dispensing fatherly advice after you and Ryan became men, but there comes a time when it is necessary. Put aside your pride and grovel."

Jeremy stared at Sheldon, complete surprise on his face. "I know you're not talking about pleading and begging."

"If it comes to that."

There was a moment of silence before Jeremy's expression hardened noticeably. "Do you want me to patch things up with Tricia because you want to retire?"

Sheldon's eyes darkened like angry clouds as he pushed back his chair and stood up. "My decision to retire is not predicated on your love life." He spat out the word. "So, don't delude yourself, Jeremy. It's just that I've been where you are right now. There were people who did not want me to get together with your mother, but at seventeen I had more of a backbone than you have at thirty-two."

Jeremy's expression was thunderous as he watched his father walk out of the room. What did Sheldon expect him to do? What more could he do? He couldn't force Tricia to remain at the farm if she chose to leave.

More important, he was unable to tell Tricia he

still loved her, because he did not want to become that vulnerable again. And given his present emotional state he did not think he would make it back from the brink of madness this time if he offered her his heart only to have her reject him.

However, there was one thing he knew for certain, which was that time was on his side. The longer she stayed the more time they had to regain each other's trust.

Two days after Gus was wheeled into the intensive care unit, he was transferred to a private room. Although oxygen flowed into his nostrils, an intravenous feeding tube was taped to the back of his right hand and his vitals were closely monitored by the electrodes taped to his chest, he was resting comfortably. His color was ashen, and what was left of his sparse white hair appeared brittle.

Tricia squeezed a dab of moisturizing hair cream into her hand, massaged it gently into his hair and scalp before she combed his hair.

Gus opened his eyes and stared up at Tricia. The last time he remembered seeing her was at the bungalow. The minute lines around his eyes deepened as he managed a tentative smile. "Hey, grandbaby girl."

She leaned over and kissed his cheek. "Hi, Grandpa. How are you feeling this morning?"

"Good." He let out an audible sigh. "I'm sorry if I gave you a scare."

"There's no need to apologize. In fact I was pretty cool," she lied smoothly. There was no way she was going to admit to Gus that she was almost hysterical by the time Ryan came to the bungalow to take him to the hospital. At that moment her medical training fled, leaving in its wake a woman who feared losing her last surviving relative.

There came a light knock on the door. Tricia turned to find Jeremy and Sheldon in the doorway. Sheldon cradled a large bouquet of flowers against his chest.

Her gaze met and fused with Jeremy's. Over the past three days they hadn't seen much of each other. She dropped him off at Sheldon's house in the morning, then drove to the hospital to spend the day with Gus. She returned to the farm at night, picked Jeremy up from his father's house and drove him back home.

They shared a bed but hadn't made love since the night they'd checked into the bed-and-breakfast, and Tricia had come to know a very different Jeremy. Whenever she cried because she feared losing her grandfather, he held her while offering words of comfort and encouragement. She had promised Sheldon that she would take care of his son, but the roles were now reversed because now Jeremy took care of her.

Gus gestured with his left hand. "Come in and sit down."

Sheldon placed the basket of flowers on the window ledge and sat in a chair in the corner, while Jeremy took a chair at the foot of the bed.

Sheldon smiled at Gus. "The flowers are from the folks at the farm." He crossed one knee over the other. "How are you feeling?"

Gus smiled at his friend and former employer. "Pretty good."

"Good enough to hang out with the Wild Bunch for our annual fall camping weekend?" Sheldon and three other men had formed a bond that went beyond employer-employee whenever they went away together. They stayed in a cabin at the foot of the Appalachian Mountains for a male-bonding weekend that included fishing, marathon poker games, emptying a keg of beer and smoking cigars.

"I'm game, but I don't know if I can smoke cigars anymore."

Tricia went completely still. "Grandpa!"

Gus stared at his granddaughter. "What's the matter?"

"I didn't know you smoked cigars."

He waved a frail hand. "I only do it once a year."

"Once a year is too much. No more cigars, Grandpa. I mean it," Tricia added when Gus rolled his eyes at her.

The elderly man's gaze shifted to Jeremy. "Does she treat you like this?"

Jeremy nodded. "All the time."

Tricia's jaw dropped. "No, I don't."

"She's even threatened me," he continued as if Tricia were not in the room.

Gus fixed a steady gaze on Jeremy. "Fourteen years ago Tricia told me that the two of you planned to marry after you graduated college."

There was complete silence from the four occupants, while the soft beeping sounds coming from the machine monitoring Gus's respiration, heartbeat and blood pressure reverberated in the stillness.

Sheldon leaned forward on his chair, his startled gaze shifting from Jeremy to Tricia.

Tricia's eyes widened as she held her breath.

Only Jeremy and Gus appeared calm, composed.

"That's true," Jeremy said.

Gus pressed a button, raising the head of his bed. "Come here, son." Jeremy pushed to his feet and approached the bed. Turning his head slowly, Gus stared at Tricia. "Please come here, grandbaby. I want you to stand next to Jeremy." Tricia gave Jeremy a questioning look and rounded the bed.

Gus took a deep breath. "I'm going to say this quickly and be done with it because I'm tired." His gaze was fixed on the ceiling. "Staring death in the face is scary. Olga used to call me a fool, and after all these years I'm forced to agree with her. I interfered with something I should have left alone." Turning his head slowly, he stared at Tricia, then Jeremy. "Jeremy Blackstone, I want you to marry my granddaughter. Marry her, protect her and give me at least one great-grandbaby before I leave this world."

Heat flamed in Tricia's face. "No, Grandpa!"

Gus glared at Tricia. "Hush up. I'm not talking to you." He ignored her slack jaw. "Sheldon, you should be a part of this." Waiting until Sheldon moved closer to the bed, Gus said, "I want you to get someone to help Tricia plan her wedding."

A grim-faced Sheldon folded his arms over his chest. He shook his head slowly. "Sorry, Gus. I don't intend to become a party to coercion or manipulation. If Tricia and Jeremy want to marry, then it must be their decision." He turned to Tricia. "The only thing I'm going to say is that I'd be honored to call you daughter."

Tricia felt like a specimen on a slide under a microscope. The energy radiating from the three men was almost as tangible as the annoyance and anger knotting her insides.

Her dark eyes bore into her grandfather's. "I love you, Grandpa, but I'm not going to allow you to control my life, and I don't need you to speak for me."

Jeremy's expression was a mask of stone. "You don't have to say anything, Tricia. Just because Gus is your grandfather, I will not stand by and let him intimidate you."

Gus reached for the buzzer to the nurses' station. Less than a minute later, a white-clad figure walked into the room. "Yes, Mr. Parker?" the nurse asked.

Gus waved his hand weakly. "Please show these people out."

The nurse folded her hands on her hips. "Gentlemen, madam, I'm going to ask you to leave now."

Tricia could not believe they had been so summarily dismissed. She was hard-pressed not to come back at Gus. "I'll see you later, Grandpa."

Gus averted his head. "Don't come back to see me unless you have a wedding date."

Sheldon patted Gus's shoulder. "Don't push it, friend."

Sheldon followed Jeremy and Tricia out of the room, smiling and shaking his head. He did not agree with Gus's scheme, but if his son did propose to Tricia, then everyone would get what they wanted: Jeremy and Tricia would marry, he would gain another daughter-in-law, and perhaps he and Gus could look forward to a new grandchild and great-grandchild respectively.

Chapter Nine

Tricia sat on the chaise between Jeremy's outstretched legs, staring up at the star-studded sky and struggling to bring her fragile emotions under control.

"Why is he doing this to me? To us?" There was a sob in her voice.

Lowering his head, Jeremy pressed his lips to her hair. "I don't know, sweetheart."

She glanced over her shoulder. Light from porch lamps threw long and short shadows over his face. "My grandfather is shutting me out because I refuse to bend to his will."

Tricia had gone to the hospital to see Gus that

afternoon, but he wouldn't talk to her and ordered her out of his room after she told him that she had no intention of marrying Jeremy.

"Gus has always been a proud man."

"My grandfather is living in the wrong century. Shotgun weddings are a thing of the past."

Jeremy traced the outline of her ear with a forefinger. "You should try to see things his way, Tricia. He blames himself because we're not together. I suppose forcing us to marry is his way of trying to right the wrongs."

She shifted and stared directly at the man holding her to his heart. "You agree with him?"

He shook his head slowly. "No, Tricia, I don't agree with him. But I do understand why he'd want you to marry me."

She was caught off guard by the husky quality of his voice. Tricia stared at Jeremy as if he were a stranger. There was only the sound of their measured breathing, the incessant chirping of crickets and an occasional hoot of an owl.

"Why?" she asked once she'd recovered her voice.

"In your grandfather's day, women needed men to protect them. To his way of thinking, as my wife you would be a Virginia Blackstone and under my and my family's protection. I don't have to tell you what that means."

As soon as she had learned to read, Tricia became

aware of the significance of the Blackstone name in the annals of horseracing. "You make it sound so simple. You get a wife, I get a husband, and my grandfather is absolved of his guilt."

"It sounds simple because it is simple."

She eased out of his loose embrace and stood up. "Nothing is ever that simple…and it…it's just too late," she said. "Listen Jeremy, I've had about as much as I can take for one day. I'm going to bed. Are you coming?"

He stared up at her. "I'm going to sit out here for a while."

She nodded. "Good night."

Tricia was awakened by the press of a hard body along the length of hers. "Jeremy." His name was a whisper.

"Why are you sleeping down here?" Since Jeremy decided that Gus would convalesce under his roof, he and Tricia had begun sleeping together in the master bedroom. He hoped they would continue to share a bed until her grandfather was discharged from the hospital.

Tricia sat up on the daybed and combed her fingers through her short, curly hair. "I needed to be alone so I could think."

Jeremy reached for her hand. "What is there to think about? You and I are going to be married."

She went completely still, unable to believe what she'd just heard. "What?"

Jeremy gathered her to his chest and rested his chin on the top of her head. "We should've married fourteen years ago. We have lost so much."

Tricia felt the slow, strong pumping of his heart against her cheek. "We can't turn back the clock," she argued softly.

He tightened his hold on her body. "Perhaps not, but we can move forward."

He still loved her, had never stopped loving her. The realization had attacked him as he sat on the porch that evening mentally playing back his life like reversing a video. He vacillated between the emotions of self-pity because of his injury and gratitude because his life had been spared, but in his selfishness he had forgotten that he was a son, brother and an uncle. He had a family who loved him as much as he loved them.

And, he had been reunited with a woman he had loved for so long that he could not remember when he did not love her. She had married another man, yet she had not forgotten him. She loved him when he had done nothing to deserve her love. He had run away and deserted her when she needed him.

Anchoring a finger under her chin, he raised her face. The soft glow from the lamp on a side table highlighted a pair of large dark eyes filled with confusion and uncertainty.

"Marry me, Tricia."

She blinked once. "Is this what you want to do?"

Jeremy nodded. "Yes. It is something we should've done fourteen years ago."

Leaning forward, she rested her forehead against his shoulder and inhaled the lingering scent of his cologne. Jeremy had asked her to marry him, yet there was no mention of the word *love* in his proposal.

She closed her eyes and prayed silently, prayed she would make the right decision. "What is there about me that makes men propose marriage when I'm most vulnerable?"

Jeremy felt her uneasiness. What Tricia did not know was he also was vulnerable, vulnerable to her rejection, vulnerable to the emotional pain only she could inflict.

"Let me take care of you, baby. I promise to protect you from all that is seen and unseen, while providing you with financial security. Gus is the only family you have, but when you marry me, Sheldon will become your father, Ryan your brother, Kelly your sister and Vivienne and Sean your nephew and niece."

Tricia did not want to think of the time when she would lose her last surviving relative. "Can we do this, Jeremy?"

"Yes, we can."

Easing back, she stared up at him. The tenderness shimmering in his smoky-gray gaze took her breath away. A sensual smile softened her mouth. "Okay, Jeremy. Let's do it."

Jeremy angled his head and brushed his mouth over her parted lips. "Thank you, baby, for giving us a second chance. Let's go upstairs. I have to give you something."

Tricia sat on the bed in the master bedroom, holding her breath as Jeremy slipped a ring with a flawless, square-cut emerald set in a band of pavé diamonds on her finger.

"My father gave this ring to my mother as a gift after Blackstone Farms's first Kentucky Derby winner. Boo-Yaw wasn't favored to come in among the three favored, but he fooled everyone when he won by a nose." Boo-Yaw went on to win many more races for Blackstone Farms, and after he no longer raced competitively, he went on to sire several more champions.

Jeremy had given Tricia a small box filled with priceless heirloom pieces that had once belonged to his mother and grandmother. There was an estate diamond ring that would have made a perfect engagement ring, but she had decided on the emerald because it was her birthstone.

Jeremy kissed her cheek. "It's a perfect fit."

She extended her hand. "It's beautiful."

He nuzzled her ear. "Not as beautiful as you are."

Not only did she feel beautiful, but she also felt complete for the first time in many, many years. She and Jeremy had so much to make up for. Once he had proposed marriage she thought about what she would have to give up and the answer was: not much. She owned property she could sell and now had a profession she could make the most of at Blackstone Farms Day School. She planned to apply for the position of school nurse. She did not have a boyfriend, lover or close girlfriends in Baltimore, and that meant her departure would be accomplished without a lot of fanfare.

Glancing up, she met Jeremy's tender gaze. "We're going to have to select a wedding date."

He rapped his knuckles on the cast. "I'd like to wait until this is off. Repeating my wedding vows leaning on a pair of crutches doesn't quite cut it."

"Then we'll wait," Tricia said softly.

Jeremy lay on his back, his gaze fusing with hers. "How about the Labor Day weekend?"

She gave him a sensual smile. "That will give me enough time to plan something that won't be too elaborate."

"We can marry here on the farm, especially since that's a holiday when everyone gets together." His gaze softened. "There are so many things I want to do with you, but I can't right now."

She crawled over his body, laughing softly. "I promise not to take advantage of you."

He curved his arms around her waist; her breasts spilled over the lacy bodice of her nightgown. "I won't say a word if you decide to use or abuse me as long as it feels good," he said teasingly. A swollen silence ensued before Jeremy said, "I've decided to leave the DEA."

Raising her head, Tricia stared down at him. "Are you certain that is what you want to do?"

Jeremy nodded. "I've been giving it a lot of thought. I know if I stay in I'd probably be assigned to a desk position, and that would turn me into a certifiable basket case. My first session with the psychiatrist was a complete disaster. He wanted me to talk about what happened to me and the other members of my team before we were rescued and I refused."

"What are you going to do?"

A slow smile spread over his face. "Are you concerned that I won't be able to support you?"

Tricia felt her face burn in embarrassment. "Of course not. It's…" His fingers stopped her protest.

"I'm going to assume the responsibility of running the farm," he said in a quiet tone. "Pop has been talking about retiring, and Ryan has been on my case for years about taking my rightful place at Blackstone

Farms." His expression softened. "If I hadn't broken my ankle none of this would've become a reality. I would not have come back to stay more than two or three days, and I probably would not have reconnected with you."

Tricia lay motionless and registered the steady pumping of her fiancé's heart under her breasts. His heartbeat was strong while her grandfather's was weak. "Hold me, Jeremy."

"I am," he said against her ear. Tightening his hold on her body, Jeremy knew this coming together was not about sex. It was about easing Tricia's apprehension about her grandfather's and their future. It was about offering his love and his protection. The fingertips of his right hand made tiny circles along her spine. "I'll always be here for you, darling."

She nodded and placed light kisses along the column of his strong neck, forehead, eyelids, nose, cheekbones, chin and mouth. She paused to remove his clothes, then her rapacious mouth charted a path from his throat to his belly and lower. And she broke her promise not to take advantage of Jeremy as she wrung a passion from him that left him gasping for his next labored breath.

Jeremy threw a muscled arm over his face and groaned in erotic pleasure that was akin to pain. "Please, please, please," he whispered over and over until it became a litany.

Tricia ignored his pleas and loved him for all of the years they'd been apart, and when he finally released his boiling passion she could not disguise her body's reaction as she moved up his chest and gloried in his hardness pulsing against her thighs.

They lay, their arms entwined and waited for the heat to fade. Tricia lay down beside Jeremy and within minutes she had fallen asleep. But sleep was not as kind to Jeremy, although he was filled with an amazing sense of completeness.

It would take time for him to believe that everything he had ever wanted for himself was about to be manifested: the girl he had spent years protecting, the young woman with whom he had fallen in love would become his wife in another month.

Tricia sat beside Jeremy on a glider on Sheldon's porch, her right hand cradled in his larger left one. They had decided to inform Sheldon of their upcoming nuptials before going to the hospital to visit Gus.

Sheldon's sharp gaze lingered on the emerald and diamond ring on her left hand. A wry smile touched his mouth. "I know Julia would have been pleased to know you are wearing her ring. It was her favorite."

Tricia stared at her outstretched fingers. "I'm honored to be able to wear it."

Sheldon appeared lost in thought as he recalled the

exact moment he had given Julia the ring. "When's the big day?"

Tricia stared at Jeremy's distinctive profile. "We've decided on the Labor Day weekend," he said in a deep, quiet tone.

Sheldon smiled. "Excellent choice." Memorial Day, the Fourth of July and Labor Day were Blackstone Farms get-togethers.

"Let me know what you want to serve and I'll have Cook put together a menu for you," Sheldon continued.

Tricia nodded, smiling. "I'm going to ask Kelly to help me with the planning."

Sheldon rose to his feet, leaned over and kissed Tricia's cheek. "Congratulations and welcome to the family."

"Thank you, Sheldon."

He wagged a finger at her. "Now that you're going to become my daughter, I want you to call me Pop."

Her smile was dazzling. "Okay. Thank you, Pop."

Reaching for his crutches, Jeremy pushed to his feet. "We're going to see Gus and give him the good news."

"Tell Gus I'll see him later," Sheldon said as he watched Tricia curve an arm around Jeremy's waist as they left the porch and made their way to Tricia's car.

A rare smile crinkled his eyes as he watched the

young couple drive away. He wasn't certain whether it was Gus's manipulation or that Jeremy and Tricia had come to their senses and realized they belonged together, but he was ecstatic about their decision.

His smile widened. Jeremy and Tricia weren't the only ones planning their future. At the end of the year he would officially retire from the day-to-day operation of Blackstone Farms and do a few things he'd put off doing for years.

Tricia found her grandfather in the solarium watching an all-news cable television station. He spied her and Jeremy as soon as they walked in the sun-filled room.

"Hi, Grandpa."

Gus glared at Tricia and Jeremy. "You got something to tell me?"

Jeremy hobbled over to Gus and sat beside him. "I've plenty to tell you, Gus. Tricia and I plan to marry during the Labor Day weekend." He ignored the older man's gasp of surprise. "And I'd be honored if you would give me your granddaughter's hand in marriage."

Gus's hand shook noticeably as he reached out and touched Jeremy's broad one. "Nothing would make me happier."

Tricia sat on her grandfather's left and showed him the ring on her finger. Her eyes welled with tears when Gus covered her hand with his, gently squeezing her fingers. Resting her head on his shoulder, she closed her eyes.

"Hurry up and get well, Grandpa."

"I will, grandbaby girl. Nothing, and I do mean nothing will stop me from attending your wedding."

Tricia and Jeremy sat with Gus until a technician came to take him back to his room for an EKG. They left the hospital, and instead of returning to the farm, Tricia headed toward Richmond. She needed to shop for a wedding dress.

Chapter Ten

Tricia walked into the expanded schoolhouse with Kelly Blackstone, awed by the spaciousness of the newly constructed classrooms. She followed her soon-to-be sister-in-law down a highly waxed hallway to the office she would occupy once the school year began.

Four-week-old Vivienne lay quietly in the carrier held in Kelly's firm grip. The baby seemed fascinated by her toes until she fell asleep during the short drive from her parents' house to the schoolhouse.

The original building, constructed for preschool children, was connected to three one-story buildings that were set up for grades one to three and four to six, and the fourth would house the principal and nurse's office, gymnasium, auditorium, library and cafeteria. The schoolhouse also boasted a square with an interior courtyard playground.

Kelly stopped in front of a door bearing a brass nameplate that read: Mrs. Tricia Blackstone, Nurse. Tricia blushed at her own excitement. It would be another two days before she would marry Jeremy and become Mrs. Blackstone, but seeing it on the door made what was to come more of a reality.

She smiled at Kelly. "It looks very nice."

Kelly returned her smile. "I told the contractor I wanted your door with your nameplate up first." The doors to all the classrooms and offices lay on dollies in the hallways.

Tricia gave Kelly a quick hug. "Thank you."

Ryan's wife had become the sister Tricia never had. Soon after she and Jeremy officially announced their engagement Kelly had thrown all of her energies into helping Tricia with her wedding plans.

Tricia liked Kelly and thought her the perfect partner for Ryan. She was kind, friendly, unpretentious and the complete opposite of the first woman he'd married. Tall and slender with a fashionably cut hairstyle, Kelly had an overabundance of energy she had channeled to become a successful wife, mother and educator.

The two women walked in and out of spaces that were to become classrooms and a science lab.

"Will everything be finished before the beginning of classes?" Tricia asked.

Kelly led the way back to the parking lot where she'd parked her SUV. Vans and pickup trucks belonging to the workmen filled up many of the spaces. "The contractor reassures Sheldon that his men will be finished a week before the start of classes. All of the furniture has been sitting in a warehouse in Richmond awaiting word when it should be delivered."

"Have you hired everyone?" Tricia asked after Kelly secured Vivienne in a car seat and sat behind the wheel.

"I still need a librarian." Her gold-brown gaze met Tricia's dark one. "Do you know someone who would be interested in the position?"

"I had a friend when I lived in New York who was studying to become a librarian. I'll have to look through some of my old telephone books to see if I can find her number."

Kelly turned the key in the ignition. "I've placed several ads in some newspapers and contacted placement offices at several colleges."

"You still have time before the school year begins, so maybe you'll get someone."

"I like your optimism, Tricia." She shifted into reverse and backed out of the lot. "I don't know about you, but right about now I'd like some ice cream from Shorty's Diner."

Tricia glanced at her watch. It was after four. "You want to eat ice cream now?"

"Yes, ma'am."

"We don't have to go into town to eat at Shorty's. Cook always has ice cream at the dining hall."

Kelly sucked her teeth. "Cook buys store-bought ice cream. I want homemade."

It was Tricia's turn to suck her teeth. "I've been counting every calorie and gram that has gone into my mouth so that I won't look like a stuffed sausage in my wedding dress, and you want me to eat ice cream." She'd dropped a dress size, going from an eighteen to a sixteen.

Kelly gave her a sidelong glance. "You don't have to eat it. You can hold Vivienne and watch me instead." Crossing her arms under her breasts, Tricia mumbled angrily under her breath about skinny women.

"I don't know whether you're aware of it or not," Kelly continued, deliberately ignoring Tricia's reference to skinny women, "but whenever you walk into a room every man has the potential for whiplash. You are the most beautifully proportioned full-figured woman I've ever seen.

"And don't forget you caused quite a stir last Saturday when you went swimming wearing that red one-piece number. The only guys who didn't hear it from their wives or significant others were the ones who were wearing sunglasses. One of the grooms was staring so hard I'm certain he popped a few blood vessels."

Tricia's dark eyes sparkled as she smiled. "You're good for a girl's ego, Kelly."

"I only speak the truth, girlfriend."

The swimsuit was the most modest one she owned yet Jeremy had asked whether she really intended to wear it. Her answer had been the affirmative, which left him in a funk for days. His bad mood ended once the cast was removed from his left leg.

A smug smile touched Tricia's mouth as she thought about Jeremy and her grandfather. Gus's attitude toward Jeremy softened once he moved into his house. He insisted the younger man call him Grandpa instead of his given name, taught him how to bluff at poker and more about horses than Jeremy had learned in the first eighteen years he'd lived on the horse farm.

Kelly drove to Staunton and parked alongside a restaurant that resembled a 1950s jukebox. Tricia nursed a club soda and watched Kelly eat a vanilla sundae topped with nuts, whipped cream and fresh berries. It was close to six o'clock when they finally got into the sport utility vehicle to return to Blackstone Farms. They were further delayed because Kelly had gone into the restaurant's bathroom to breastfeed Vivienne once the baby woke up crying to be fed.

Kelly maneuvered into a parking space at the dining hall and turned off the engine, while Tricia got out and gathered Vivienne from her safety seat. She was now able to hold the infant without losing her composure. Vivienne looked as much like her mother as Juliet had Jeremy.

"She probably needs to be changed, and I don't have any more diapers with me," Kelly said, as Vivienne woke up fretfully. Tricia handed Kelly her daughter, who returned the baby to the safety seat. "I'm going back to the house. Go on in. I won't be long."

Tricia waited for Kelly to drive away before she made her way to the entrance of the dining hall. She opened the door and went completely still as a roar of *"Surprise!"* greeted her.

Her shocked gaze lingered on Jeremy leaning on a cane, grinning from ear to ear. A large, printed banner reading Congratulations to Tricia and Jeremy! hung from a wall under which a long table overflowed with gaily wrapped gifts. Covering her face with her hands, she squeezed back tears. Now she knew why Kelly delayed coming back to the farm.

Leaning heavily on his cane, Jeremy limped over to Tricia, curved an arm around her waist, lowered his head and covered her mouth with his. Her arms circled his neck and she kissed him back.

"Get a room!" someone shouted. The dining hall erupted in laughter.

"Save some for the wedding night," came another deep voice.

Jeremy ended the kiss and gave Tricia a sensual smile. "I hope someone took a picture of you when you walked in because the look on your face was priceless."

Tricia rolled her eyes at him. "I have to assume you were in on this."

He nodded. "Guilty as charged. Come sit down and eat before you open your gifts." He led her over to the table where Gus sat with Sheldon.

She kissed her grandfather's cheek, then Sheldon's before he pulled out a chair for her. "How long have you guys been planning this?"

"Actually it was Kelly's idea," Sheldon said. "When she overheard me and Ryan talk about making arrangements for the moving company to pack up your house she said they should catalogue the entire contents including color schemes. She made up a list of things she thought you'd like and set up a wedding registry."

Tricia stared at Jeremy. "To say I was clueless is an understatement, because I've never known anyone at Blackstone Farms to keep a secret for more than twenty-four hours."

"I beg to differ with you," Sheldon countered. "I

had no idea you and my son were keeping company as kids."

Jeremy stared at his father. "We didn't begin, as you say, 'keeping company' until we were eighteen."

Tricia glanced across the table, meeting her grandfather's solemn gaze. There was no doubt he was thinking about his own daughter, who had dropped out of school and became a mother before she was eighteen.

Tricia's gnawing need to know about the man who had fathered her and the whereabouts of her mother had eased after Gus's heart attack. The fear of losing her grandfather forced her to reexamine herself and those she loved. If Patricia Parker wanted to see her, then she would've made the attempt. After all Patricia had had thirty-two years to reconnect with Tricia.

A waiter approached the table, pen and pad in hand. "Is everyone ready to order?"

Tricia reached for the printout of the dinner choices and perused it as Sheldon, Gus and Jeremy gave the young man their selections. The dining hall's furnishings were reminiscent of upscale New York City restaurants: dark paneled walls with stained-glass insets, plush carpeting, linen-covered tables and Tiffany-style table lamps. Breakfast and lunches were buffet, but dinners were always served. The exceptions were pre- and postrace celebrations. Weather permitting, these functions were held outdoors.

Tricia glanced up at the waiter. "I'll have the Caesar salad with grilled chicken."

She redirected her attention to Jeremy and reached for his hand under the table. He looked nothing like the heavily sedated man she'd been reunited with after more than a decade. He'd gained weight and there was a sprinkling of gray in his close-cropped black hair.

Jeremy shifted his chair closer to Tricia's, silently admiring her delicate profile. "Do you know how hard it has been not to sneak upstairs and climb into bed with you?"

She lowered her gaze, enchanting him with the demure gesture. "I thought you liked having Grandpa as a roommate." Her voice was as hushed as Jeremy's.

"Believe it or not he's a real cool dude."

Tricia smiled. She'd heard people call Gus a lot of things, but never a "cool dude."

Conversations faded as waiters and waitresses began bringing out dishes from the kitchen for the more than thirty people filling up the dining hall. Gus and Sheldon exchanged a knowing look before Gus pushed back his chair and stood up. A hush fell over the room.

Tricia stared up at the man who was both father and grandfather. He'd managed to put on a little of the weight he'd lost when hospitalized and although still gaunt he appeared elegantly serene.

He cleared his voice and smiled at Tricia. "I'd just like to say a few words before we begin our meal. I have so much to be grateful for—for Tricia being at the right place at the right time when I suffered a heart attack, for her putting up with her cantankerous grandfather and for Jeremy who helped make me aware of the power of forgiveness."

Gus closed his eyes and when he opened them they glistened with unshed moisture. Sheldon rose to his feet and gave the older man a rough embrace as applause filled the space.

Ryan and his family walked into the dining hall and sat at a nearby table. He snapped Vivienne's carrier into the high chair, pushing it under the table. Leaning over, he tapped Jeremy's shoulder. "What did we miss?" he whispered.

"Gus becoming maudlin."

"No!" There was an incredulous look on Ryan's handsome face.

"Believe it, brother."

Tricia hid a smile when she heard the exchange between Jeremy and his brother. She didn't know whether it was Gus's brush with death or her agreeing to marry Jeremy and live at the farm that had changed him, but whatever the catalyst, she hoped the change was permanent.

Tricia felt slightly tipsy from the champagne that had been served with delicate pastries and petit fours prepared for the occasion by the pastry chef. She rose unsteadily to her feet as a few of the farm residents began chanting her name.

Jeremy touched her hand. "Would you like to use my cane, sweetheart?"

She ignored his remark and made her way to the table laden with gifts. She sat on a chair decorated with streamers of white satin.

There was a pregnant hush when she picked up the first package. Decorative paper, ribbon and bows were discarded as she opened boxes containing gourmet cookware, silver and crystal picture frames, exquisite Egyptian cotton linen, plush bath towels, scented candles, hand-painted flowerpots, bathroom accessories, an espresso-cappuccino machine, personalized stationery imprinted with both her and Jeremy's names and an antique soup tureen from Kelly.

When she'd admired the fragile china piece, circa 1850, she'd never thought Kelly would give it to her as a wedding gift. Smiling at Kelly, Tricia mouthed "Thank you very much."

Tricia sat on the floor of the porch between Jeremy's outstretched legs, her elbows resting on his knees. They'd returned from the dining hall, put Gus to bed and then retreated to the porch. The mercury was in the low seventies, the night sky ablaze with summer constellations.

Jeremy leaned forward on the rocker and toyed

with the curls on the nape of her neck. "Are you nervous?"

"A little." Tricia's breath was a hushed whisper. "I take that back. I'm frightened, Jeremy."

His fingers stilled. "Why?"

"I keep thinking something is going to happen that will prevent us from getting married."

Leaning down, Jeremy pressed a kiss to her fragrant curls. "Nothing's going to happen, sweetheart. Saturday, at exactly four o'clock you and I are going to stand in front of Judge Campbell and take our vows with our family and friends as witnesses.

"We're going to hang around long enough to share a toast, eat cake, then we are going to disappear for the next three days."

Tilting her chin, Tricia stared up at Jeremy. The soft light from porch lamps flattered his deeply tanned face. His white linen shirt was unbuttoned to his waist, and each time she glanced at his furred chest she found it hard to swallow.

"I feel guilty leaving Grandpa."

"He's going to be all right staying with Pop. He has already made arrangements with a registry to have a nurse come out and check on him."

Tricia nodded. She and Jeremy planned to spend three days at Sheldon's cabin near the West Virginia border. Reaching up, she grasped his hands and squeezed them gently.

"I love you, Jeremy."

There was a pulse beat of silence before he said, "I love you, too."

Her eyes filled with tears, but they didn't fall. It was the first since they were reunited that he admitted to loving her.

Tricia felt as if she was on a runaway roller coaster that had no intention of stopping as she drove to Richmond for the final fitting of her dress. She had chosen a sleeveless, full length, silk-lined, off-white lace sheath dress covered with seed pearls from the scooped neckline to the scalloped hem. A single strand of opera-length pearls, matching earrings, a garland headpiece made with miniature white roses and a pair of wispy lace shoes with sturdy embroidered heels rounded out the former turn-of-the-century romantic ensemble. The seamstress made the adjustments and informed Tricia that the dress would be delivered to Blackstone Farms before noon on Saturday. She left the bridal shop for her scheduled appointment at a day spa.

Dusk had descended on the farm when she returned, feeling as good as she looked. Her skin glowed from a European facial, her hands and feet soft and dewy from a hydrating manicure and pedicure and her body supple and relaxed from a full body massage. She'd had her hair cut and styled so it framed her face in feathery curls.

Her pulse quickened when she spied the pale-blue streamers fluttering from the poles of the large white tent set up in a grassy meadow. The blue matched the yards of organza-swathed chairs lined up in precise rows under the tent. A portable stage for a band and dancing was also in place for the reception that would follow the ceremony.

Tricia maneuvered her car into the driveway behind Jeremy's SUV. A day after the orthopedist removed the cast, he began driving again.

She got out of her car and mounted the porch steps. Pausing on the top step, she stared at her fiancé sprawled on the chaise. Moving closer, she leaned down and kissed him.

A slow smile tilted the corners of Jeremy's mouth upward as he straightened and patted the cushioned seat. "Come sit down."

Tricia sat between his legs and pressed her back to his chest. "Where's Grandpa?"

Jeremy kissed her ear. "He went to bed early. He said he wanted to be rested for tomorrow."

Gus had openly expressed his relief once Tricia revealed she did not want a formal wedding. He had worn a tuxedo for his own wedding, swearing he would never look like a penguin again. The wedding party included Ryan as best man, Kelly as matron of honor and their son, Sean, as ring bearer.

Curving an arm around Tricia's waist, Jeremy shifted her effortlessly until she straddled his lap.

"You look fantastic." There was no mistaking the awe in his voice.

She smiled demurely. "Thank you. I've decided I'm going to treat myself to a full body massage at least once a month." The hands cupping her hips feathered up her ribs to cradle her breasts and she drew in a sharp breath. Her head fell limply to his solid shoulder. "What are you doing, Jeremy?" she asked in a trembling whisper.

He laughed deep in his throat. "Offering you a sample of my special massage. You have a choice between the basic, all the way up to the deluxe package." His thumbs caressed her breasts in a sweeping back and forth motion, bringing the nipples into prominence.

Gasping, she breathed heavily against his ear. "What are you charging for the basic package?"

Jeremy's fingers stilled. "The rest of your life."

Easing back in his embrace, Tricia studied his features in the encroaching darkness. "How about the deluxe package?"

"The rest of your life."

Tricia ran a finger down the length of his nose. "You should be reported for price fix—"

Her statement died on her lips when his mouth covered hers in an explosive kiss that sucked the breath from her lungs. She melted into Jeremy's strength, loving him with all of her senses.

They'd promised each other that they wouldn't

make love until they were married, but each time he touched her, kissed her, silent screams of unexploded passion roiled with nowhere to escape. Nothing had changed. All Jeremy had to do was fix his smoldering smoky gaze on her, touch her, kiss her and she dissolved into a trembling, heated mass of wanting.

Her lips parted to his probing tongue as she drew it into her mouth. In that instant everything about Jeremy seeped into her and made them one—indivisible. It had been that way the first time they'd become lovers. It hadn't been planned, nothing said, but both had known it was time their friendship had to change. There had been too much awareness of the other, too much sexual tension between them.

Tricia moaned softly when she felt Jeremy's sex hardening under her bottom. She tore her mouth away from his, her smile as intimate as the kiss they'd shared.

"What are you trying to do, seduce me?"

He nodded and offered her a grin that was irresistibly devastating. "I don't plan to go all the way. Just a little kiss here." He pressed his mouth to the area under her ear. "And one here." His voice had lowered seductively as he moved to the fluttering pulse in her throat. "And a little feel here." He gathered the flowing fabric of her dress and slipped his hand under the silken material of her bikini panties.

A shudder shook Tricia. "I think we'd better stop and continue this tomorrow. Same time, different place."

Jeremy released her hip and reached around his back. "I bought you a little something as a wedding gift." She stared at a small square package wrapped in silver paper and tied with velvet ribbon. "Take it, Tricia."

She took it, slipped off the ribbon and peeled away the paper. As soon as she saw the black velvet box she knew it contained a piece of jewelry. She opened the box and went still. Jeremy had given her an exquisite filigree bar pin with a sprinkling of diamonds surrounding a brilliant blue topaz.

Her eyes filled with moisture and she blinked it back before the tears fell. "It's beautiful."

Cupping her chin, he raised her face. "You're beautiful. I gave you my mother's and grandmother's jewelry, but I wanted you to have something from me that no other woman wore before."

Curving her arms around his neck, she breathed a kiss under his ear. "Thank you. I have something for you. Do you want it now or tomorrow?"

"Give it to me tomorrow."

Tricia dropped her arms and slipped off his lap. "I'm going upstairs to turn in early. No one wants to see a bride with bags under her eyes."

Reaching for his cane, Jeremy propelled himself off the chaise. "I'm going in, too."

She held the door open for him and they walked through the entryway and into the living room. Corrugated boxes labeled Living Room were stacked in a corner near the curving staircase.

"They were delivered while you were out," Jeremy explained.

Tricia nodded. Her future father-in-law had arranged for her furniture to be stored in a warehouse in Richmond until she decided what she wanted to use or give away.

"I'm not going to open one box until after we get back."

"You don't have to put everything away in one day."

"I'd like to have them done before the school year begins."

"Tricia, baby, you have the rest of your life to decorate the house however you wish."

She knew he was right, but there were changes she wanted to make in the overtly masculine home. "You're right." She kissed his cheek. "Good night."

Jeremy's lids came down, shielding his gaze. "Good night." He watched Tricia walk up the staircase, knowing he would not see her again until she was to become his wife. He planned to rise early and go to his father's house. He, Sheldon, Ryan and Sean would leave together, while Kelly would accompany Tricia and Gus.

He'd asked Tricia to hold on to his heart a long time ago, and in less than twenty-four hours he would claim the only woman he had ever loved as his partner for life.

Chapter Eleven

It was a picture-perfect day for an outdoor wedding in Virginia's horse country. Tricia rose early, showered and pulled on a pair of shorts and a T-shirt. Gus was up when she went downstairs, and she decided to prepare breakfast for them instead of ordering it from the dining hall.

Gus sat across the table from Tricia in the large kitchen, his gaze fixed on her face. "You've been asking me about your mother for a long time."

Tricia felt her heart lurch. "If what you intend to tell me is going to make me upset, then I don't want to know. Not on my wedding day, Grandpa."

He reached across the table and his large veined

hand covered one of hers. "You don't want to know?"

She shook her head. "Not anymore. I don't need to know where my mother is or who my father was, because the only daddy I know is sitting in front of me. And if my mother wanted to find me all she had to do was come back to Blackstone Farms." She chewed her lower lip for several seconds. "I don't hate my mother, but in all honesty I can't say that I love her because I don't know her. And if she couldn't take care of me, then she did the next best thing giving me to you and Grandma. If I ever meet her one day, then that's something I will tell her."

Gus smiled and character lines deepened around his dark eyes. "You've made me proud, grandbaby girl."

"Thank you." Tricia returned his smile. "I love you, Grandpa." Gus withdrew his hand, dropped his head and stared down at his plate. It was a full minute before his head came up. Pride and tenderness shimmered in his gaze.

They lingered at the table, reminiscing until the doorbell rang. Tricia glanced up at the clock over the stove. It wasn't quite eight o'clock. She got up and made her way to the door.

A young man stood on the other side, holding up a plastic-covered garment on a hanger. It was her dress. She thanked him and returned to the kitchen.

"Do you want to see my dress?" she asked Gus.

He shook his head. "I don't want to see you in all your finery until I'm ready to give you to your young man. I know," he said quickly when he saw Tricia's expression, "his name is Jeremy. He's nice, Tricia. And he's good for you."

She flashed a wide grin. "I hope so, because he's going to become my husband in less than eight hours."

Kelly buttoned the tiny covered buttons on the back of Tricia's dress, then placed the garland of miniature roses on her head. It was the perfect complement to the vintage-style dress. "Make certain you have something old, something new, something borrowed and something blue."

Tricia admired the pale-blue slip dress caressing the curves of Kelly's slim figure. "The pearls are old, my dress is new and the pin has a blue stone." She had affixed Jeremy's wedding gift to the bodice of her dress.

"What about borrowed?"

Her eyes widened. "I don't have anything borrowed." Lifting the hem of the lacy dress, she crossed the room and opened the door to a massive armoire. She pulled out a drawer filled with handkerchief squares and took one. "This will have to do." She refolded the handkerchief, pushing it between her breasts.

Kelly laughed. "There was a time when I used to

fill my bra with socks and tissues to make me look bigger. Thanks to Vivienne I no longer need a Wonderbra."

Tricia wanted to tell Kelly that her own breasts had increased during her pregnancy and breastfeeding, but hadn't returned to their former size. She hadn't begun weaning Juliet when she lost her.

A clock on the mantel of the fireplace chimed the quarter hour. It was 3:45. Waiting until Tricia pulled on a pair of lace gloves, Kelly picked up a bouquet of a combination of creamy-toned roses, hyacinths and astilbe and handed it to her. The stems were wrapped in a long piece of wide white silk ribbon and tied in a bow at the neck of the bouquet. A blue pearl stickpin at the center of the bow held it in place.

"Are you ready, girlfriend?"

Large near-black eyes sparkled like polished onyx. "Yes." The single word mirrored the confidence flowing through Tricia. She had waited a long time for this day.

Kelly pushed her hands into a pair of lace ice-blue gloves, grasped a bouquet made up of blue and white flowers and walked out of the bedroom, Tricia following. They descended the staircase and found Gus, resplendent in a dark-gray suit waiting for them. His smile spoke volumes.

He extended his arm to Tricia. "You look beautiful, grandbaby girl."

Resting her head on his shoulder, Tricia smiled. "Thank you, Grandpa."

Gus covered the gloved hand on his jacket sleeve. "The car is waiting for us." He led her out of Jeremy's house that would soon become Jeremy and Tricia's home to the chauffeur-driven limousine parked in the driveway. The driver assisted Tricia, Gus and then Kelly into the car.

Tricia forced herself not to chew her lower lip and eat away the lipstick the cosmetologist had applied earlier. She closed her eyes and took in deep breaths in an attempt to slow down her runaway pulse. All too soon the ride ended. She opened her eyes and under the tent were rows of chairs occupied by full-time, part-time and resident employees of Blackstone Farms and several neighboring horse farms. At the opposite end of a white carpet littered with white and blue flower petals Jeremy waited with Judge Campbell, Ryan and Sean.

The driver opened the rear door, extending his hand to Kelly. Gus followed and held out his hand to Tricia. She placed hers trustingly in his, smiling.

"Are you ready, Grandpa?"

He raised an eyebrow. "Are you ready, grandbaby?"

She inhaled, then let out her breath slowly. "Yes."

All heads turned to stare at Tricia and Gus when a keyboard player began to play the familiar chords of the wedding march. Kelly led the procession over the carpet, and less than a minute later Gus escorted Tricia over the flower-strewn path to where Jeremy stood, a stunned expression freezing his handsome features.

Jeremy did not want to believe that Tricia could look so innocent and wanton at the same time. The lace skimming her curvy body made her appear ethereal in the streams of diffused sunlight coming into the large tent.

Don't lose it, he told himself over and over as she drew closer. He, who had lost count of the number of times he'd been in situations where his life hung in the balance, was unnerved by the image of a woman he'd loved for so long that he could not remember when he did not love her.

She was now close enough for him to detect the dewy sheen on her flawless face, the scent of the flowers in her bouquet and the soft sensual smell of her perfume.

The judge squared his shoulders under his black robe. "Who gives this woman in marriage?"

"I do." Gus's voice carried easily in the warm air. He took Tricia's hand and placed it in Jeremy's. "Be happy," he whispered before he stepped back and sat down in the chair that had been left vacant for him. He looked across the aisle at Sheldon and smiled.

Sheldon nodded and mouthed, "Boo-yaw!"

Grinning, Gus pumped his fist in the air. He and Sheldon had begun their association as employer and employee, but since his retirement Gus counted Sheldon as a friend and now, with his granddaughter's marriage to Jeremy, family.

"We are gathered together in the sight of God and man to reunite two families in matrimony." Judge Campbell's sonorous voice captured everyone's attention.

Tricia barely registered the judge's words as she stared up into the sooty eyes staring down at her. Jeremy was incredibly handsome in a charcoal-gray pinstriped suit, white shirt and robin's-egg-blue silk tie. His close-cropped raven hair lay neatly on his well-shaped head.

When it came time to exchange vows and rings, she smiled at Sean who stood ramrod straight holding a white pillow with the wedding bands secured with silk ribbon. She handed her bouquet and gloves to Kelly before Jeremy repeated his vows and slipped a band on her hand. Her voice was steady but her hands were shaking when she repeated the gesture.

She heard the judge telling Jeremy he could kiss his bride, and she knew then it was over. Her wish had been granted. She'd waited fourteen years to become Tricia Blackstone.

Her smile was dazzling as she and Jeremy followed Sean, Ryan and Kelly down the carpet to receive the best wishes of those who had come to witness the joining of another generation of Virginia Blackstones.

Tricia curved her arm around her husband's waist inside his suit jacket to steady him. "Careful, hot-shot," she teased softly. "Cut another step like that and you'll be on your face."

Jeremy swung her around. "What I want to do is cut out of here."

They had planned to leave right after cutting the cake, but Sheldon offered a toast, a toast that was echoed individually by every farm employee. Teen-agers and the young children who now knew that Tricia would become their school nurse offered their own reticent toasts.

"Do you think it's safe to leave now?"

Jeremy glanced over Tricia's head. He met his father's gaze and smiled. He released his wife's hand long enough to pantomime a wave. Sheldon nodded and returned the wave.

"Let's go," Jeremy whispered, leading her out of the tent. They skirted several couples and managed to make it to an area where he had parked his SUV. Their luggage had been loaded in the cargo area earlier that morning.

"How's the ankle holding up?" she asked once Jeremy removed his jacket and sat behind the wheel.

He gave her a quick glance. "It's okay."

"Do you want me to drive?"

"No. I can make it. Sit back and relax, Mrs. Blackstone. I don't want you to plead a headache or fatigue later."

Tricia folded a hand on her hip. "Have you ever known me to plead a headache, Mr. Blackstone?"

Jeremy turned the key in the ignition and shifted into gear. "Nope," he said after a lengthy silence.

Tricia did as Jeremy suggested and closed her eyes. She hadn't realized she had fallen asleep until he shook her gently. "Wake up, sweetheart. We're here."

The house in the mountains was larger than she had expected. Rising two stories in height, it looked more like a chalet than a rustic cabin. It was surrounded by towering pine trees growing so close together that she doubted whether light reached the earth even during the daylight hours.

Jeremy touched her shoulder. "I'll be right back."

Tricia watched as Jeremy made his way to the front door. He hadn't used his cane, and his gait was off. He was scheduled to begin intensive physical therapy the following week, and she hoped the exercise would strengthen his ankle so he would not be left with a limp.

Within minutes golden light blazed from every window so like the many jack-o'-lanterns on display at Blackstone Farms during its annual Halloween celebration.

Jeremy returned, unloaded their luggage and minutes later Tricia found herself in the middle of a large bedroom with an adjoining bath that resembled a European spa with a massive sunken tub with enough room for four people, a free-standing shower and a steam room.

She shivered slightly as warm breath feathered over her nape. Smiling, she said, "So this is where the Wild Bunch rough it."

Curving his arms around Tricia's waist, Jeremy lowered his head and trailed kisses along the column of her long neck. "It's not so rough, is it?"

She rested her hands over the dark-brown ones pressed against her belly. "I see why they like to come here and hang out. It's better than those overpriced spas in California and Arizona."

"Will you share a bath with me?"

Tricia closed her eyes. "Yes."

Turning her in his embrace, Jeremy cradled her face between his palms. "I love you so much, Tricia." His voice was pregnant with emotion. Her lids fluttered wildly before she met his heated gaze.

"I have to give you your wedding gift."

A hint of a smile touched Jeremy's mouth. "You are my wedding, birthday, Christmas, New Year's and every day and holiday gift. I don't need anything—only you."

Leaning into him, Tricia's lips brushed against his. "And you're all I'll ever need, Jeremy." She kissed him again, then turned in his embrace and presented him with her back. "Please unbutton me."

Jeremy made a big production of undoing the little buttons. With each inch of flesh he bared he kissed. The top of the dress slid off her shoulders and the handkerchief fell to the floor. He bent over and picked it up. Tricia quickly explained the significance of something borrowed, eliciting a laugh from him.

"I thought you wanted to plump up your—"

"Don't even go there, Jeremy Blackstone," she said, cutting him off. "I have enough, thank you."

Slipping his fingers under the straps of her slip, he eased it off her shoulders before unhooking her bra and baring her chest. Her breasts were large and firm like ripened fruit, fruit he wanted to suckle, fruit he wanted to feast on.

Tricia felt the heat of her husband's gaze on her chest, and the area between her legs responded immediately with a rush of moisture that left the nether region pulsing with a need that only Jeremy could assuage.

Jeremy's eyes widened until the dark centers fused with the sooty gray. His nostrils flared as he detected the scent of Tricia's rising desire. She was ready for him.

"I'll be right back." Turning on his heel, he walked stiffly out of the bathroom. He had to get away from Tricia before he ripped the clothes from her body and took her on the tiled floor. He wanted her just that much.

But this was their wedding night, a night in which their coming together would be special enough for them to talk about when they were too old to do more than kiss and hold hands.

Tricia filled the large tub, undressed, hanging up her clothes in a corner closet and opened her vanity case. She'd managed to brush her teeth and cleanse the makeup from her face before Jeremy returned.

He was naked, and recessed lighting shimmered over a tall, lean dark body that reminded her of an African totem representing fertility.

Jeremy pushed a knob on the tub and water pulsed from the many jets. Smiling, he reached for her hand and led her down four marble steps into the swirling water. Warm water lapped over Tricia's breasts as she floated buoyantly until her toes touched the bottom of the concave tub.

Curving her arms around her husband's strong neck, she kissed him deeply, her tongue curling with his, the scent of mint wafting in her nostrils from his toothpaste and mouthwash.

It had been too long—weeks since they'd made love and Tricia responded like a cat in heat. Her hands swept over his shoulders, chest, breasts, belly and still lower to the hardness bobbing against her inner thigh.

Jeremy threw back his head and groaned loudly. The touch of Tricia's hand squeezing his flesh was like a heated branding iron. He had wanted this coming together to be slow and leisurely, but knew it was not to be. Moving back to a depression built into the tub, he sat, bringing Tricia with him as she straddled his thighs.

Wrapping an arm around her waist, he lifted her easily and she guided his sex into her body. They sighed in unison as flesh closed around flesh.

Bracing his back against the marble ledge, Jeremy watched desire darken Tricia's eyes and face. Cupping her breasts he lowered his head and suckled her, nipples and areolae hardening like tiny pebbles. She met each of his powerful thrusts, giving and receiving in kind.

The passion he had withheld from every woman he had ever known he surrendered to Tricia.

The love he was unable to give any other woman he had ever met he surrendered to Tricia.

The children he'd hoped to have but never risked creating with any woman he surrendered to Tricia.

Everything he was and hoped to be he surrendered to the woman in his arms: his wife.

Tricia melted against Jeremy and her body and world was filled with him. Nothing mattered. The pain and loss of Juliet faded as she lowered her head to Jeremy's shoulder and prayed for the beginnings of new life in her womb.

The pain, hurt, lies and deceit faded completely as a desire she had never known gripped her mind and body, setting them on fire. Her husband became flesh of her flesh, heart of her heart and soul of her soul.

She breathed in deep soul-wrenching drafts as waves of ecstasy throbbed through her lower body. Her hips quickened, moving against Jeremy's in an age-old rhythm that sent scalding blood through her veins.

She was on fire!

Tricia's eager response matched Jeremy's. He felt his flesh hardening, swelling until a familiar sensation signaled their passionate lovemaking was nearing its climax.

He closed his eyes, threw back his head and growled deep in his throat when her pulsing flesh squeezed him tightly. His breath came in long, surrendering moans at the same time Tricia's fingernails bit into the flesh over his shoulders. He welcomed the pain as he succumbed to *le petit mort.* He had faced death again, but this time it was in the most exquisite way possible. It was in the scented embrace of a woman he would love forever.

A moan of ecstasy slipped through Tricia's clenched teeth. She had wanted it to last longer but her body's dormant sexuality was starved for a desire long denied, and she was hurtled beyond the point of no return as a lingering pulsing passion burned like smoldering embers. She clung to Jeremy like a drowning swimmer, her head resting on his shoulder while she waited for her pulse to return to normal.

She closed her eyes and smiled. "I love you," she whispered hoarsely.

Jeremy tightened his grip on her waist. "Love you back."

Tricia and Jeremy returned to Blackstone Farms enveloped in a glow of love and contentment that was obvious to all who glimpsed them. They had spent three days cloistered in the cabin, making love, cooking and planning their future.

Jeremy maneuvered into the driveway to Sheldon's house and cut off the ignition. Shifting, he smiled at Tricia. He had wanted to take her home, but she insisted they stop to see Gus.

Resting his right arm over the back of her seat, he leaned over and brushed a light kiss over her parted lips. "You're still glowing."

Tricia nuzzled his neck. "That comes from being in love." She had lost count of the number of times they'd made love with each other. It was as if they were insatiable and wanted to make up for the time they were apart. And each time she opened her arms and legs to her husband she opened her heart to accept all Jeremy offered.

Jeremy stepped out of the vehicle to assist Tricia

when he spied the familiar figure of his father sitting out on the porch. He waved to the older man.

"Hey, Pop."

Sheldon pushed off the chair and came down the porch. A warm smile softened his sharp features. "Hey, yourself." He offered Jeremy a rough embrace before he leaned into the open passenger-side window and pressed a kiss to Tricia's cheek. "You look wonderful."

Tricia returned his rare smile. "I feel wonderful. We came by to check on my grandfather."

"Gus went out."

"Out!" Tricia practically shouted.

"He went to the movies," Sheldon said quickly. "His nurse thought he would do better if he didn't stay home so much, so she took him to the movies to see a romantic comedy about two middle-aged couples who find love after they join a group for widows and widowers."

Jeremy leaned against the bumper of the SUV and crossed his arms over his chest. "You should've gone with them. You could use a few pointers about getting back into the dating scene."

Sheldon's eyebrows drew together in a scowl. "Tricia, please take your husband home." Turning on his heel, he mounted the porch stairs and went into the large white house.

Tricia knew Ryan wanted his father to remarry,

but this was the first time she'd heard Jeremy mention it. "Jeremy, let's go home."

Jeremy shifted and rested his arm over Tricia's hip. "Do you think I pissed Pop off?"

Tricia opened her eyes and stared out at the shadowy darkness. "You know your father better than I would ever know him, but I suspect he resented your intrusion into his personal life."

"Pop has been alone for too long."

Tricia turned and faced her husband. "He's single by choice, darling. Your father is a very handsome man whom many women would find attractive and consider a very good catch. Once he meets the right woman he'll want to change his marital status without his sons insisting they know what's best for him."

Jeremy's arm tightened on her waist, bringing her body flush against his. "Are you telling me to mind my business?"

She smiled in the dimness of the bedroom. "Yes, my love. No, Jeremy!" she gasped when a hand reached down and covered her feminine heat.

Her protests were short-lived once she found herself sprawled over her husband's chest, and the only thing that mattered was that she loved the man in her arms as much as he loved her.

Chapter Twelve

Tricia sat on the floor in the living room opening cartons. It had taken her two days to empty the boxes containing items for the kitchen and put everything she intended to keep away. Another day was spent unpacking china, silver and stemware that had once graced her dining room. She preferred her own dining room furniture to the style that Jeremy had selected. When she told him she wanted to make the switch he told her that the house was hers to change, decorate or renovate.

He had begun the responsibility of taking over the reins of running the horse farm from Sheldon. Jeremy, Sheldon and Ryan had established a ritual of meeting after breakfast to discuss the farm's finances and the projected sale of existing stock to increase cash flow. Expanding Blackstone Farms Day School from preschool to sixth grade had strained the farm's cash reserves. It would take more than two years of tuition from the non-farm students to recoup the expenditures.

Tricia glanced up when she heard familiar footsteps. Jeremy stood over her, smiling. He tightened the knot to a wine-colored tie under the collar of a stark-white shirt. Her wedding gift to him of a pair of white-gold and onyx cufflinks were fitted into the shirt's French cuffs. He and Sheldon were scheduled to go into Richmond for a breakfast meeting with a banker to apply for a short-term loan.

"I have some money," she said without preamble.

Jeremy's hands stilled. "What are you talking about?"

"I have some money," she repeated, "you could use to ease the farm's cash flow." The first time Jeremy discussed the farm's finances with her she thought about the money sitting in a Baltimore bank collecting interest. The money she had received as a settlement and the proceeds from the sale of her home was more than the amount Sheldon intended to borrow.

Jeremy eased his tall frame down to the sofa, his gaze fixed on an open box. Resting atop a sheet of bubble wrap was a photograph of Tricia cradling a baby. At that moment he was grateful he was seated, realizing he could have fallen and reinjured his ankle.

Tricia looked the way she had before she'd left the farm. Her hair was long, and instead of the single braid it flowed around her shoulders in curly ringlets. The child staring out at the camera was an exact replica of the images in his own baby photographs.

She had had his child and not told him!

Rage swelled not permitting him to breathe. "Why didn't you tell me?" The question was squeezed out between his clenched teeth.

"What are—" The words died on Tricia's lips when she noticed the direction of Jeremy's gaze. Sitting atop the box she'd just opened was the only photograph of her with her daughter she'd kept. In her grief, she had cut up all of the others before realizing she would want one tangible memory of her beautiful baby.

She reached out to touch Jeremy's knee, but he jerked away as if she were carrying a communicable disease. Rising to his feet, he glared at her. "Don't touch me."

Tricia went to her knees, her eyes filling with tears. "Jeremy, please. Let me explain."

His hands curled into tight fists as he glowered at the woman he wanted to hate. He shook his head. "No, Tricia. I don't…I can't. Not now."

The tears filling her eyes fell, streaking her face,

and she collapsed to the floor not seeing her husband when he walked out of the room. However, she did hear the front door he'd slammed so violently that windows shook. She cried until spent, and when Gus found her she was still on the floor.

He managed to convince her to get off the floor and sit on the sofa. Curving an arm around her shoulders, he pressed a kiss to her short hair. "What's the matter, grandbaby girl?"

Tricia told her grandfather about Jeremy seeing the photograph of her and Juliet. "He hates me, Grandpa."

Gus patted her back. "No, he doesn't. He's hurt because you didn't tell him that he had become a father."

"I have to make him understand that I didn't deliberately deceive him."

"Jeremy loves you, Tricia. And because he does he'll come around."

She wanted to believe her grandfather, but the look on Jeremy's face and his "Don't touch me," said otherwise. Easing out of Gus's protective embrace, Tricia stood up and headed toward the door.

"I'm going out."

Lines of concern creased Gus's forehead. "Are you going to be all right?"

She stopped, not turning, and flashed a wry smile.

"Yes. I'm going to wait for my husband to come home, then I'm going to tell him about his daughter."

"You can tell Jeremy about Juliet after I tell you about Patricia and your father." Gus saw Tricia's back stiffen, but she did not move. "Your mother got a part-time job at Sheffield's Hardware the year she turned sixteen. Olga warned her about Sheffield's son, who did not have the best reputation with young women. Patricia wouldn't listen and snuck out nights to meet him.

"Patricia thought he was going to marry her once she told him she was carrying his baby. Of course that never happened because his father had made plans for him to go away to college. She dropped out of school, had you and took up with him again. It all ended after Morgan Sheffield left Staunton to attend college. You were a year old when Patricia put you in my arms and asked me to take care of you. The next time I saw my only child was three months later when I had to go to Tennessee to identify her body. The police told me she'd died of malnutrition. It was apparent she had starved herself to death. I brought her body back and had her cremated.

"I know your pain, grandbaby, because I know how it feels to lose a child. Raising you offered me another chance at parenthood. But once I realized you were involved with Sheldon's son it was like déjà vu. The difference was that Jeremy loved you and he still loves you."

Her shoulders slumping, Tricia nodded. "Thank you, Grandpa, for telling me about my mother. Now I have closure."

She walked out of the house and made her way toward the road that would take her to the north end of the horse farm. A sad smile touched her mouth. The Sheffields had abandoned their business more than ten years ago, after a Home Depot was erected in a strip mall several miles off the interstate.

Her past behind her, Tricia knew she had to right her future.

The first person Jeremy saw when he returned home after his meeting with the bank president was his wife's grandfather. "Good afternoon, Grandpa."

It actually wasn't a good afternoon because he hadn't been able to concentrate on anything since seeing the photograph of Tricia with his child. The image of the baby with black curly hair and large gray eyes would haunt him to the grave.

Gus nodded, his expression impassive. "Good afternoon, son." He gestured to a nearby chair. "Come, sit down."

"If you don't mind I'd like to talk to Tricia."

"Tricia's not here. Sit down."

Jeremy went completely still. "What do you mean she's not here?"

Gus saw naked fear on Jeremy's face. "She didn't run away, if that's what you're thinking."

"Where is she?"

"She went for a walk."

Turning on his heel, Jeremy retraced his steps off the porch. "I'll see you later."

Gus nodded, watching the tall figure as he walked to his vehicle and drove away. It was obvious Tricia was not her mother because she had fallen in love with a man who loved her unconditionally.

Jeremy let out his breath in a ragged shudder as he stopped and cut off the engine. She was there, sitting under a weeping willow tree, her bare feet in a narrow stream. He had driven to the section of the farm where they'd once picnicked and made love. He walked over to where she sat staring up at him. Her gaze was unwavering as she rose fluidly from the grass.

"If you want a divorce, then I won't contest it."

Jeremy moved closer until they were only inches apart and slipped his hands into the pockets of his trousers to keep from touching his wife.

"There will not be a divorce, Tricia. Not now, not ever. Unless…"

Her eyelids fluttered. "Unless what?"

"You're ready to give me back my heart."

Tricia stared at the man with the luminous eyes that had the power to reach inside her and hold her heart captive. "No, Jeremy. I can't give it back because I don't want to."

A smile softened his mouth. "And I don't want you to." He pulled his hands from his pockets and reached for her. Burying his face in her hair, Jeremy pressed a kiss there. "I can't believe I did the same thing I did fourteen years ago—walk away from you rather than staying to face the truth."

Clinging to her husband, Tricia told Jeremy everything from the moment her pregnancy was confirmed to when she placed a single red rose on the tiny white casket before it lowered into a grave and her subsequent decision to marry Dwight.

"If I had come back to the farm, she never would have died."

Jeremy placed his fingers over her mouth. "Maybe all she was given was three months, darling. She's an angel now." His mouth replaced his fingers and he kissed her. "Our little angel."

Tricia clung to Jeremy, feeding on his strength. "I love you so much."

He smiled. "Love you more."

"I don't think so," she countered.

"Would you like to place a wager, Mrs. Blackstone?"

Easing back, Tricia smiled up at him. "What would I have to wager, Mr. Blackstone?"

"Your heart."

She felt a warm glow flow through her. "I accept, but only if you're willing to wager the same."

"You have it, Tricia. I gave it to you a long time ago."

"How long ago?"

"The first time I peered through the bars of my crib to see you staring back at me."

Leaning back in his embrace, Tricia tilted her head and laughed uncontrollably. Jeremy's laughter joined hers and they were still laughing when they walked into their home and smiled at Gus, who watched them climb the staircase to the second floor.

Jeremy lowered his wife to the bed with the intent of reconciling in the most intimate way possible. They took their time loving each other with all of their senses.

Sated, limbs entwined, hearts beating in unison, Tricia and Jeremy were filled with the peace that had surrounded them from the moment they'd acknowledged their love for each other. It had taken a long time, but they were now ready to plan for another generation of Blackstones.

* * * * *

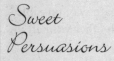